# INFALLIBLE

## VOL 2

TJ SPENCER JACQUES

# NOVELS BY
# TJ SPENCER JACQUES

NINE NOTCHES

BURGUNDY DOUBLOONS SERIES

INFALLIBLE SERIES

This is a work of fiction created by author TJ Spencer Jacques. All the characters, organizations, and events portrayed in this novel are either products of the author's imagination or used fictitiously.

Infallible - VOL 2. Copyright © 2018
Self-published under Raegan Publishing LLC. All rights reserved.

Printed in the United States of America.

For more information visit tjnovels.com

ISBN 978-0-9903732-6-1  Paperback

First Edition: August 2018

# NOVELS BY
# TJ SPENCER JACQUES

## NINE NOTCHES

## BURGUNDY DOUBLOONS SERIES

## INFALLIBLE SERIES

This is a work of fiction created by author TJ Spencer Jacques. All the characters, organizations, and events portrayed in this novel are either products of the author's imagination or used fictitiously.

# INFALLIBLE

## VOL 2

TJ SPENCER JACQUES

# CHAPTER 1

Madden Thursday
March 30, 2017
Noonday

## MONICA

Yesterday was my birthday, but it stormed all day with flash flooding. Today there isn't a cloud in the sky—go figure. We're the middle of winter and it feels like autumn. Sweater weather. There is truly no place like home, and if it's time to receive news that the first of eight chemo treatments will kick off within three weeks, then I can think of no other place I'd rather be than New Orleans—come what may.

He said it so fast:

*To battle your cervical cancer, my treatment protocol calls for a regiment of chemo-radiation within the next three weeks. Week one will start in twenty-one days, but your youth is your strength, and I have every confidence in you.*

My doctor has every confidence in me, but I have none in myself—not even enough to put the car in drive. I guess I'll just sit here, in the parking lot of the doctor who just confirmed twenty minutes ago that I have cancer. And why am I even surprised? My sister had it, two of my aunts died of cancer-related illnesses, and it killed my mother. My mother: a woman who was so full of life, who shopped every opportunity she could, who could light up a room with her colorful outfits and her Chanel Number Five . . . just like that, she was gone.

And now it has come for me.

*Mommy, where are you?*

Why put myself through the misery of a full dose of chemo when cancer is only going to kill me anyway? I can't believe I said that. There goes my mind. I must guard my thoughts. My mind is all I have.

My daughters will be teenagers pretty soon, and even though I know my husband is a wonderful father, they still need me; they still need their mother. Meanwhile, I still need my mom. Caring for someone with cancer is like having cancer—you feel the side effects, you feel the life passing through your fingers, and you feel the moment when hope dies. I'm not sure where my mom found the strength, but she smiled through it all . . . for me.

For us.

Only sickness has the power to transform a daughter into a caretaker and a mother into a child, but I was charged with that draconian responsibility.

*To resuscitate Momma or not to resuscitate?*

My sisters couldn't handle watching the slow drip of death, and I couldn't handle the thought of funeral arrangements, but add us together and the sum total still equaled strength. I was by her side when she coded, and I was there when they dragged her back to me. I was there to see the disappointment in her eyes. She was ready to go, and I was forced to place my need to be nurtured to the side and let her go spend some quality time with her mother. What a painful dilemma.

And my poor husband . . . life is so unfair.

If I would have known the earthquakes in my pelvic region

were due to cancer, I would've had one more dance with Jarvis at the Zulu Ball—I may have already attended my last ball. I was so pretty that night, I felt pretty, and he made me feel prettier. I guess in all the haste to look pretty for my husband, I lost my meds. If only I'd had my meds, I could have enjoyed one more dance that night. Instead, that night marked one full year of suffering.

All the tests confirmed it, all the additional opinions confirmed it, even a specialist in Cuba confirmed it—I have it. I was in denial until today. I figured the longer I sought second, third, fourth, fifth . . . fourteenth opinion, just maybe one of them would say the words I so needed to hear: *You're going to be just fine. You're going to live.*

But I thank God for my sister Connie; she beat breast cancer, and I'm not sure where would I be without her and my niece. Connie wanted to be here today, but I asked her not to come, but rather to meet me afterward for pralines and coffee, because that's our thing.

Sugar.

Sweets.

Support.

Strength.

I started my car ignition and my will to fight, then drove to meet Connie. My favorite niece might join us. Where would I be without the two of them? What would I do without my sister keeping my girls on the days I was too sick to get them off to school and cooking for me like she was Octavia in *The Help*? Where would I be without my niece cleaning and doing laundry? I didn't ask them to do any of those wifely chores; they appear three times a week, and my girls have never missed one day of school. Hell, my husband and I are still amazed—my daughter's grades improved during the watchful care of my sister. Ain't that some shit?

There I go again, laughing and crying—that's all I seem to do. I think of my support and my silly husband and I smile. I think of cancer and I . . .

I pulled up to my favorite place of solace; the place where my sister and I always retreat to during times of trouble. She doesn't see my car, so I sit for a second and enjoy the picturesque view of my sister. Look at her, submerged in prayer, under the same oak we sat under during our freshmen year when grandmother was ill. Our special oak. Our place to be alone with God, yet together. St. Katharine Drexel Chapel is unique, not just in the interior design—the octagon-arranged pews in the sanctuary and a ceiling that carries prayers directly to God—but also in its outward appearance. It looks like one of my mother's crystal salad bowls.

All either one of us ever had to say was, *Meet me at the chapel.*

A white rosary lies serpentine between her fingers. She's dressed in a peach suit with cream pants, and she has Anita Baker's hair. Only once I exited my car did she see me, and I saw her worried eyes and arms that wanted to hug me from forty yards away. Anxiety lifted her as she searched my face for any signs of hope. The good news—the only good news—is my desire to fight this cancer. Not able to stand the unknown another second, she walked toward me: her worry held in a single tear that was in no hurry to fall.

Arm in arm, we walked back to my favorite bench. I'm not perfect—God knows I've made mistakes—but thank God my sister never judged me, not even for that Atlanta situation. She has always protected me like a big sister should. I'm blessed to have her—all my other sisters, too, but especially Connie, who has stood so close by my side. So blessed.

We sat and talked, laughed, and prayed. That's when I noticed a familiar scent.

"Connie, when did you start wearing Chanel Number Five?"

"Monica, I was about to ask you the same question!"

We were overcome with joy and inhaled as much of her as we could hold in our lungs. Then, we welcomed her in unison.

"Hello, Momma."

# CHAPTER 2

Friday, March 31, 2017
7:20 p.m.

## BIYELL

I'm in Baker, Louisiana, a little outside of Baton Rouge, to see GiGi. Not to rub on that soft booty, not to squeeze those thick thighs, not to make her cum on this pipe—not tonight, though I would love to. I'm here for one purpose and one purpose only: to end my relationship with GiGi. The thought of never making love to her again, never watching her step out of the tub in that little leopard-print two-piece cami, is enough to make me throw up.

I can't believe I'm doing this to a woman I love, and I still can't believe Glenn received his settlement. Then again, I can, because he's a good dude. I know what I'm about to say sounds like some corny shit, but that's what I want to be—a good dude like Glenn.

Over the past four years, I've told so many lies I can't remember them all. I can't even remember everyone who I lied to.

All I know is it's harder to lie, and I'm getting tired of getting busted. There was a time I could tell a woman just about anything and she took it at face value; now they Google it. It's aggravating. And the fucked-up thing about this is I love GiGi, and I love my wife. I want to keep GiGi, but it's time to let her go. That's the hard part, and that's the part I'm here to do. I'm here to let her go.

Easier said than done.

Though I hate to admit it, Uncle Glenn is right that this is no way to live. Since last night, I've felt pains in my chest—it hurts so bad. The thought of breaking up with GiGi has me hyperventilating. I'm connected to her in both mind and body; I feel what she feels. I love her, I do. She is more than just my baby mama; she is my friend. She is my *other wife.* Yeah I said it and I'll say it again—GiGi is my other wife, and I need two wives. I do, and that's real shit.

We shot pool on Mondays, which was our date night; she was that kind of girl. And she was horrible at shooting pool, but it didn't matter. She made the nights fun. GiGi made life fun, and my mind and body associate her with pleasure and happiness. Whenever Tamera worked my last fucking nerve, I stormed out of the house and drove an hour to GiGi. I liked having somewhere to go that was away from Tamera. In some ways, I'm more compatible with GiGi than my wife, but my wife outranks her in years, and it's those years that make it difficult to leave Tamera.

I should give Uncle Glenn his check back. That's what I should do. I know I'm in her driveway, but I should turn around. I'm out of my mind thinking I can go through with this. I mean, look at my forehead—I'm sweating like a pig and it's not even hot. This shit is crazy. I can't do this. I can't hurt her. I should forget this bet with Uncle Glenn. I should put this truck in reverse and haul ass back to New Orleans. Even with the traffic, if I leave now, I'll make it back around nine p.m.

I can't drive back.

I've got to put an end to this.

I have to stand like a man and do the right thing.

I'm tired of lying. I just want some peace. I just want rest. The only way I'm going to get some rest is to walk through that door and end this relationship. But what if she shoots me in the face? I know it sounds crazy, but what if? She has a gun and knows how to shoot it. I'm tripping again. She's not going to shoot me, but she may stab me. Her family always jokes about her *hot head,* telling me, *she'll cut you up like an onion.* Maybe those weren't jokes? I'm trippin'.

Fuck it, let's just get this over with.

When I entered the house, she was in the bathroom bathing my daughter. They don't see me standing behind them, and I don't want them to. When I break her heart, I'm also going to break my child's heart. I'm active with my daughter. And it's not that I won't see my babies, it's just that I can't have any interactions with their mother—Glenn said until I'm strong, there should be a mediator. For a whole year, a mediator? Glenn said it's the only way to *detox from hoes,* but she's not a hoe; she's my other wife.

Fuck, my chest hurts so bad. She's such an awesome mother, and she's carrying another child for me. I have dogged her life. I treat her like a queen and pay bills, but I've still dogged her life. Maybe I should marry GiGi and divorce Tamera; after all, I am tired of her snooping through my shit. Being married to Tamera is like being married to a probation officer or a prison guard who makes you spread your ass cheeks to check for contraband. And another reason I should text Glenn a new name is because Tamera only has one child, but here, there are a total of three hearts I will break in one night.

The child in the tub.

The mother kneeling on the side the tub.

The baby that's showing in her belly.

I'm not heartless, even though you think I am. I'm in a jam; a tight spot. I have two good women, and for almost four years I couldn't decide, but today I must.

She's scrubbed a day of *raising hell* off my daughter. The end is near, but when it's the mother of your children, is it ever truly over?

"Shit!" GiGi yelled. "Boy, I didn't even see you standing there. Are you trying to give me a heart attack?" she asked, but it feels like I'm the one on the verge of a heart attack.

"Shit!" my daughter repeated.

"Don't say that . . . bad word," she corrected my daughter, who has developed a fondness for the word *shit*.

"Sorry, I was appreciating the view. Checking you out, that's all."

"Umm-hmmm, every time you check me out I end up with another baby . . . knock it off."

"Daddy, daddy, daddy!" My soapy daughter reached for me from the center of the tub. I smiled at her and waved.

"Once you finish with the baby, come meet me in the living room."

"Okay, I'll be right there, just give me ten minutes. If you're hungry, I have a lasagna plate in the microwave for you."

I still have a chance to back away from this deal with Glenn, but if not tonight, then when? There will never be a good time to crush GiGi. I'm delirious. I've been up for twenty-three hours worrying about how she's going to take this news. In a few minutes, I will find out.

Breathe. I have to breathe.

# CHAPTER 3

7:55 p.m.

## BIYELL

From down the hall, I heard the flopping of her slippers as she approached the kitchen with my daughter on her hip. GiGi removed my plate from the microwave, inserted a pink bowl for my daughter, then pressed *start*. Braylyn wasn't interested in the food—only the Elmo sippy cup filled with juice—but her mother insisted. Braylyn has her mother's temper; not even thirty seconds after GiGi placed the bowl in front of her, the lasagna spattered across the floor. I hurried over to clean the mess while GiGi grew frustrated with Braylyn.

"It's okay; Daddy will clean it up." I wiped up the spill, then calmed my daughter.

GiGi heated up another bowl of lasagna, then rolled the high chair into the living room, where I offered to feed my baby. Around this time of the evening, I always had more success with feeding Braylyn. I was also the one who gave them a needed break from each other.

"Choooo-chooo, here it comes." Right before the spoonful touched her mouth, I ate it, and Braylyn smiled with all teeth.

"Choooo-choooo, here it comes." Right before it touched her lips, I gulped another spoonful. "Emmm, yum, yummy— that's so good." My daughter giggled out loud. "Okay, here it comes. Chooooo-Chooooo," went the spoon, but this time she opened wide and gulped it down like Daddy.

"Well, I'll be," GiGi said.

"It works every time."

"And that reminds me . . . we're taking family pictures on Wednesday. I'm not rescheduling again. Okay?"

I nodded.

"And one more thing: After I didn't hear from you in time yesterday, I took the liberty of putting a deposit down on the house I found off Manhattan Avenue. It's close to my new office."

"You put a deposit down without discussing it with me first?"

GiGi rolled the highchair over to her. "Yes, but only after I called you, left voicemails, and sent several emails. The house wasn't going to last, so I made an executive decision."

Once again, Braylyn rejected the spoon from her mother.

*The time is now.* I have to come out with it, because it's getting more difficult by the minute . . .

"Oh, and I almost forgot—I also placed a deposit for the movers. They will pack us up next week. My cousin Jeff in Houston would like to move home, so he agreed to rent this place. We're all set!" she said in an elated voice. "You should be proud. I handled everything without stressing you out with the annoying details you hate. I know I've hit you with a lot, but you know how you are after I feed you then fuck you . . . it's snoring after that." Her focus shifted back to Braylyn and the lasagna.

"Tyra, I have to end our relationship." There, I said it.

Her body became encapsulated in a block of ice. She didn't turn; she didn't lower her arms. It took her brain a minute to reboot. In the high chair, my daughter cried for her juice.

"What did you say?"

"I said I have to end our relationship."

"Did I do something?"

"No."

"Then why? I don't understand."

"It's hard for me to say it, but—"

"Hard for you? Without any warning? You're breaking up with me? I have your child, and I'm carrying your child! Biyell, where is this coming from? Why are you doing this? What did I do to you?"

Her questions were back to back before I could get a chance to answer.

"Biyell, I am seven months pregnant, and you're breaking up with me? Braylyn is still a baby—not even two years old." She handed Braylyn the Elmo sippy cup.

"Bae, this is not what I—"

"Don't fucking *bae* me. This is about another woman? Have you met someone else?"

After I hard swallow, I said, "Yes . . . and no."

"What?"

"Yes, it's about another woman, but I haven't met anyone."

"Biyell, if you don't stop talking in riddles, I swear to God . . ." She searched the room for something to use as a weapon.

"Tyra, I'm married."

I watched her slowly rise to her feet in rage. I can't believe I said it, but I did. I finally said it.

*I'm married.* Those are the words I should have said the day I met her. I was pumping gas on College Drive in Baton Rouge, and she was at the gas pump on the other side. She was Jill Scott-thick, with deep curves, a small waist, and a flat abdomen area. Her hair was jet black and bone straight with a center part. She had perched lips, flirting eyes, and even though she tried to ignore me, I couldn't let her simply pump her gas and drive away without knowing her name. I needed to know her; she was my type. So I spoke to her, and she smiled back.

"Can I have a second of your time?" I stood close enough to force her to look upward.

"Sorry, but I'm a little busy."

"Since you're busy, then why not take my phone number? Instead of listening to the radio, you could listen to me tell you why you're the most beautiful woman in Baton Rouge."

"Only Baton Rouge?" Her eyes rolled. Those suckable lips smiled.

I knew then that I had her, so I quickly wrote down my number. She accepted it and drove off. Five minutes later, she called me.

"You have ten minutes to explain why I'm the most beautiful woman in this country. *Tick, tick, tick.*"

I should have told her then what I said just now, but I didn't. Instead, I reeled her into my fantasy world where I pretended to be single while having a wife eighty miles south in New Orleans. The fantasy continued even after Tamera gave birth to my child.

*It's better late than never.*

I guarantee that whoever coined that phrase never watched a woman cry without making a sound. That same individual never watched a heartbroken woman press the sides of her temples to keep her head from exploding. That same person who created those shallow words never watched the ears, face, and neck of his woman blister red from heartache.

"When did you get married?"

"I was married when I met you . . ."

At that point, she let out a cry that was similar to my daughter's cry for the sippy cup, only deeper and packed with more sorrow. Then after about five minutes, she calmed. An ire calm, like the perimeter inside the eye of a hurricane, where the sun shines through for a while and the skies are clear.

"*Bruh,* you're married?"

The only other time she ever called me *bruh* was when she caught me in a lie. For her to address me as *bruh* was her way of withdrawing and transitioning into a defense posture—that distant place where we no longer interacted as lovers, where she wasn't my girl and I was no longer her man. Here, we were common strangers.

"Bruh, you fucking played me?" The eye of the storm moved.

"Your wife sent you out here to end it? All this talk of marrying me once you bought a house was lies and games?" She leaned into my face. "So this is the part where you skip out on my kids?"

"I never said that. I never said I wasn't going to take care of my kids."

"You better believe you will!"

"There were so many times I wanted to tell you . . ."

"I can't fuckin' believe this! For real Biyell, you played me?" She moved closer to me. "So all of it was lies? All the working overnight in different cities? You weren't working in different cities, you were right in New Orleans with your wife?"

"I'm sorry . . ."

"So when I slept down there for Christmas, whose house was that?"

"My sister's home."

"*You dirty . . . motherfucker. You dirty motherfucker!* Oh, I get it, I'm the dumb country bitch out here in Baker! Do I look like a *hump and dump* bitch to you? Is that what you took me for?"

"Tyra, I never meant for things to get out of hand like this, but—"

"You pop me off with two kids and then vanish? Is that how this goes? I'm supposed to walk this shit off? Is that how this goes? Was all that bullshit about how much you love me also a lie?"

"I never said I didn't love you. I wanted this relationship and—"

"That's right, because I'm just a relationship, and she is the wife. What's it called . . . a *side bitch?* I'm your side bitch, Biyell?"

It was then that GiGi snatched my daughter out of the high chair and stormed out of the house. I knew where she was going—her mother lived next door. It was time to evacuate.

The area where GiGi lived was a parcel of land that was developed as a large cul-de-sac. All ten of the homes in the cul-de-sac were built by her family members. When GiGi returned, I was in the process of snapping my seat belt. I locked the door just as she pulled on the door handle. I looked over GiGi's shoulder to see her mother trailing her with my daughter on her hip.

GiGi turned to address her mother. "Mama, please go back in the house with my baby. The mosquitoes are bad; I don't need your help."

"Tyra, I don't know what's going on with you two, but you will not have your business in the streets."

"Mama, please go back inside!" GiGi yelled before turning her rage toward me. "Where are you going? Call your wife, maybe the bitch will extend your curfew! Ask her if I can have you for a few more minutes."

"I knew he was married. I kept telling you that man *was married!* You didn't want to listen," GiGi's mother called as she escaped the mosquitoes with my daughter.

"Don't go yet, Biyell." GiGi pulled the door handle so hard the truck rocked like a bassinet. "When you drove your ass out here to *fuck me* you had all night; don't leave so soon," she taunted me in a condescending tone before her voice switched back to rage. "Open this got-damn door, Biyell, before I jump on this hood."

"Tyra, you're trying to cause a scene. I'm leaving."

Every front door in the cul-de-sac cracked; every porch light clicked on.

"I'm not causing a scene, sweetie pie!" she yelled around the cul-de-sac. "There's nothing to see here, folks. Just a married man and his side bitch having a wholesome conversation about some bastard children . . . that's all. Nothing to see here." Violently, she pulled at the door. "Biyell, open this fucking door."

I raised the window to just a crack.

"Tyra, you don't want to talk, and you know it. You want to fight. I'm not going to jail out here." She is related to half of the Baker Police Department. "I just wanted to come out here like a man and tell you face-to-face, not over a text."

"Like a man?" she fussed through the crack at the top of the window just to make sure I heard every insult. "You thought by coming out here and confessing to my face that you've lied for almost four years is something a man would do? A man would stand out here like a man."

"Tyra, I'm sorry . . ."

"Who is she?"

"That's not important—what's important is telling you the truth. I'm married, and you needed to hear that before you relocated."

"Biyell, I am still relocating, so if that was your reason for driving out here tonight then you wasted good gas." She started to elbow the window, then suddenly looked up like someone had inserted a flash drive into the top of her head. "I know who it is! It's the name that always appeared on your phone late at night! When I searched for the number, it came back to *Tamera Baltimore.* When I asked you about it, you said that was your sister and y'all had a family plan. But that's not your sister, that's your motherfucking wife!"

I slowly backed out of the driveway into the street.

GiGi walked on side of my truck holding the door handle, refusing to let it go. Suddenly, neighbors poured out of their homes—the homes of her relatives. What I didn't want to happen was now happening. We had caused a scene.

Someone asked GiGi's mother what was going on. It was her

aunt.

"Oh nothing, she just found out he's married, that's all."

Just like that, the family turned on me.

Out of nowhere, a cousin appeared in front of my truck. He told GiGi's mom that I would not drive off with GiGi holding onto the truck. I asked him to help me.

"Nawww, playa, I'm not here to help you." His hand was under his shirt, gripping something that looked like a pistol. He looked to be about twenty years old, and had a build that suggested he'd played a lot of football in high school and college. He was a Suge Knight kind of a dude with a shiny dome and a beard dripping with testosterone. "I'm here to make sure you don't drag my cousin."

GiGi's mother approached again, with my daughter screaming on her hip. "Tyra, what you're not going to do is fight in the street over a husband that ain't even yours. Let him go. Do you hear me, Tyra, you let him go!"

GiGi released the door handle, but her cousin was still standing in front of my truck, wishing for a reason to blast my chest open. Just as he yielded the right of way so I could finally leave, I heard GiGi's mother scream.

"No, Tyra, put that down!"

"You dirty bitch!" GiGi growled behind my vehicle.

Her cousin didn't have to shoot me, because the brick that shattered my window sent sharp shards of glass into my neck and eye before they swiped the side of my head. A cut opened and blood poured out. Dazed and wounded, I drove through a chorus of laughter and applause.

"Tyra busted that nigga in the head!" the Suge Knight cousin welled with laughter. "That'll teach his dog-ass—he should have asked the last nigga who tried to run game on Tyra. He's still missing."

The neighborhood laughed.

That was the last thing I heard as I drove off out of the cul-de-sac with one eye and a tail between my legs. GiGi had every right to hit me with that brick, but I wish her cousin would have shot me—that would have felt better than hurting GiGi. The good news is, I kept my end of the deal with Glenn. The bad news is, I left my heart in Baker with GiGi.

I arrived home much later than anticipated. I needed stitches, but a bag of ice from the gas station had to do. I got it from the same gas station where I met GiGi. About ninety minutes later, I came to a rolling stop in my driveway with my ice pack pressed again my eye and the bitter aftertaste of lies in my mouth.

Before entering my house, I sent GiGi a text from my new phone—the one Uncle Glenn gave me, the one that represented a new beginning.

*I'm sorry and I do love you.*

Almost as soon as I sent over those words, my new cell phone alerted me of a text:

*And you changed your phone number? Since you're trying to delete me, I would have you to know that I am aware that you and Tamera Marie Baltimore were on food stamps last year. I also have your current address. I also know she was hired with us last month. I'm your wife's supervisor—you're fucked LOL!*

# CHAPTER 4

Saturday, April 1, 2017

## JARVIS

THE TRUTH - It's Saturday night, or better yet, one day left before I have to break things off with Briana: the best sex I have ever had in my life. What was I thinking joining in on the challenge with Uncle Glenn? That's right: a shot at that two-million-dollar check. That money could help me get my manuscripts to Hollywood. Still, she's the best sex I have ever had in my life, and that's not an exaggeration. Don't get me wrong, I've had my share of women, but none like Briana. There is no comparison. So why am I ending the best thing I have ever had?

The money.

I would've said my wife, but why lie? If Uncle Glenn had never proposed this deal, then there's no way I would have quit Briana. Even before my wife was diagnosed with cervical cancer, sex with her was average at best. Women are notorious for giving us the *show-off* pussy until we're deep into the marriage—then it turns into the *roll-over-here* pussy. You figure it out. Nevertheless, I feel like shit for fucking her niece. Then again, it's her niece who's fucking me.

Take, for instance, the thirty-minute round we just finished. I was sliding in and out of Briana, just minding my own business, when she says:

"Give it to me on my stomach."

"But I'm almost there."

"You will thank me."

The understatement of the year.

She turned over onto her stomach like a mermaid and arched her back. Then she waited. As I humped like a chihuahua, I barely heard her moan until I said *I'm cummin!* That's when she pressed that soft ass against me in a way I've never felt. I volcanoed in her for five minutes. Then I collapsed. Correction—I fainted. For real, I passed the fuck out. And Uncle Glenn is asking that I give this up? And fuck who? I've been to the mountaintop of pussy and looked over and seeeeeeeeeeen Briana. Her pussy is the pinnacle. The thought of never sucking her breast again is enough to make me tell Uncle Glenn *thanks, but no thanks.*

Why not marry Briana?

I thought about that question all week; I even had a vision of a wedding, of lifting up a veil and kissing her in a stunning white gown . . . that's when I snapped out of it. But I could marry her, and if anything ever happened to my wife—God forbid—I could make Briana full time.

*But it looks so bad.*

It looks horrible.

Fucked up.

I know.

She's Monica's niece. Hell, I was at the hospital when she was born! *Fuck,* that sounds horrible. I mean, Briana cleans and babysits for my sick wife.

In fairness to me, I didn't know my wife had full-blown cancer, because she never gave me a direct answer. Yesterday it was confirmed, and here I am at Briana's house today. Fucked up, huh? I know, but you've done some fucked up shit in your life, too. Who are you to judge me? Huh? But anyway . . .

I have to end this thing with Briana, especially now, since my wife is going to need me more than ever. Maybe Briana will understand, being that she knows the situation. Maybe she'll respect me more as a man for taking this step to be there for Monica. And it's not like she'll have to run on side of a railway car as I head off to war; I'll still get to see Briana once a week when she comes over to help out around the house. Maybe then she'll see it my way and we can still remain close?

It's been a little over two months since that night Briana invited me to her apartment, and every night since, I have looked forward to seeing her at the end of my day. I have become accustomed to her, accustomed to how she makes me feel, accustomed to her proofreading my thoughts. She loves to read what I have written, and when I ask her to read my rough drafts out loud, she acts out each section of dialogue like an audition. Maybe it is an audition? Maybe I have fallen in love. *Damn, I can't believe I just said that.*

Why did I accept that money from Uncle Glenn?

Quit Briana and do what?

Beat my dick for a year?

It's been a very long time since I allowed myself to feel this way, to fall for a woman in the most carefree way imaginable. Damn you, Uncle Glenn and your money! Look at that perfectly shaped ass. I deserve this; I deserve Briana more than any man her age, A guy her age wouldn't know what to do with this silky body. I don't want to quit her, but I need that money and Uncle Glenn is only asking for one year of total commitment. What's one year without being inside of Briana?

Forever.

Forever and a day.

Shakespeare must have had a Briana, too:

*What angel shall*

*Bless this unworthy husband? he cannot thrive, Unless her prayers, whom heaven delights to hear; And loves to grant, reprieve him from the wrath, Of greatest justice . . .*

—*All's Well That Ends Well*, Act III, Scene 4

Monica is sexually shut down, with no guarantee of regaining her full health, but I must remember my vow. I will be there for her, but here is one thing you can count on: after this year is up and I win that prize money, I'm returning to this bed, to Bri-Bri, to caress this soft, cotton ass, to keep her for the rest of my life.

*Pow.*

*Pow.*

Look at it jiggle.

I just need to convince Bri-Bri to wait for me, that's all. I believe she will. It's time to wake up my little love kitten and ask her. Here it goes.

With soft kisses on her neck, "Bri-Bri. Wake up."

Her eyes opened with a moan and a smile. "You want some more, baby?" Her eyes fluttered into focus.

"I wish, but I'm empty and satisfied."

"I think you have a little bit more in there . . ." her warm hand clutched my shriveled jewels.

"Trust me, baby, I'm empty."

"Good, that means I've done my job," she purred in my armpit, where I leaned down to kiss her bangs.

"There is something I need to talk to you about."

"I already said yes, I'll give you five sons." The things we ask for during sex.

I chuckled. "Not the five sons, Bri, it's something else."

I have to get this right; if I do, then I can have the best of both worlds in one year and one day. I'm turning forty in a few weeks, and every man in his forties has earned the rights to the spoils of life. Having a mistress like Briana is the best gift I could have given myself. A life of money, success, trips to the Oscars, and a body like hers . . . Do I deserve that life? Hell yeah, I do!

"Briana, you know I care about you, right?"

"I do . . ."

"Do you trust me."

She rose on her elbows. "Yes I trust you, Jarvie-babe."

THE LIE

"Briana, as you may already know, it was confirmed yesterday that Monica has to undergo chemotherapy. And, I-I was thinking that we should take a break for a while so I can be there for my wife."

"We're breaking up?" She inflated from her elbows to face me from an upright position in the middle of the bed. "A break? For how long." Briana's voice was filled with dread.

"I don't know; I'm thinking at least a year. That should be long enough to get Monica through her therapy."

"But what do her treatments have to do with us? I don't see a need to break up?"

"Briana, deep down I feel the same way. You are everything to me."

"Then don't pause what we have—we can support Monica together, as a couple," she pleaded.

"We can't, we have to pause."

"Not really."

"But Monica is going to need me, and I don't want to hurt you in the process as her day-to-day care becomes more demanding."

"No, I'm not hearing you right now."

Those were the last words Briana said before barreling out of the bed. I watched as she picked up her panties and bra off the floor, then drummed into the bathroom. I followed as far as the door would allow before it slammed.

"Briana, you know how I feel about you, and I'm not asking for a permanent breakup. I only need a year. That's all . . . a year."

The bathroom door opened. her body was wrapped tight in a plush, purple robe. Her hair was tied under a purple scarf.

I love her hair.

I love the way it changes every week like her mood. This week it's a jet-black Michelle Obama style with the bangs. Last week it was Beyoncé blonde, and the week before that it was a maroon afro. She wore that maroon comb-out with that maroon bra and maroon panties; even the lights in her bedroom glowed a deep rouge as she leaned against the doorway. Thinking back, I just realized that those panties and that bra were the same style and design my wife wore on my birthday two years ago, before her illnesses stripped her of everything seductive and sexy. *Briana has been studying us like a calculus test.*

"No, no, no! We're not ending like this. A year will turn into two years, then you'll stop taking my calls."

"Bri, don't make this difficult for me, I'm only asking for a year."

"I said no. There is no need to take a break. I have made plans for our future, and I intend to keep those plans."

"Plans? How could you make long-terms plans without discussing those plans with me? Have you forgotten that I'm married?"

"I know you're married, but we are a couple. Taking a break from our relationship is not fair to me."

"Bri, this is not about you . . ."

"I know it's not about me, but I'm willing to support you and Monica."

"I have made myself clear. I'm not asking you; I'm telling you that we need to take a break. I was counting on you to be more understanding being that you are—"

"Related to your wife? Being that I'm her niece?" She pushed past me to the closet. "Fuck that, Jarvis. You're not dumping me. I'm not falling for that. This is about another bitch, isn't it?"

"No, I have no one else but you."

At this point, the argument was rumbling from room to room as I trailed behind her with outstretched arms. Briana wasn't open to a compromise, nor was she open for a rational conversation—breaking up wasn't in her plans. As for me, I have no choice. I mean, I do have a choice, but not if I want a shot at winning two million dollars. The way I look at it, none of the guys in my *Madden* crew will last one year without fucking up. That means I am the frontrunner to take home the grand prize—if only I can survive this conversation with Briana.

I cornered her by the breakfast table, which sat just to the left of the electric range and particle board cabinets. That's when she disappeared. Not all of her—only her sensory processors, her consciousness, those inner parts needed to connect with. She was gone, and I was alone with her avatar. With her index finger, she scribbled invisible graffiti across the eggshell latex as if I wasn't there at all, as if our conversation was never spoken at all. Then I heard several hard sniffles and a bubbling of anger as her head osculated in disbelief.

"Briana, how could you be so understanding when it comes to fucking a married man, but when I tell you I need a break to take care of your dying aunt, then you flip the fuck out?"

"BECAUSE SHE'S DYING!" Briana screamed as she ran past me to the bedroom closet. In a thunderous rampage, she collected an arm full of stilettos—the kind with the razor heels—and pitched them at me like she was pitching darts at the back wall of a bar. I bobbed and weaved. One scratched me across my back, but I lived.

"It's the curse of this family! It's what we do, we die of cancer—first the great aunts and now the young." Briana slumped in front of the bed with her hands covering her eyes. "One of my cousins—my age—just announced on Facebook today that she has it. This relationship with you may be the only happiness

I enjoy before it's my turn—before cancer finds me!" With one foot in front the other, she drew nearer. "There isn't anything you can do to save Monica—it's over for her—but we have a chance. Can't you see it?" She dried her damp face on my chest.

"On that note, I'm leaving."

She hooked my arm. "Jarvie-Babe . . . I'm sorry, please forgive me. Believe me when I say I love you."

"And I love you too," I replied.

"Then let's work through this; we're perfect for each other." She placed her palms flat on my chest.

"Briana, if you love me the way you say you do, then you will give me the time I need to care for Monica."

It was then that she walked over to her dresser and opened the bottom drawer. In her hand, she held what appeared to be two bottles of pills.

"Remember the night your wife suddenly fell ill at the Zulu Ball?"

I nodded, then she tossed the pill bottles to me one at a time—both were prescribed to Monica. In a rage, I gathered my clothes off the floor. "Did you—did you—t-take her meds out of her purse?"

The only sound was her breath, which *swooshed* and *swooshed* and *swooshed* like a steam press across wrinkled denim.

"DID YOU STEAL MONICA'S MEDICATION OUT OF HER PURSE?"

The only reply I received was the bang of her cherrywood dresser drawer, and the subsequent tumbling of a rack of fingernail polish.

"That's fucked up! You are really fucked up! You don't play around with someone's medication."

"And you don't play around with my heart. We're not taking a break. I've spoken."

"That's really fucked up, Briana. Who does that?"

"A winner," she said as she picked up the bottles of fingernail polish. "Jarvis, I have some say in how things are going to go between us, and we're not taking a break, or cooling off, or having a pause, or whatever the fuck you want to call it. You break it, you own it."

Bri pulled the tie on her robe and unwrapped her body. "After you calm down, we will devise a plan to care for your wife as a couple, because that's what we are: a couple. Monica's days are numbered, but you and I will have a lifetime together. I know that sounds insensitive, but it's the circle of life." She stood kissing distance from my lips.

"Briana, stay the fuck away from my wife, and stay the fuck away from me." I stormed out of her apartment, got into my car, and bucked over every speed bump that led out of her apartment complex.

\*\*\*

I couldn't believe it. Monica didn't leave her pills at home that night—Briana swiped them out of her purse. How dirty could you be? It's your aunt, and you steal her pills? I knew I shouldn't have gotten involved with her, I fucking knew it.

*What have I done?*

How could I do this to Monica? I know she was sick and unable to make love to me, but how could I do this? It's her niece, for God's sake. If this shit ever gets out, I will look like the biggest asshole in the country. Hell, the biggest asshole in the world. Surly I can't be the only man who has stepped out on his wife during times of illness? But I stepped out with her niece, a child she christened as a baby. I was at the christening. How could I be so vile?

Bri will not tell a soul about this, because it makes her look just as bad. If I go down, then she's going down with me. To confess that she's having an affair with me looks bad across the board—for that reason I think my secret is secure. But what happens when she resumes cleaning the house? What happens if Briana causes a scene in my house? And if I stop her from cleaning our house, then what would be my reason? *We broke up, and now her presence around my wife makes me uncomfort-*

*able?*

I'm in a fucked-up spot, but I did end it like I promised Uncle Glenn. Bitches come and bitches go, but I did keep my word. I'm still a part of the challenge, and I could still win that prize money.

I entered my home to find my wife seated in a dimly lit room with the sounds of Diana Ross glittering from the corner. She was singing the theme from *Mahogany*. Straight away, my eyes focused in on an empty bottle of white wine, but I couldn't make out the label. Then, my gaze drifted back to Monica.

*"Do you know where you're going to, do you like the things that life is showing you . . ."*

She's in another time and place, and I know where. Her mother was an R&B backup singer who worked with everyone from Stevie Wonder to Quincy Jones, but never got a shot as a solo artist. "Mahogany" was her mother's favorite song, and when Monica's missing her, she plays it—really loud.

It takes at least five glasses of wine to destroy a bottle like that; she was holding number five loosely in her hand with her feet propped on the armrest of the sofa. She turned and finally saw me. "Hi, *baaabay-bee.*"

"I see you have a party going without me tonight."

"I think you better get accustomed to being without me. I'm shutting down like K-Mart."

"Monica, don't talk that way." I placed my laptop bag on the floor at the base of the lampstand, raised her legs as I took a seat, then lowered her legs across me. "You're not going anywhere."

"Oh, I'm going. It's just a matter of when, that's all."

"We have to think positive. I believe if anybody can beat this cancer, you can."

". . . and when I go, you better not have a mean bitch around my daughters, burning them with cigarettes."

I laughed, but she was serious. "Monica, please . . ."

"Jarvis, you hear me, your new bitch burns my girls with cigarettes, I will haunt you and that hoe!"

That was Monica's biggest fear about dying: me getting remarried and my new wife burning my daughters with cigarettes. Like I would marry a woman who smokes. Like my daughters would stand perfectly still while she burned them with a pack of Salem 100's.

"You hear me, bitch?" she yelled at the ceiling fan. "You burn my girls with a fucking cigarette and see what happens!"

"Monica, no one is going to burn our girls with cigarettes, okay?"

"And you better know it! I'll come out of that grave like that *Thriller* video on her ass. *Is this the Thrillerrrr . . . Thril-ler night, and no one's gone to save you, bitch. Thrillerrrr . . .*"

"Babe, I think it's time to help you to the shower."

"I'm good; you go take a shower. *Creatures crawl in search of blood to terrorize yawls neighborhood.*" She clawed her fingers like the "Thriller" dancers.

"Monica . . ."

"Okay, okay . . . help me up."

I slid the glass out of her hand and escorted my wife to our bedroom, where she fell back on the bed. I unbuttoned her jeans, and she lifted her butt just a little. With her jeans and socks in hand, I clicked on the light in the bathroom and got the bottles going in the tub. Once the tub had filled about halfway, I forklifted her into my arms, just like when we'd crossed the seal of our apartment for the first time. Instantly, my mind went back there—back to a time when our only concern was the light bill.

After a few short paces, I lowered her into the warm suds. No sooner did her head find a comfortable resting place did I hear the doorbell.

"Were you expecting someone?" I asked.

"No, that's probably that bitch coming to burn my daughters with those cigarettes. *Drag her ass back here.*"

"I doubt it, seriously. Don't slide under that water; I'm going to check the door." I kissed Monica on the forehead.

"*Is this the Thrillerrrr . . . Thril-ler night . . .*"

When I made it to the door, there was no one there. When I looked down, I saw a little gift bag with a bow. I opened it; there was a card directly on top.

*Do you remember what you asked me for the other night? I'll remind you. You asked me for a son, and I said I would give you five sons.*

In the bottom of the bag there was a white box, and in that box was one of those pink and white pregnancy sticks.

*Here's the first of those babies you asked for. Congratulations to us.*

# CHAPTER 5

Sunday, April 2, 2017

## RASTA

I must love this girl—seriously. It's been nearly fifteen years since I last stepped foot in a church, but it's the only place to see her. She's not taking my calls or returning my texts, and she blocked me on Facebook. She's erased me out of her life . . . but I've changed. I know it's hasn't even been a full month yet, but I've changed. At first, the reason I eased off the weed was for LaDeisha—to show her I was capable of making a change, that I wasn't an addict. However, this new me is now something I'm doing for myself. I want to prove to myself that I'm not an addict, and that I can present a more professional side.

Yes, I'm still Rasta Man; minus the locks, that's all. And I have allowed LaDeisha to reduce me down to a stalker, but I have to see her. She has to see the new me. The person she is refusing to talk to is the old me. I'm putting in the work.

As for Shameka, she was never an option—not at all. Some

women argue with their man like he's some chick in the projects she's about to fight. Shameka's that type.

You're only going to call me a bitch so many times before I slap the lips off your face, so to keep it from getting to that point, it's best to go our separate ways. If you have reduced me to the point that I now longer have words to express how pissed off I am . . . then you're the wrong woman.

The only problem that remains is the friends we have in common on social media; the group that constantly provides me with updates about Shameka and her Facebook posts. I tried to explain to them that they're not obligated to tell me when she trashes me online. The lesson I've learned is never tolerate someone you can't stand just because you need them. I am guilty as charged.

Then there's LaDeisha; she's the woman I've chosen to be my wife, if I can just convince her that I am not a weed-head thug. And she's right—I will never pass a background check once they start digging into my past. All my weed charges, traffic arrests, and child support warrants will stick out like a black dude at a Trump rally.

Despite all of that, I deserve to be happy with the woman I love, and I can't think of any other than LaDeisha.

She just walked right past where I'm seated.

My eyes followed her as her parents ushered her to the front of the church. She's in the section reserved for the important folk, while I'm holding it down in this last pew. In terms of relevance, her pew is a who's-who of New Orleans politics and business. That's what it's like attending any event with LaDeisha; she knows everybody, or they know her and want to meet her in person. Rarely did we have an uninterrupted dinner. Most men would find the popularity of a woman like her too much to deal with, but I wasn't intimidated by her. She inspired me.

I remember the first day I met her in the French Market; she was giving a tour to several members of Congress when they made a stop at my booth. I was surrounded by a bunch of snotty congressmen who asked a million and one questions but didn't buy shit. Then LaDeisha stepped through the crowd to ask me about one of my tribal carvings.

"Wow, you carved all of this yourself?"

"Yes, on a good day I can crank out about four."

"This amazing," she said as I wrapped her charging elephant in a sheet of shipping foam. "A man who can make things with his hands, I like that."

"You should feel the same hands on your shoulders at the end of a long day, squeezing that tension out of your body. Digging and pulling on both sides of your neck. That good hurt in the center of your back. You just felt it, huh?"

She shrugged with a smile. "A little, a little."

"Well, I thank you for your business, and my number is inside. Call me, and I'll personally deliver these hands."

"I will hold you to that, and you better not stand me up when I call."

"I promise."

She called, and what started as a back rub turned into passionate lovemaking that never faded or dipped. She gave me her entire body like a full course meal, with dessert. LaDeisha is smart and spicy, nasty and nerdy, feminine and freaky . . . then I lost her. Like that old Teddy Pendergrass song, "The Whole Town's Laughing at Me," I lost her. I lost her because my name is shit in the public records search. I lost her because I am not qualified to go where she's going. I lost her because I don't fit in or look the part. But now I'm halfway there.

With some of the money from Uncle Glenn, I had Telly expunge my record on those misdemeanors, which left only the current charge. Telly had the case moved to a judge he campaigned for last year—he feels confident we can get the charge reduced to personal use instead of intent to distribute. If only I could rewind the clock ten years, I would have never seen the inside of a jail. My carefree life cost me a chance to have the woman of my dreams, but I haven't given up yet.

After the service, I made a fast break for the front door. I wanted to steal her away from her parents just for a minute. I waited as worshippers waved goodbye on both sides of me. I didn't hear one word preached today, and if I did, then it was in one ear and out the other.

For LaDeisha, leaving the church was also a campaign stump opportunity, and she made the most of it. She held every baby she could pry away from its mother's arms and wrapped her arms around every lifelong member in her path.

"Mrs. Taylor, can I count on a pot of your beans for my announcement dinner? Pretty please?"

"Deisha, I was your catechism teacher—whatever you need will be there, simmering in the pot." Smart move on LaDeisha's part because I know Mrs. Taylor, and everyone know she can cook.

That's when LaDeisha appeared at the top of the stairs. She was wearing pearls and a congressional dress and held a Jackie Kennedy purse. As she reached for the railings that aided churchgoers four steps down, I held her hand. Her smile went from welcoming to *whoa* in less than two seconds. She'd never seen me without my braids or the stench of weed in my clothing. This was her first time meeting this Roderick, and I only had a minute to make an impression.

She smiled at me. "Have we met before?" she asked in a startled but impressed voice.

"I don't believe we have." I kissed the top of her hand. "Hi, my name is Roderick Ross, people use to call me Rasta."

"Nice suit, Mr. Ross." She wasn't lying; it was a dark blue cut with a blue and silver tie and royal blue shoes. "So, what did you think of the sermon?"

"It inspired me to live my best life."

"Oh really."

"Yes."

"Interesting," she nodded. "When did you cut your hair?"

"That night I left your house."

"You did that . . . for me?"

"I did it for us; I want to be where you are."

"I live in a cruel political world."

"Then allow me to play the back."

"Let's talk about it tonight."

"At your place?"

"No, over the phone."

"I'll take it."

And just like that, she was whisked away into a sea of greetings that was exhausting to watch. But from the midst of the waves, she smiled at me. That was the hope I needed. A piece of LaDeisha is better than going straight to voicemail.

"I agree, Ice Cube; today was a good day."

# CHAPTER 6

Madden Thursday
April 6, 2017
7:35 a.m.

Today was Diana's last day on the job, and a huge party was planned for her in the labor and delivery ward. She had worked with many of the nurses there for well over thirty years. Others she had mentored right out of nursing school—they called my wife Momma D. There wasn't a dry eye in the room. The way some of the new girls were crying, you would have sworn that my wife was dying, but Diana brings life to a room—it easy to see why they will miss her so much. She had even worked a few days longer than her two week's notice required, just to help out the others when they were short-staffed.

Diana had also told the director that if he ever has a Level 5 emergency, she will remain available should he need her. That's a Level 5 Hurricane Katrina-type crisis. When Hurricane Katrina hit, Diana worked the entire shift—even her director couldn't believe it. At that moment, she became a nursing legend at West Jeff Hospital. Today I wore my prosthetic because I want to walk her out the front door for the last time, and I thank God I am accomplishing this goal fifteen years ahead of our projected retirement.

We walked out of the labor and delivery ward arm-in-arm to the elevator; the nurses lined on either side of the corridor and showered my wife with flowers and tearful goodbyes. One of those nurses was a lady my wife called Emma B—she was present on that nightmarish day when my wife delivered my daughter. Diana once revealed to me that it was Emma B who told her to stay with me.

*Love can survive the greatest pain.*

Emma B was right: our love today is stronger than ever. I only wish I could see my daughter. That's my biggest regret in life.

That was our morning, and we just arrived home about an hour ago.

Even with all of our dough, we're still living in the same apartment, where we plan to be until we build our house. Only recently has Diana warmed up to the idea of looking at plans, and my delight has been watching the gleam in her eyes as the builder presents the many possibilities. What's funny is she can't seem to make up her mind, and that's okay with me—I want to stay here a little while longer, anyway.

As far as our interactions over the past couple of weeks coming off that bloody fight, we're getting better, one day at a time. That painful flashback set us back, but the difference this time was we talked it through—as compared to previous fights when she would hold her resentment in for months.

Between you and me, Diana's gotten into this challenge I have with the guys. We even have a little score sheet and have placed our own bets on who we think will win. We also have a side bet on who we think will get knocked out first. I'm betting on Jarvis going down first, but Diana seems to think Shameka is going to trip up Rasta. I know Rasta, and he's done with Shameka, but I haven't shared my reasons. I think what Diana likes about this challenge the most is that these guys are putting forth the effort to live a committed life. All of them except Telly. He was the one who caught Diana off guard, but I wasn't surprised.

Before I issued this challenge, Telly talked to me a lot. Not just on Thursdays—he called me throughout the week and confided in me about everything. The biggest crisis in his life: *Yolanda or Erica?* He likes Yolanda a lot, but he loves Erica. With all things considered, I don't see Telly as a man who can be with one woman. It's not part of his DNA. He loves Yolanda's legal mind, and Erica submissive manners. Yolanda stimulates his mind, and Erica stimulates his ego. It's a shame he is too afraid to commit to either one.

Some guys will always have a woman on the side, and that's Telly. In any case scenario, I'm hoping he can get his stuff together, but it breaks my heart that he didn't even try. All he had to do was make a decision.

*Yolanda or Erica?*

Only one!

Telly got as far as texting me Yolanda's name, but once he heard the terms, he couldn't follow through.

This is not high school where you have invited two girls to the same prom; this is real life, with real feelings and real hurt. And I'm not going to sit here and act like the thought never crossed my mind to get a mistress—mainly because of this threesome fantasy I had about a year ago—but Diana iced it with one counterproposal:

"Glenn, if you want a threesome, I'll grant your wish."

"Really? Can I have it for my birthday?" I was so excited.

"Yes, but under one condition . . ."

"Yes, just name it! Anything."

"I will give you the threesome of your wildest dreams . . . but the next day you have to watch me fuck two men."

That was the end of my threesome fantasy. She lost me like Gillian.

But that's why I love her.

I married a woman that I feel is undisputed; no other woman

compares to Diana. Some may feel that other women are prettier, but not to me. Some may feel that other women are sexier, but not to me. I have eyes for one. I see her as the ultimate—the absolute best woman that God created. Yea, I'm pussy-whipped, I admit it, but I love it.

Last night we were lying in bed. She was next to me lying on her stomach, and I started rubbing my hands across her panties. I didn't want anything. She offered, but I just wanted to rub my hands across her panties. That is what happiness is, and that is what I want for all five of these guys; four out of five at least gave it a try.

Madden Night
6 p.m.

I offered to rent a room for our Madden Night, but Diana insisted that we do things as we did prior to her retirement. So, she's going to take the evening and have a girls' night out with some of her friends, and it's guys' night out for us—same place, same time. Around five-thirty, I kissed Diana as she headed out the door, and at six o'clock on the nose, all the guys entered through the front door—all except Telly.

The guys embraced with hugs, and then we fell into our usual seats. It was quiet like child support court. It was quiet like when I'm trying to listen to my neighbors fuck. There was no weed, nor was anyone in the mood to smoke. It was in that first ten minutes that I began to realize just how much Crowd Noise meant to our brotherhood. The first one to break the silence was Rasta—or should I say, Roderick Ross.

"What I don't understand is why can't he still come on Thursdays? He's not participating in the challenge, and we let Yonnis hang out with us."

All eyes were honed in my direction.

"I thought about it, too, but the reason I implemented that rule was for the integrity of the group. I no longer want to be the host of a seminar on how to cheat and get away with it. This can't be the place to swap strategies on how to fuck over unsuspecting women. At some point, we need to have a bond that is built on keeping our word, and if you can't keep your word to the woman you sleep next to every night, how can I trust you? How can any of us trust you?"

"The way I look at it, Uncle Glenn, you can give me that check right now because I don't see any of these guys winning it," Timothy said.

"The fuck you mean you don't see any of us winning it? Everybody in this room has already committed to winning it. Have you proposed to Tootsie yet?" Jarvis asked.

"No, but I plan to."

"When?" Jarvis demanded to know.

"Soon, real soon."

"See, that's some bullshit right there! Uncle Glenn, we need to resolve this tonight." Biyell took offense to the rules. "Timothy can bullshit around for a whole year single and still win this challenge. I think he should be forced to work things out with Kayla or he can get the fuck out of this bet!" Biyell suggested.

"Hold up nigga, how can you tell me who I should or shouldn't be with?"

"Because you're technically single and this challenge is for married niggas who fuckin' up, not whiny-ass dudes who throw perfectly good women away."

"*Whiny?*" Timothy stood. "*Whiny?*"

Jarvis came at him from the left. "At least you should be required to propose." He turned to me. "But if she doesn't accept his proposal, then he's out."

"What about Rasta?" Timothy asked me.

"Why you pulling me into this shit? I don't have anything to do with this conversation. I'm here to play *Madden*," Rasta shot back at Timothy.

"Because you're in between women; you're not with LaDeisha or Shameka, so I think we're in the same boat," Timothy said.

"That's hoe shit, Timothy, and you know it." Rasta was pissed.

"Call it what you want to, but the word on the street is LaDeisha don't fuck with you. Her status on Facebook was changed to *single*."

"Actually, what's going on is LaDeisha and I are working things out."

"Prove it" Timothy yelled. "Call her right now and put her on speaker phone. We should hear a conversation that sounds like she's working things out with you." Timothy put Rasta on the hot seat.

"What's going on with LaDeisha and me is really none of your business. You're the one that's divorced, and we've never met this Tootsie. She could imaginary or a Tootsie Roll for all we know. At least LaDeisha is a real woman—but let's Face-Time Tootsie." Rasta stood nose-to-nose with Timothy.

It never failed: Timothy's egg-shaped ass always started altercations with people twice his size. I swear he has this tall man mentality in a fat, midget-sized body.

"All right, guys. Let's cool it. Let's cool it. Cool it for a second," I interjected while Jarvis separated Timothy and Rasta.

Both guys made valid points. Neither Timothy nor Rasta was in a relationship, but both had submitted the name of the person they planned to be faithful to for the entire year. Timothy had committed to Tootsie, and Rasta had committed to LaDeisha, but neither relationship was qualified as monogamous. It was time to give both of these guys an ultimatum.

"Rasta, you raise a good point . . . as do you, Timothy. From the way I see it, your situations are parallel. Neither of you are in a solid one-on-one relationship. So, here's what I'm going to do. You guys have a month and a half to proof up that you're with the woman you claim to be with. In the meantime, the challenge is between Jarvis and Biyell.

"So we're out?" Rasta asked.

"I'm not saying you're out. You have forty-five days to proof up that you're in a real relationship. The official deadline will be the Madden Night closest to the forty-five-day mark. If you can't proof up by then, you're out."

"But proof up how, Uncle Glenn?" Timothy asked.

"Either with a marriage proposal, or you bring her here and introduce her to the group as your official woman. Either way, it's not fair to have a partial situation while Jarvis and Biyell are giving it their all."

"You're goddamn right." Biyell removed the bandage above his eyebrow to reveal a row of stitches that looked like a black caliper.

"*Damnnnnn*, she fucked you up!" I said.

"Dude, you sure that was a brick? Looks like she shot you in the face," Rasta laughed. "Boy, put a tampon in your eye and plug the hole."

"What I still don't understand is how you get hit in the face with a brick while you're sitting in a truck full of gas?" Jarvis asked. "You caught a cramp in your foot and couldn't press the gas? You thought she picked up a brick to kill a roach? That brick was for you, nigga."

"I told you, her cousin was standing in front of the truck."

"Dude, sounds like that shit was well rehearsed. I'm wondering how many niggas got their asses beat down on that street fuckin' around with GiGi. Yo' ass should be in church tonight," Timothy joked.

"You just made my point—this challenge has cost me thirteen stitches, temporary vision loss in my eye, and a busted window on my truck. So if you think you are going to pussyfoot around while I'm getting bricks thrown at my head, think again, *playboy!* The money goes to the men who prove they can cut the drama out of their lives. You're either all in or you're out like Telly."

Biyell's altercation in Baker last week was ugly. None of us could have imagined it would go south so quickly. Yet I'm proud of him. I didn't think he could do it, but he pulled it off.

"I had to do it because I didn't want to lose my Tamera, but since I confessed to Tyra that I was married—"

"Wait, who in the fuck is Tyra?" Jarvis looked puzzled as he powered up his laptop.

"GiGi's real name is Tyra. May I continue now?" Biyell clarified.

"Then nigga, call her by the name we gave her. We don't know a Tyra . . . fuck! For a minute I thought you had developed a case of *hoe-nesia* and lost count of a bitch." Jarvis roasted.

"Mannnn, fuck you. But anyway," Biyell was perturbed with Jarvis and shot him a look. "I need you guys to help me work through something."

"That's what we're here for," I said.

"Tyra, or shall I say GiGi—"

"Stick with GiGi! We don't know her as Tyra and you fucking me up by calling her Tyra," Jarvis complained.

"Run this by me again, why was she given the code name GiGi?" Timothy asked.

"Well, according to what I wrote, he said her pussy was so tight he couldn't get his dick in, so he started talking to his dick, saying *Get in there, Get in there, yeah, yeah, big girl, back it up!* And from that day forward, we've referred to her as GiGi." Jarvis appeared to be reading from his notes.

"Nigga, you wrote that down? Why?" Rasta asked.

"For a little something I'm working on," Jarvis answered.

"Can I please get back to what I was saying?" Biyell yelled.

"Yeah, go ahead, go ahead," the group said.

"Thank you, fuck!" Biyell blew out a deep sigh. "GiGi has gone on the attack! She's taking her anger out on Tamera. She's coming in next week to do evaluations at Tamera's location—but her location just had an evaluation last month. Tamera doesn't know it, but GiGi wanted to make sure I knew about it."

"Did she call?" I asked just to see if he'd spoken with GiGi since his breakup. "Biyell, it could've been just a threat to freak you out."

"GiGi is as serious as a heart attack; it's not threat. She copied me on her agenda for Monday; she will be there. Tamera's meeting is at four o'clock."

"Whoa, are you serious?" Timothy sounded concerned.

"Four o'clock is when a manager says to you, *let's take a walk outside*. Four o'clock is when they fire yo' ass. At least that's been my experience," Rasta said.

"If I give Tamera a heads-up, then that's another confession, and she will leave my ass."

"Which means you're out of the challenge," Timothy said.

That's when I figured out why Biyell was rattled. "You're forced to remain silent and watch Tamera walk into a trap set by your mistress."

"Uncle Glenn, I'm fucked!"

# CHAPTER 7

11:58 p.m.

## TYRA

I'm so happy Braylyn has decided to go to sleep—finally. Nights like this, she wears me out. I can't play with her at the pace that she played with her daddy; running up and down the hall, him tossing her gently into the air and letting her fall on a bed of pillows . . . he would get her so worked up that she fell asleep with no problem. Tonight, my baby is looking for her daddy. That is what pisses me off—that my child has to look for her daddy, but *Tamera Marie Baltimore's* child doesn't.

He's there with them, but soon my children will not be the only ones looking for their father. Believe dat.

Yes, I heard my mother loud and clear: *You cannot fuss and fight over someone else's husband*—but I didn't know he was someone else's husband. He lied to me. I'll be honest, I never asked him if he was married, but that sweaty nut-fucka should have told me. That information should have been offered up on day one; as a matter fact, he should've never approached me on day one. And I should have never given him the time of day.

But who am I kidding?

Physically, Biyell would get my ass again; you could go a month and not see a man like him. And that dick! That dick. That dick. That DICK! His dick is like getting two income tax returns; like a vacation with a weekend before and after, like that shampoo tech who scratches your scalp and makes your toes crack, like someone eating your pussy with four tongues. That dick got me—the curve, that meat, that *awwwww*.

He was everything I liked in a man; I liked his smile, his body, his manly aggressiveness. I should have known he was too good to be true. Women are competitive, and no woman is going to allow a man like that to walk around unattached. A man that fine with no woman is gay! There's no such thing as single and not fucking. You can fly a kite with that church bullshit; if he's as fine as Biyell and not fucking, then he's getting fucked by a dude. But I digress. I didn't ask him; I was horny that day he approached me, so, you know, I just went along for the ride . . . with a married man.

So here I am alone on a Thursday night, and knowing him, he's probably by Uncle Glenn's house. They're probably laughing at me, and how I fell for that lie. They're probably saying, *you could tell a bitch anything and she will believe it.* They're probably saying, *that bitch can take care of our own children, charge it to the game, hoe.* Well, I'm not a dumb bitch. I may have gotten caught slipping, but I'm not a dumb bitch.

Men never grow out of it—running game. The players will be with us always, but that Biyell picked the wrong one to fuck with. I copied him today, so he knows Tamera and I are going to have a little conversation come Monday. I'm about to do a little homework first; time to check out a few databases around the state. Time to see what Mrs. Tamera Marie Baltimore has been up to over the past seven years. Bitch, you better be so clean your breath smells like Ajax.

Hmmm.

Let's enter her Social Security number into the HUD database to see if she has applied for any form of Housing Assistance. Sometimes people are not one hundred percent truthful on their applications, and the only way to know for sure is to take a little peek at Mrs. Tamera Marie Baltimore. After all, I'm going to be her new supervisor, and I should at least know the quality of person I'll be working with, right? Exactly.

Well, look at that, *Ha! Ha! Bay-Bay.* Mrs. Baltimore applied for Section 8 Housing four years ago, and she listed her marital status as single on her application.

Hmmm.

So let's open another browser and log into Vital Records for the State of Louisiana. I need to know exactly when Tamera Tucker and Mr. Biyell Baltimore got married. *Well, suck my big toe, hoe!* They have been married over ten years. And yet when she filled out this application, her status was single. Hmmm.

If she forgot she was married on that application, let's see if Tamera forgot she was married on the food stamp application. *Shut the front door, hoe!* Mrs. Tamera Marie Baltimore likes being single on paper. No husband, none of his income listed . . . He makes $3,580 a month, I have one of his stubs, but she didn't mention his income. And they're still getting the food stamps; she just renewed last month.

Hmmm.

I think this is a good time to pull the Medicaid records on her child. I have a strong feeling she forgot to mention Biyell's income, and since I know how much he earns every week, let's see if the State of Louisiana Department of Health knows. *Tamera. Tamera. Tamera,* you are *a fool with it, girl.* Biyell's information is missing in the field assigned to father's information, and she has indicated that she's single again.

Wait a minute.

Her daughter, Bylisha Baltimore, was born two days after my daughter! That low-down motherfucker! He told me he had to leave the hospital because of an emergency on the job—a crew member fell off a building. That too was a lie. The emergency was Tamera went into labor.

Biyell, you fucked with the wrong one. You will pay. I'm going to punch your wife in the face and watch you cry. Tamera, since you like being single on paper, I'm about to make your dreams come true. Biyell's doggish ass will not wait until you get out of federal prison.

You're going to jail for fraud on Monday at four o'clock.

Bitch.

# CHAPTER 8

Monday, April 10, 2017
8:30 a.m.

## TELLY

I gazed out of the oversized windows at the joggers who raced against themselves as streetcars the color of candy apples centipeded in the morning sun. Our meeting place was a little diner on St. Charles Avenue called The Trolley Stop; one of my all-time favorites in New Orleans for breakfast. Surprisingly, I arrived on time, but Yolanda just notified me that she's a few blocks away. I'm still amazed at how the owners of The Trolley Stop converted a vintage gas station into a restaurant that serves hot pancakes around the clock; it has to be the greatest location in the city.

The server greeted me from the pick-up window as she clutched a handful of cloth-wrapped utensils. Her walk wasn't sexy or graceful, but more like that of a llama. She was equally as luminous, with pale skin that twinkled beneath excessive ink. Under closer examination, I'm willing to bet she's one of those retired gutter punks, with the fuck-the-world piercings in places where earrings were never intended to go. But she's cute.

Yeah, I'd fuck her.

Now that I think it about, I've never fucked a white girl.

I remember when Rasta was fucking Katie Couric—not the real Katie Couric, that was the code name for his neighbor's wife. She was the super-friendly type, the kind who couldn't hide their sexual attraction if their life depended on it. I swear I saw the bitch leap over Rasta's fence one time when she noticed us pulling into his driveway. Then she came in just relaxed and bold like a white peacock—even smoked a blunt with us. Me, on the other hand? I was nervous like a slave in the movie *Roots*— like *Massa betta not catch us and diz white womanz.*

Rasta, well, he felt the same way in the beginning, but once he got over the fear that the Klan was going to hang him by the dick on the levee, he said the sex with Katie was pretty fucking awesome.

I wonder if I would enjoy a white girl?

If I ever decide to date outside my race, then I want a lily white girl to be my first—not one who grew up in the hood and knows the lyrics to every trap song. No, no, no! When the day comes that I integrate my dick and gift my interracial virginity to someone special, I want the whitest Britney Spears-type bitch I can find. Cream of Wheat white—like my server.

Her name is Stacy.

From the resolve in her eyes, I can tell that she's just crossed the defining age of thirty and decided that it's time to give this grown-up thing a try. She placed a glass of water on the table and shot me a generic smile with eyes the color of a rich mocha latte. I returned the smile. Emerald tattoos splashed with maroon serpentined up her lanky arm from her knuckles to the thin skin on her neck. I wonder if she has tattoos on her ass cheeks.

No wedding ring?

If not for this breakfast with Yolanda, I would make a bid for her soul. That's the difference between a man like Biyell and a female connoisseur like myself. For Biyell, a female's body is sufficient enough, but not for me. I have to consume a woman and flood her neuroreceptors, to and strip her of the ability to feel pleasure without me; that blurred area where she becomes conjoined to my every need and desire. I'm in it for her soul.

If I had an opening, I would ask Stacy out, but my roster is full with Yolanda and Erica.

She's probably tired anyway; tired of intrigued assholes like myself, settled men who pivot for her attention because they've never fucked one like her. Even though Stacy has gone out of her way to look unattractive in the traditional sense, she's failed miserably. I see clean through her artistic mutilation, her wall of abstract nonsense, her deliberate deflections.

Oh, my God.

*She's still innocent.*

Unlike many of the women I've met in the halls of the courts—the ones appalled by the epiphany of forty and single, but present with affectionate abandon—Stacy, this gothic little princess, has never been gutted to the studs. Not fully, at least, because the mystery man left her soul intact—she has more love to give, I can see it in her eyes. *Stacy, you're lucky I'm meeting my girl this morning; you get to hold onto your soul a little while longer.*

I ordered two coffees while I waited for Yolanda. I am a little agitated this morning because of an argument with Erica; it was our first major fight over something that no couple should fight over—*giving up my apartment.* And yes, I agreed to move in, but I wasn't counting on her pressuring me to do it at this very minute. Erica feels like I'm holding onto my apartment because I don't have confidence in our relationship. As in, I'm retaining it as an escape clause. That's not the case, but I am comfortable where I have lived for the past five years, and unfortunately, my studio is way too small for her and the girls.

The other part of it is Yolanda.

She has a key to my place—I gave her one as a symbol of my commitment—but Erica has never seen my apartment. I love getting those calls from Yolanda at the end of her day when she says, *I'm about to grab some takeout . . . and find a good movie on Netflix.* Minutes later, she walks through the door with a bag from Café Dauphine filled to the top with everything from fried catfish platters to crawfish stew. If I cave to the pressure to move in with Erica, that will mark the end of my relationship with Yolanda, and I'm not ready to make drastic changes in my comfortable life.

But Yolanda is ready to get married.

I will not be able to dodge her that much longer. I can't marry a woman who makes more money than I do. Relationships with massive income deficits always crash and burn, leaving the man shattered and nut-less.

I like my nuts.

That's why I avoided that challenge from Glenn, and Lord knows I need the money, but I'm trapped by my circumstances. I can't get my finances together. It'll take me another three years to come close to Yolanda's pay grade, but I'm grateful for Erica—she always repairs my damaged ego. *What if I landed a big contract that paid me a third more than Yolanda makes, would I marry her?* That's a great question. Do you want the ugly truth or a pretty lie?

The ugly truth is I would marry Yolanda and keep Erica as my well-kept mistress. She would have to quit me, because I can't quit her. Erica would like to continue our heated discussion at lunch today, so after this breakfast, I'm off to court, then after court, it's round two of the fight from this morning. My eyes were barely open when she sucker-punched me:

"If you feel the way you say you do, then what's the hold up?"

"Erica, there is no hold up. I'm trying to mentally prepare for it, that's all."

"Telly, I have opened my entire world to you, and you're the only man who has ever met my children except for their father.

Am I missing something here?"

"Erica, you have gone far and beyond to prove your commitment to our relationship—"

"But have you?" Her words rained down on me as she paced alongside the bed. "I don't see a matched effort; a deeper commitment, an emotional investment from you. It feels like I'm the only one trying and you're cool with being some guy I'm dating—a boyfriend. Yesterday made two years. *WHAT ARE WE DOING HERE?*"

There was that question again; the same one Yolanda asked me just over a month ago, and I still don't have an answer because I don't know. As it relates to me, I know what I'm doing: I'm enjoying two very beautiful women, more than my fair share. I am holding onto Yolanda and Erica as long as I can, because I love them the same and in some sick kind of way, they're sister wives who have not been formally introduced yet.

There have been times when I was making to Yolanda and I wished Erica was in bed with us, or I pictured the two of them under my comforter locked in a passionate kiss. That's the ugly truth—my happiness up to this point has been contingent on maintaining an intimate relationship with both Yolanda and Erica.

And one of them just arrived.

From across the restaurant, I watched her at the hostess table, and every man in the room did the same. She wore a gray mini-skirt suit with a single-button blazer and a black crewneck blouse that featured a lace trim across her cleavage. Yolanda is the kind of fine that you can tell from her front view that the booty is thick.

The booty's thick.

The legs are thick.

The thick breast fits perfectly in my large hands.

I have never scored a touchdown in a Super Bowl, but watching all the men's eyes follow her to my table is the equivalent. Trailing Yolanda is Stacy with our coffee. The procession was done in perfect timing, Yolanda's eyes smiled at me.

Next to my table is a frail man with a brown rice beard; he never looked in my direction the entire morning until Yolanda approached my table. I felt his imposing eyes like flies at a picnic. I moved around the table to pull her chair back; she kissed me. With her thumb, she removed a trace of lipstick from my lips. I angled my chair to block the line of sight of Mr. Rice with the single cup of coffee and no woman.

"You look scrumptious this morning; I am blessed."

"Why, thank you, Mr. Ned."

"I only ordered coffee because I can't predict your early morning appetite."

"With the full run of things I have on my list today, I'm going light. Just coffee."

"Just coffee?"

"Only coffee for breakfast?" I was bracing for her to swallow fifty dollars worth of pancakes. "Are you sure, because I'm not sharing my food with you this morning."

She giggled. "I'm sure."

"On that note, I'll order one pancake for you and three for me. Just in case."

When the waitress returned, I placed our order, then looked up and felt an unusual pressure from Yolanda's eyes. She never blinked. *A weighted gaze.* For a minute I thought she was on the verge of a seizure. Then her head dipped into her chest for about ten seconds, and when our eyes reconnected, I saw sadness.

"What's on your mind this morning? You have that look." She didn't reply.

"Earth calling Yolanda, come in Yolanda." Another passing streetcar caught her attention.

"I don't know about red for a streetcar on St. Charles Avenue. I'm more of a New Orleans traditionalist, and I like my street-cars grass-green." Her voice was as sad as her eyes.

"This sudden shift in your mood, I know it wasn't brought on by the changing of the streetcars from red to green. Talk to me, baby, what's bothering you?"

"I may as well get on with it . . ."

"With what?" I asked.

Just as Yolanda was about to share what was on her mind, Stacy returned with our food. In front of us were some of the best pancakes in New Orleans. Those pancakes, stacked next to eggs fluffy like cotton and a fried link of smoked sausage shot-putted me back to grandmother's house on a Sunday morning.

"I have met someone else."

Those words felt like Mr. Rice's beard behind me had dislodged one of the table legs and whacked me across the back of my head. It was like she was speaking in a foreign tongue, like I needed Rosetta Stone to translate. In my entire career of dating and whoring, I have never heard those words before—not spoken directly to me, not in my face, not ever.

The room whirled.

My head started to whirl.

My entire life started to whirl.

*Did she just say what I think she said? Has she met someone?*

"A man?"

"Yes, a man. He's someone from my firm."

"So you met a man romantically? I'm just trying to make sure I follow you."

"Yes, romantically . . . but not at first."

"But it has gotten to the point where you feel you needed to tell me."

"Yes."

"Is it someone I know?"

"No, we went to Harvard Law together."

"So this started at Harvard and continued all of this time?"

"No Telly, he never gave me the time of day at Harvard, but, but we recently took on some projects together—"

"Projects together? You and I have a project together with the police union—where do you find the time?"

"I know, but when the opportunity was presented to possibly

argue a case before the Supreme Court, I couldn't pass it up . . ."

"So you outsourced the police work to me. Was that the call you took when we had lunch at Neil's a few weeks back?"

"Yes, that's when he made the offer. Look Telly, I have not had sex with him or anything, but he is interested in marriage, and in building a life together . . . a firm with two Harvard lawyers."

I fell back in my chair and looked for one of those red streetcars, but there were none in sight. Nothing to see but a guy walking his dog, a beautiful morning, and table full of cold pancakes.

"Telly, I asked you repeatedly if you were sure I was the woman you wanted. You jerked me around; played with me like your PlayStation. The country has changed a president since our first date, and here we are—*still boyfriend and girlfriend.*"

"Yolanda, I gave my all to you, I was faithful! And you dump me? You invited me to our favorite breakfast spot . . . for this?"

With her arms folded symmetrically on the white tablecloth, she leaned in. "I thought it was appropriate to end our journey where we started. No harm no foul. A place where we could agree to continue our friendship . . . at least."

"What you really mean is, a place where you could continue to outsource work from the police union while you and *Mr. Harvard Man* fly away to Washington. Fuck that, Yolanda."

"See, I didn't want this conversation to go there, but you took it there. You may not like how it feels, but I did the right thing by not cheating on you. The right thing to do was to sit you down and tell you I no longer want to be your girlfriend. Look at me." Yolanda leaned across the table and tightened her lips.

"I am a grown-ass woman . . . with the needs of a grown-ass woman. Telly, do you know what those needs are? If you think it's dick, then a girlfriend is all you deserve. I don't need dick. I need security, my own man, someone who can lead me and teach me a few things. Instead of being angry, you should thank me."

"Thank you? Thank you?! Are you fuckin serious? Because

you found another guy behind my back . . . I should thank you?"

"Telly, I didn't find shit behind your back. I am an unrestricted free agent. This is my life and my time you've wasted. You should thank me because I held enough respect for your feelings to tell you face-to-face, but make no mistake about it, Cyrus Cochran was going to take me from you one way or the other. Do you know why? Huh? Do you know? Because he knows what he wants, he can make up his mind, and he has a fucking plan! What's your plan, Telly? Do you have one? Let's hear it." Her hand cuffed the back of her ear.

"You have no plan! Just smoking weed and video games. Games are for girlfriends. Women get married. Check, please." The eyes that had followed Yolanda to my table watched me fumble the game-winning ball.

Yolanda pointed to a window that faced the side street. "Do you see that black GL550? That's Cyrus; he's waiting for me like a limo driver . . . the way I waited for you. Enjoy your breakfast." Impatient with the waitress, Yolanda reached into her purse, flicked a hundred-dollar bill on the table, and bolted for the door.

About halfway to the hostess station, she turned back to me.

"And by the way, tell *Erica* I said hello, and good luck with your broke ass."

With that, Yolanda ran out of my life and into the arms of Cyrus Cochran.

A busboy spoke through a tight fist as if he held a microphone. "Did sister-girl just dump dude like that? Damn, she's gangster!"

The bus boy continued to roast me, which caused every guest in the restaurant to bend sideways in laughter, including the old dude behind my table. I'm sure he heard every word of our conversation; in fact, his smirk confirmed it.

"That's a lot of losing in one morning." Mr. Rice Beard said. "Pass those pancakes."

# CHAPTER 9

Monday, April 10, 2017
3:55 p.m.

## TYRA

Only one more meeting, and then I can get to the real reason for my visit to the New Orleans district office—the bitch who sent her husband to my house. The bitch who robbed me of my happiness. I stood in the middle of the street and watched my man—who I thought was my man, her husband—drive off into the night. I'm here for Tamera Baltimore. That bitch has it coming.

*Hoe.*

But first I have to wrap up this meeting with Motormouth Marla, who feels her six measly years on the job are worthy enough for a state level promotion. For the last thirty minutes, she has yapped away without taking a breath. What Marla lacks in size (she stands no higher than this computer monitor) she overcompensates for with her mouth.

"Overall, Marla, I'm very happy with your job performance

and the number of cases you're processing in our crisis queue. I have ranked you in the top tier in the state."

"Thank you so much, Dr. Thibodeaux, for recognizing me."

"Let's have a meeting again in ninety days, and I will have a more thought-out career path for you." Deep down I'm thinking, *the way you talk everybody's* business, *I wouldn't be surprised if they tossed your mousey ass out of this fifth-floor window.*

"Dr. Thibodeaux, you have no idea how happy it makes me to know that you're mapping out my long-term opportunities with Social Services. I pride myself in being a team player and I always make the goals of the department my number one priority. Because these children need us, and I know that God called me to work here, it's more than just a job—this is my ministry. And I have risen so fast from first tier social worker to department case manager, and I have been able to improve the quality of life for so many kids that it blows my mind to think of what I could accomplish at the state level under you. I'm so appreciative of you . . . did I ever tell you how much you inspire me? You, Dr. Thibodeaux, are like the only person with a doctorate in social work I have ever met . . ." Like I said, Marla could talk Jesus to sleep on a sunny day, but that's Marla.

"Marla, I appreciate all you're doing for this department. Let's talk more in July, okay?" Her lips are always moist from overactive saliva glands, and her braces only add to the electricity in her mouth, but I like Marla. "On your way back to your station, could you send in Mrs. Baltimore, please? She's my last one for the day."

"I sure will, Dr. Thibodeaux, and in case I don't see you again before you leave, have a safe trip back to Baton Rouge," Marla said as she skipped down the center aisle toward Tamera's cubicle.

With Motormouth Marla finally out of my office, I reached down into my briefcase and retrieved the red dossier I had prepared over the weekend for my last evaluation of the day. Of course you know I plan to fire that bitch, but not before I break her down, make her roll around on the floor, and beg for her job. I know it's not fair, but point out one thing that happened to me that was fair. Point out one thing!

It is what it is, and that's life.

I live, I learn, and I never fall for the same shit twice.

Because of Biyell, I have to rethink my entire life plan—a plan that I created once I became involved with him and became pregnant. On some days I look at Braylyn and cry. Because I didn't do my due diligence on Biyell, she's caught in this hell-hole called single parenting.

I promised myself in my teens that I would never have a baby without a husband first, but here I am. After avoiding fake love my entire adult life, I'm pregnant plus one. The other reason I look at my baby and cry is because I owe her an apology. When I discovered I was pregnant, my first thought was to send the code to my girlfriend—a Bat-Bitch signal shining on dark clouds, a SMS of despair. The code is a text comprised of four digits; a pin code of regret. Only one person on Earth knows the significance and the urgency. If she receives the code, her reply is immediate.

*When?*

*Monday.*

*Time?*

*10 a.m.*

*Consider it booked. I'll be there for you.*

That's all the info needed, and that's the way it's always been between us—me and my best friend who's closer than a sister. She was the one who created the code because she was the one to get pregnant first. He was married, and she didn't know until his wife knocked on her door. I was her ride home from the abortion clinic. One year later, on the same day in June, the twenty-seventh of the month, she was my ride home.

Code 0627

A true story.

I thank God that was my one and only time having to send the code. Unfortunately for my best friend, there were two other occasions for her. Before one of these occasions, her boyfriend was a young up-and-coming pastor, and after two years of dating, he proposed. I was so happy for my BFF—the rock on her finger could not outshine the sparkle in her smile, all day, every day. One day we arrived at his house and she used her key. We made our way to the kitchen and started to prepare a romantic dinner for him, a little something special to announce that she was pregnant.

There we were in the kitchen, all giddy like little twelfth-graders when I heard it. Then she heard it, then we cautiously approached the guest bedroom. Then we saw it. In that instant, we discovered the meaning of the term *beard*. It became clear that my best friend Brittany was the young pastor's cover for a down-low lifestyle. We were too shocked to speak. A man who I recognized as a pastor of another local church was deep between her fiance's legs making raw, passionate love to him—the way a man makes love to his woman. In my life I've never been fucked like that or kissed like that during sex. That was the last view my friend had of her man—getting fucked missionary style by another man.

Brittany, this beautiful young woman with so much hope of happily ever after, never recovered from that scene and opted out of men completely.

After the code and the vomiting and the guilt, we never discussed any of the residual feelings from that experience, nor did we notify the potential baby daddy that we decided to use the code. In each case, however, the relationships ended officially the day the code was sent.

I never judged Brittany, and she never judged me. I'm not justifying our code in any way, but we made executive decisions to protect our careers and each other. A year later, I received my Doctorate in Social Work from Tulane, and my best friend received her doctorate six months later. When I became pregnant with Braylyn, I agonized for a full day. I wanted to send the code, but I couldn't bear to haul another sack of self-reproach. I couldn't do it, and for the first time, I wanted the baby. I wanted Braylyn, and I want the baby I'm carrying.

My daughter, with her silly little self, has brought so much joy to my life that I couldn't imagine life without her. If only she didn't look just like her father, but after all, he is her father. She has his smile, his broad shoulders, and his big hands, and they have the same birthmark on their necks. The only difference is Braylyn's is the size of a dime and Biyell's is the size of a quarter. I still can't believe Biyell played me like this. I can't fucking believe it. The motherfucker was at every prenatal checkup, at every Lamaze class . . . he was the one who drove me to the hospital when my water broke. When my daughter was delivered after fourteen hours of labor, Dr. Barabino handed Braylyn to Biyell first, but gave him some stern words before he placed her in his arms.

"I'm handing this baby to you because you are responsible for her first and foremost. It is your responsibility to make sure she has shelter, food, safety, and the best education money can buy. Do you understand?"

"Yes. Yes, sir." Biyell was scared like a deer at a gun convention.

"Before I hand you this precious little girl, I demand a promise that regardless of your relationship with her mother, you will never abandon this baby. You will never walk out of her life, and you will always put your personal feelings aside to support the mother of your child."

"I promise, sir."

"Despite and regardless, you are committed to this baby for life."

"Yes, sir—"

Dr. Barabino cut him off. "Repeat my words: *Despite and regardless, you are committed to this baby for life.*"

"Despite and regardless, I am committed to my baby for life."

"Congratulations on the successful delivery of a healthy little girl."

I watched the entire interaction; it was so precious it moved me to tears. Doctor Frank Barabino was a seasoned OB-GYN who delivered my entire family. He retired after Braylyn was handed off to Biyell. Biyell did everything in his power to make Braylyn's first day special. Then he drove us home from the hospital as one happy family. How in the fuck did he do all of that with an identical family eighty miles away?

Since that day, I have to give Biyell credit for one thing: though he wasn't faithful to me, he never broke a date with my baby. But he still ain't shit, because he gets to ride off to the next town and slay the next unsuspecting woman who has a glimmer of hope that true love is real and all of the bullshit we absorb as women is an anomaly.

Suddenly, there was a soft tap on my door. I invited the person in. It was Tamera.

There was a cordial handshake between us, and then a gesture from me welcoming her to have a seat. Strategically, I positioned her between two pictures of Braylyn that I placed on the desk. The pictures immediately caught her attention. The one thing that was crystal clear to me within the first ten seconds of meeting Tamera was that her husband had a type of woman he loved. I was his type, and Tamera was his type.

We have the same bronze skin, we're the same size—about a fourteen—and we have the same hips. I have on a black and white, plaid, ruffled skirt (with a paper bag waist draped on the sides) with a black blouse and black heels. The entire outfit was purchased from Eloquii.

*Thhhhis bitch* has on the exact same outfit, except with red heels. I have to give credit where it's due—her shoes are fire! But anyway, she's wearing my dress and the resemblance is freaking us both out. We could be sisters.

"Mrs. Tamera Baltimore, this is our first time meeting,

but definitely not our last. I am Dr. Tyra Thibodeaux from the State Office of Supervisors over Social Services, and my visit here today is a part of our random compliance and case load evaluations. It's nice to meet you."

*She looks nervous, as she should be.*

"Nice to meet you too, Dr. Thibodeaux, and I love your dress."

"Same here, love the red shoes, by the way." *This bitch* has the same color foundation, the same lip gloss, and the same bone-straight hairstyle. I wear this hairstyle because Biyell loves it. It's painfully obvious that he's been controlling us through preference. He's morphed us into the same woman in different locations.

"Mrs. Baltimore, I understand you have been with our department nearly forty-five days?"

"Yes, that's correct."

"Are you aware of our integrity policy relating to forms and applications?"

"Yes. Yes, Dr. Thibodeaux."

"And did you know the state takes it very seriously when employees, at one time or another, have been less than truthful when applying for social services?"

Tamera doesn't know it, but I always have a state trooper on standby in case we need to walk someone out in handcuffs.

"Umm, umm, yes, Dr. Thibodeaux."

She's scared. I can hear the pattering of her heel as it connects with the floor. The taps come in quick succession like Gregory Hines. She's folded her hands in her lap, one over the top of the other. She had a slight tremble in her jaw. I should call Jake Barrett at TV 6 NEWS and see if he's interested in this scoop. I can see the headline now: *State Employee Tamera Marie Baltimore Arrested for Section 8 and Medicaid Fraud.*

"Mrs. Baltimore, is there anything you would like to share with me?"

"Umm, umm, not that I can think of at the moment."

"I'll give you some time to reflect." I pretended to scroll

through my phone in search of a police officer to respond. "Officer Rayne . . . no, Officer Vincent? Officer Moore . . . no. Do I know any state troopers who work this area?" I murmured.

"Am . . . I in some sort of trouble . . . Dr. Thibodeaux?" Tamera's eyes watered.

"That all depends on you and how you answer my questions."

"Dr. Thibodeaux, could you excuse me just for a second? I need to text my husband to have him pick up our baby from daycare."

I think she knows her ass is going to jail.

"Not a problem," I replied in a cold, raspy voice.

And now I have her right where I wanted her—scared to fucking death and calling Biyell. He knows I'm here, and he knows what's about to go down. It's time to text State Trooper Vincent and let him know I may have a felony arrest for him in about thirty minutes. Trooper Vincent has a crush on me. When I call him to walk out one of our employees, he normally arrives with sirens blaring and fifteen cops. Biyell will learn a valuable lesson today. The next woman he plans to fuck over, he had better choose her carefully.

When Tamera returned, her eyes were like two peppermints. Her nose was swollen, and her hands scrubbed and rotated inside each other. Suddenly, Officer Vincent responded to my text. I replied back to him with a speech-to-text message.

"Stand by, Trooper Vincent, I may need your assistance."

"Roger that, Dr. Thib."

It was then that I watched Tamera's neck give out. Her head slumped forward and came to rest in her palms. Around her wrist, supported by a yellow elastic coil, was her keychain. On that keychain was a locket. On the outside of the locket was a picture of her daughter, Bylisha. My heart sank. Heat seeped out of my body.

Our daughters were twins delivered by different mothers. On my desk was Tamera's resume. I glanced at it, and noticed that she just recently graduated over the summer from an online university. Before that, she had worked at the airport for TSA for ten years. Before TSA, she worked for Walmart, and prior to Walmart, she worked for Popeye's.

"Dr. Thibodeaux, I don't know what's going on, but I would like to make a statement. I have always wanted to be a social worker because I was a foster kid. No one adopted us once we hit the system, and my siblings and I were separated and forgotten. I became a social worker because I know how it feels to be the kids you have assigned to me, and if I were financially secure, I would work here for free. I love my job. About a year ago, my husband started bringing home less money on each paycheck, and things got really hard. His checks were always short $800 to $1,200, and with child care, it was hard. I'm not sure what this meeting is about, but—"

"Tamera, what is your extension at your desk? I have a trooper in the lobby I need to speak with for a minute, and I will buzz you back when I'm done."

"My extension is 0627."

*No fucking way.* "Great, give me a few minutes."

I watched her mosey back to her desk with five hundred pounds on her shoulders. That's when the tears fell. Not Tamera's tears, but my tears.

*I can't do this. I will not do this. Lord, please forgive me. Please take away this anger in my heart, Lord. I can't destroy her for something her husband did to me. That $1,200 she mentioned was the amount Biyell gave me on monthly basis. Tamera started on drive thru at Popeye's, worked night shifts at the airport, and still found a way to graduate from college. I will not destroy her.*

I need to dry my eyes and buzz her back.

I dialed extension 0627. "Tamera, I'm ready to resume."

"I'll be right down, Dr. Thibodeaux."

That four-digit extension. When I need someone who isn't going to judge me, I press the same four digits. I used that same numerical combination when I needed another woman to lift me out of the gutter of guilt in the painful days after my visit to the clinic. Whenever I enter that code on my phone, my girlfriend Brittany always arrives with open arms.

Tamera timidly entered the office and returned to the same seat. It was time to have a woman-to-woman—or better yet, a *sister-to-sister* talk.

"Tamera, I came here today to crush your entire world, and I think you know where this was going."

"Yes, Dr. Thibodeaux."

"Just call me Tyra."

She agreed with a nod.

It was time to reintroduce myself the best way I knew I could without being malicious. So, I handed her one of the pictures of my daughter. "This is my daughter Braylyn; her sister is your daughter."

Tamera's hand covered her mouth. Her eyes swiveled back and forth, from the pictures of our daughters back to my watery eyes. She brought the picture closer to her face.

"Oh my God! I knew it when I sat down. At first glance, I thought it was a picture of my child. There's something I think you can clarify for me." With her other hand, Tamera scrolled through her phone in search of something. Soon, she found it.

"Did you receive this picture?"

I looked down. It was a picture of Biyell's dick, taken in a bathroom. I scrolled through my messages going back two months and found the same picture. We held his dick in our hands—the same dick. There was nothing more that needed to be explained. Tamera extended her hand to shake; we hugged with our hands.

"Hi Tyra, I have wanted to meet you for nearly four years."

"Hi Tamera, your husband just confessed the other day after four years that he was married, but Biyell didn't have a choice, because I forced the truth out of him. Actually, it was my mother's plan—to tell Biyell I was transferring to New Orleans and watch his reaction. She said, *Tyra, a hit dog will holler every time.* She was right—Biyell panicked. That's when I knew you were out there somewhere."

"So you gave him that third eyebrow? That suspicious injury he claimed happened at work?"

I raised my right hand. "Guilty as charged! I tried to decapitate his ass with that brick." Tamera asked for a high five; our hands met high above my desk.

"Tamera, there's something else." Her eyes stretched to full capacity. "I'm pregnant with my second child for your husband."

I watched her chin fall into her chest. How I hated to push her into the endless depth of her husband's deceit, but if I were in her position—and I am—I would want to know. But I couldn't help but wonder what she felt in that moment—*is her experience somehow different because she's his wife?* I know our experience must be similar; I had what she had, minus the title of wife. When all the lies come crashing down, does the sense of knowing pacify the sting of infidelity? I sighed. *There's no victory for me here.* Only my mother gained a sense of triumph from our saga; her relentless belittling was fulfilled because I gave my all to the wrong man. Why am I sitting here as if what Tamera is feeling is any differently from how I felt as I drove here? We're both victims of that selfish-ass bigamist.

Slowly, her head started to nod, as if all the pieces were falling in line and Biyell's warm quilt, which had covered every one of his falsehoods, was snatched away. The truth is often naked and cold.

"Like I said, I didn't know you were married, and he has left me with two kids to raise without their biological father as my husband. Biyell was married when he approached me four years ago, and if I would have known, you and I would have met on a sunnier day."

"You are carrying his child as we speak?"

"Yes." I stood so she could see my belly. "Over seven months.

I'm due at the beginning of June."

"It's so over when I get home!" Tamera spoke to the ceiling. "It's so over. Biyell told so many lies. Everything was a lie."

"Yes, so many lies I've lost count," I confirmed. "He lied about things that were not worth the lie."

"It's how he props himself up," Tamera nodded. "His lies supplement his deficiencies—then he starts to believe his lies, then he forgets he told a lie. I've watched him lie to other people, then we would laugh about it later—about how the person fell for it—but all the while he was probably laughing at me as he drove to your house in Baker. I believed it all. Until recently. I know this is going to sound crazy, and I don't mean to come off as deeply spiritual and all, but I felt it. I mean, I felt you in my spirit, I felt the moment you entered his heart. But I'm not angry with you—not at all. My husband is not the man I thought he was."

I actually witnessed the time frame she released him; it happened in a deep sigh.

"So what are you doing after work? He has harassed me for a threesome for three years." Tamera's humor was like the sun that shone during a thunderstorm.

"Gurrrl, you too?" I folded my arms and slowly reclined.

"Yes, I say we give him a threesome he will never forget. In my living room."

"Tamera, that is a wonderful idea. Like Shalimar, *let's make it a night to remember*."

# CHAPTER 10

Monday, April 10, 2017
6:30 p.m.

## BIYELL

I arrived home before Tamera. She's working late tonight, which I take as a good sign considering the text I received from GiGi—the text about their meeting. Hopefully, I dodged a bullet. Uncle Glenn and nosey-ass Jarvis have drained the battery on my phone trying to get an update, trying to make sure GiGi hasn't busted open my other eye, but I don't know if they've met or not. The one thing I know for sure is if GiGi and my wife had their meeting, then one of them would have cussed my ass out by now.

No new is good news.

I entered my house carrying a plastic bag containing fresh seafood, along with a diaper bag on one shoulder and a very hyper Bylisha on the other. It was like the daycare fed my child cotton candy all day then sent her home with me—this little girl is wired. Kicking and turning and yelling for no reason at all. Off the fucking chain.

"*Wannnnnnne! Wannnnnnnne!* Juuuice. Juuuice. Mommy."

"Mommy is on her way." I tossed the diaper bag on the sofa.

"Juuuuuicee."

"Bylisha, chill.

"*Juuuice. Mommy.*"

"Bylisha, come on now. Please be a good girl for Daddy. You don't cut up like this for Mommy." That wasn't true.

I'm convinced that somewhere on her body, hidden under her back, are six fat Duracell batteries, fully charged. Once inside, I filled her sippy cup with juice. Then, I reached for the remote, clicked on the DVR, and scrolled to Elmo.

Bylisha smiled. "Juuuice."

She thanked me with a few poorly executed claps as I sat her in front of the television. Thank the Lord she's quiet. Next, I shot Tamera a text.

*Hope you had a great day. We made it home, and I'm preparing dinner.*

*You just made me moist*, she replied, followed by a pucker-lipped emoji and a purple eggplant.

In the kitchen, I grabbed a large bowl, filled it with water, then baptized the large catfish fillets. My momma said, *Always wash your food and mustard greens and stop eating from everybody because folk is nasty.*

Our dinner tonight is lemon-baked catfish with creamy crawfish pasta and oven-hot buttered rolls, and for dessert we have banana ice cream topped with hot caramel. It's a meal I normally cook for Tamera on a special occasion like Mother's Day or her birthday, but this week marks a new beginning, which makes this a special occasion. I've given up my double life and for the first time in a long time, I'm faithful. But I miss the fuck out of GiGi already.

I preheated my oven to 350 degrees and laid out my fillets on a deep baking pan. Once each fillet was perfectly spaced, it was time to apply my seasoning mix. In the microwave was a sauce bowl that contained a chip of butter along with garlic, parsley, and diced green onions. I poured the blend across the catfish. Just in time, the oven notified me that the temperature inside was a go. In went the fish. Now on to the crawfish pasta.

That's when my inner thoughts appeared on each of my shoulders in the form of two guys; one I call Pimp B, the other is a miniature Uncle Glenn.

**Pimp B:** That creamy sauce in the pasta—don't it remind you of somebody?

**Me:** It does sort of look like GiGi when I used to hit it from—

**Lil Glenn:** Focus on Tamera. Focus on her creamy pasta. Stir your wife, and she'll give you the creamy pasta, too.

**Pimp B:** Check out those dinner rolls. Those rolls are fluffed up just like GiGi's ass. Like that time she stripped naked in front the television during the season finale of *Game of Thrones* . . . You remember that?

**Me:** Oh yes, I remember that . . . she made the booty clap for me.

**Pimp B:** Exactly! We've been married to Tamera for how long?

**Me**: Going on eleven years.

**Pimp B**: Has she twerked one ass cheek for you? Has she shaken anything for you? A tittie? An earring? Anything?

**Lil Glenn:** Every woman comes with her own unique way of showing affection, and sometimes it's just an issue of communication. Have you ever expressed to Tamera the things that turn you on?

**Me:** No, I haven't.

**Lil Glenn:** She's your wife, not a psychic friend. Tamera has the same freaky thoughts, but you have yet to make her feel comfortable expressing that side of her personality. She's afraid you might think less of her, so she's waiting for you to merge the marriage into those lanes.

**Pimp B:** Shut the fuck up, Lil Glenn! If she's not hoeing out for her husband, then who in the hell is she saving the good shit for? That's why you get married, to hoe out with your husband. He shouldn't have to ask for lap dance. Now like I was saying before that pussy-ass nigga interrupted me, GiGi has a pussy that never quits. It don't stop; the harder you pound her, the wetter she gets. Let her go? And let another dude eat all that delicious pussy? You better click the block button on Lil Glenn.

**Lil Glenn:** And your wife has an ass just like that—it's the same ass. When will you see that you've been chasing the same thing? Beating your dick to every porn video online, even the videos of a woman fucking a dog?

**Me:** Hold the fuck up! Don't bring up the woman and the dog, I was curious, okay? That's all that was. Curiosity.

**Lil Glenn:** That's your story, huh? Are you sticking with that?

**Me:** Yeah, I nutted to it—a few times—but in my defense, I was horny that night. And if you think back, the dog videos phase was that week that Tamera and GiGi's periods synced up. I get a pass on the dog videos, okay?

**Lil Glenn:** Hey, I'm not here to judge you. If you're into that kind of thing, then it is what it is. The point I want you to realize is you're chasing this super-nut from a galaxy called Nutstovia, and all the while, you have a woman alongside you who would love to go on a fantastic voyage. Invite your wife to that land *far, far* away. Take your wife to Nutstovia.

It feels like I'm losing my mind. I can't control my thoughts. *Awwwwww.*

Who am I kidding?

I miss the fuck out of GiGi.

I should ask her to dinner. I should have a good relationship with GiGi. After all, she is the mother of my child, and she's pregnant again. I can't go a year without interacting with her. But the only way I can interact with her is through a mediator. I get why Uncle Glenn forced that requirement, because it's easy to fall back into the same lifestyle, but my circumstances are different from Jarvis, Rasta, and Timothy's. I need to hear her voice. Even if she's pissed off. I need to hear all of it, even if every other sentence starts with *fuck you*. Negative attention is still attention when you're possessive. She's mine.

My phone just alerted me of a text. Maybe it's GiGi?

*I'll be home in five minutes. Love you.* It's from Tamera.

*I love you too.*

Sure I fucked around on my wife, but it wasn't because I didn't love her. I was bored out of my fuckin' mind. I'm bored right now. GiGi was the best thing that happened to my marriage. Being with Tamera is like being married to a corrections officer. If she isn't shaking down my cell in search of contra-bitches, she's telling me what to do and when to do it. GiGi posted my bail and freed me from Tamera State Penitentiary.

But I can only ever do GiGi for two days before she works my last fucking nerve with her facetious attitude and innuendos. That's when I start to miss the stability of Tamera. It's fucking madness. Absolute madness. My mind associates Tamera with home, my dick associates GiGi with pleasure.

I want what I want when I want it.

Then there are the women I encounter during the work day. My pre-pussy before I get to GiGi. My confirmation that my dick is still Good Dick. My diagnostic pussy. That check engine light pussy. That zero-to-sixty in twenty seconds pussy. That's why every once in a while, I'll dick down a seventy-year-old widow. That's my Social Security pussy. Hear me out, hear me out—I know I'm fucked up, but I've kept my street life far away from my home life, and I keep the Magnums in my cable truck. At no point during this marriage has another woman knocked on this door for me, nor has one ever called Tamera's phone.

Not one time. I deserve some credit for that, right? I was able to take care of my household and still support GiGi, which is more than most deadbeats can say.

I plan to win this bet with Uncle Glenn and win back GiGi

on the same day. I'll shower her with diamonds and clothes. If I consider her pussy *my pussy*, then I take care of her. I own GiGi, and I'm not letting her go. Not like this, not ever. We're simply in *time out* mode, that's all. I think I hear Tamera's car pulling into the driveway.

I check my crawfish pasta.

I remove my dinner rolls.

I check my fish.

From the living room, I hear my daughter starting to whine again, so I run out to her with a cup of Cheetos Puffs, and that does the trick. Tamera entered the house to fine a happy little girl and a husband in the kitchen cooking her favorite meal.

"Is that hot dinner rolls I smell?"

"Yes it is, baby . . . welcome home."

She closed the door behind her, slung the purse, and lifted the child. Together they approached me in the kitchen, and it was then that I saw what Lil Glenn was trying to convey. The scene nearly moved me to tears. *This is that feeling he Uncle Glenn described; he feeling he gets when Lady Diana walks through the door.* This is that stress-free feeling that comes from doing the right thing.

"My favorite meal?" Tamera looked pleasantly surprised, yet confused. "But it's not my birthday."

"I know, but I felt like doing something special for you."

She lifted Bylisha to kiss me. "And you set the dinner table with candles?"

"Why not? Every day is a special occasion while married to you."

"Hmm, is that so? Well, I appreciate it, I do." She moved back into the living room where she performed her usual inspection of Bylisha's diaper bag. She was able to detect the care and attentiveness of the daycare workers by counting the Pampers. I could never figure that one out, but Tamera believed it like scripture. If she sent six pampers and Bylisha came home with four, then she knew our baby had been pissy all day. Tamera removed two diapers from the bag and was very pleased. She's an awesome mother.

The food was done, and it was time to set the table.

"How was your day?" I asked her. "Anything out of the ordinary?" *Like, did you have a meeting with my baby mama from Baton Rouge?*

"Out of the ordinary? Like what, sweetheart?"

"You know, any new cases or unusual meetings?" I placed her plate on the side of a chilled class of red wine.

"No, today was just another day in the Office of Child Protection." Tamera placed my daughter in a booster seat and angled the seat in her direction.

I lit both candles, and she smiled.

"Biyell, you really know how to make a girl feels special."

"Well you're not just any girl, you're Mrs. Baltimore." I inched my chair up to the table, closer to the baked fish that sizzled on the side of the creamy pasta. "You are my beautiful wife."

"That's right . . . I am your wife. Which makes you my loyal, committed husband."

"That's right, the happiest husband on Earth."

"On Earth?"

"Yes, on Earth, and tonight I'm taking you to a land far, far away."

"*Far, far* away like Atlanta?

"Even farther . . ."

"You're taking me to New York?"

"Even farther than New York . . . we're going to *Nutttttstovia.*"

"We can go right now; my bags are packed." She sipped her wine. "And who else have you taken to the land of Nutstovia?"

"You will be the first, but I went to prepare a place for you." I lied.

"Well, aren't I a lucky little piggy?"

"We're blessed. The Bible says if a man has found a wife,

then he has found a good thing. I found you, and you're my good thing."

"Preach, pastor." Her hand turned into a Mahalia Jackson fan. "Well lay me out on the floor, *honey child* . . . I'm your good thing?"

"Yes, you are." That part was true.

Tamera is the hardest-working woman I've ever known. She will take on any job to make ends meet. At the TSA, she worked the three a.m. to eleven a.m. shift and never complained—not one time, not even when they asked her to work a double. She did it with a smile. I placed the money on the dresser and she paid the bills. I never worried about grocery shopping, because she shopped for us. I never worried about the laundry, because she folded it, and still found the energy to get the kitty-cat wet for me at the end of my work day.

"Umm, hmm. So I'm your good thing?"

"Yes, you are baby. Don't I make you feel special?" I asked.

"Oh, I never said you didn't, I'm just taken aback to hear you say it so boldly. That's all."

"Tamera, I know I have been emotionally inconsistent, but all of that has changed—"

"*Oh really?*"

"Yes, you will love this Biyell, the new me."

Her forked sliced into the buttered fish. The moment it touched her tongue, her eyes closed. "Um, um, um, that's so good I lost my thought. Oh, yeah . . . and which Biyell did I have in the past?"

"Let's just say I could have been better to you, but here's to this Biyell." I offered a toast from across the table. "To a new beginning."

Suddenly, there was a knock at the front door.

"Who could that be?" I wondered aloud.

"Crap, I almost forgot."

"Forgot what?"

"I was in such hurry to get home when you sent that text

about dinner that I left a sensitive file on my desk. Marla agreed to drop it off for me."

"Oh . . . okay."

"Can the new and improved Biyell run Bylisha's bath water while I get this file from Marla?"

"Not a problem." I was only halfway through my dinner, but no problem, I will run the bath water.

I sprayed 409 cleaner around the tub and scrubbed it good. After that, I filled Bylisha's tub below the halfway point with warm water and threw in several of her floating toys. The toys were just as important as the soap—no floating toys, no bath. It was then that I thought about Braylyn. No less than two nights a week I ran her bath water; no less than two nights a week I tossed in the same bath toys, then watched from the hallway as her mother kneeled on the side of the tub.

*I can't do this.*

I have to withdraw from this challenge.

I still have time to win GiGi back if I put in the effort.

I grabbed a large towel to dry my hands. Halfway up the hall from the bathroom, I caught a glimpse of Marla seated at the kitchen table, curling a fork full of pasta.

"Gurl, you are blessed to have a man who can cook like this." She washed down the pasta with a slow sip of wine.

"Gurl, he said every day with me was a special occasion, that's why he cooked all of this food."

"And all those nights I cooked for him, I never knew he could cook like this." Marla was GiGi.

For a moment it felt like I was loaded on some new type of weed. There they were, seated at my kitchen table, wearing the same outfit. GiGi was wearing the dress I bought for her birthday. It looked so good that I'd ordered another for Tamera. Like girlfriends, they chatted as if I wasn't there at all. The one thing I had worked so hard to prevent was happening. These two woman were to never cross paths—not even at my funeral were they to be seated less than four feet apart.

It was the type of eerie feeling I imagine occurs when a man on death row takes the last bite of his last meal; the type of fear I imagine occurs after a flight attendant says *brace for impact*.

"Honey, I reheated your food while you were running the bath water for our daughter. Please join us."

"What's going on here?"

"Dinner," Tamera said. "The special meal you cooked for your wife. Remember?"

All I could do was shake my head and repeat the same question.

"What's going on here?"

Tamera half-turned with a homey expression. "Honey-boo, you prepared this wonderful meal, and since my supervisor was in town, I invited her over for dinner. *Dr. Tyra Thibodaux* is our guest for the evening. What an honor. I hope you don't mind?"

With a wave of a hand, GiGi invited me to have a seat at my kitchen table.

"So you two planned this out."

"Planned what?" GiGi asked as the fork slid out of her full lips.

"You know what the fuck I'm talking about; you planned this little meeting to set me up."

"Since you mentioned a meeting . . . I walked right into a meeting today, one that you were fully aware of. I figured I'd return the favor." Tamera held my daughter, who'd drifted asleep on her shoulder. "You knew Tyra was coming—you knew I could have gotten arrested on the job—and you never said a word."

"Not one word," GiGi agreed.

"So you two have met."

"*Obviously,*" Gigi scoffed.

"How did you sleep at night knowing she was in Baker with one child on the hip and another in the belly?" Tamera demanded.

"How about I bring this little investigation to a close?" If I'm going down, then I plan to go down swinging. "Fuck it. I'm busted. Cold fucking busted. We all can agree on that. I was married to both of you—you legally, and you illegally—and I loved every minute of it. I had my cake and my pattie-pie and licked the fuckin' spoon. You two can talk until you get laryngitis, I'm done. Count me out of your little game."

"Tamera, excuse me while I address this," GiGi began.

Tamera nodded her approval.

"A little game? You fuck over my life, and you call this meeting a little game? Motherfucker, I was this close to sending your wife to jail today. Her face would have been all over the news tonight, and you have the nerve to catch a *fuckin' attitude*. I'm sitting in another woman's house because it is the only place I am guaranteed the truth from a man who claimed to love me. And you have the nerve to act pissed off? *Nigga, suck my dick!*"

GiGi threw her glass of wine in my face.

The alcohol burned my eyes.

"My husband had unprotected sex with both of us for nearly half of this marriage." Tamera was right. "And you have the nerve to make this about you?"

"What the fuck do you want me to say?" My head oscillated between GiGi and Tamera. "You already know everything there is to know. *I'm caught! It's over.*"

"Biyell, if you think you're getting off this easy then you're dumber than a mop bucket. My breaking into your phone days are over. I knew you were cheating on me. I couldn't prove it, but I knew it. I had you with that dick picture."

GiGi held the picture in front of her face as confirmation.

"You lied to me that night, and you will lie again because you love her." Tamera was right.

GiGi thanked Tamera for the food and reached for her purse. "I came here tonight just to see your face when you saw me at your kitchen table. That's all I needed to see. In a split second, all of my questions were answered. It was never going to end. Once things calmed down with your wife in New Orleans, you were coming back to Baker to reel me back in."

"I wasn't."

"*Oh. So.* You're admitting that I didn't mean shit to you?" GiGi's anger lifted her from her seat with that same look in her eye as when that brick crashed through my truck window.

"Tyra, I am not saying that—"

"Then say what the fuck you mean." I heard the sound of knuckles cracking from her fist as she stood over me. "Say it."

"What I'm saying is, I wasn't going to come back for you, at least not for a year, because that was the bet."

"*WHAT BET?*" They asked in unison.

"The challenge—that we couldn't be faithful to one woman for one year. Uncle Glenn got tired of us bragging all the time, so he put forward this bet, for two million. That's why I had to break it off with you."

"Not because you love me, but because of a fuckin' bet?" Tamera asked as she stormed out of the room carrying my daughter.

"A bet, Biyell? That's all I was worth? You left me pregnant over a bet?" GiGi's steamy tears fell one after the other.

"I was going to come back for you once I won the money."

Tamera heard that entire sentence. She swiftly reentered the room as soon as she put my daughter in her crib. "And then resume cheating on me? You're making confessions to your mistress in front of me?"

"I'm not his mistress, I'm just some chick he fucked over." GiGi tried to step around me, but I held her arm. "Good luck with your bet, Biyell, I hope it was worth Braylyn and her brother, because my son will grow up around his uncles, who are real men. You will not pass that hoe disease down to my son." She swung her arm from my grip and continued to the front door.

I didn't hear anything after she said *your son.* GiGi is carrying my son.

"Oh, no-no, Tyra, you can't leave yet. You forgot something,"

Tamera called after her.

GiGi turned with a confused look before she reached the door.

"You forgot to take this motherfucker with you. This marriage was over when he said after a year he was coming back for you."

That's when Tamera moved around the table and into my space in the worst way. "Leave with her."

"I'm not leaving; this is my house, too."

"LEAVE!" Tamera yelled in my ear like a Marine Corps drill instructor.

"I'm not leaving my—"

"Oh, you're leaving. There will be no peace in this bitch until you're gone!" Suddenly, her hands tried to lock around my throat with deadly intent. "You will leave right now. Leave here and don't ever come back. Do you hear me?" Her fingernails cut into the thin skin on my neck. In the corner of my eye, I saw GiGi weep her way out of the house.

When I finally managed to free her hands from my neck, my wife stomped to our bedroom. Then came the snapping sound of hangers.

I was faced with a decision: Go to the bedroom and calm Tamera, or let GiGi know how much I love her before she drives away.

I ran after GiGi.

As soon as she made it to her car, I grabbed and pulled her to me under my carport. She buried her face in my chest. Her sobs were deep and heavy. I felt the pain I had caused.

"I'm so sorry; I tried everything to keep from hurting you."

While I held GiGi, just over my shoulder, I heard my clothes flying through the air and landing on the front lawn. Tamera was on a new level of pissed off, while GiGi could barely stand, let alone drive herself home.

"And another fucking thing!" Tamera yelled at me from the front door. "If that two-million-dollar bet with Uncle Glenn was contingent upon me, you're shit out of luck and wifeless." Then she slammed the front door.

Then I drove GiGi home.

She cried the entire ninety miles back to Baker, Louisiana. Little did she know, we cried together.

# CHAPTER 11

Madden Night
Thursday, April 20, 2017
6:55 p.m.

It's still Madden Night minus Telly and Biyell, but nevertheless, we're here. I never anticipated that my challenge would change the dynamics of our group as much as it has: we're unrecognizable. Telly doesn't call me anymore, nor has he spoken to Rasta much over the past few weeks. Rasta said that every time he tried to check on him, the call went directly to voicemail. It hurts, but in the end, I don't think Telly is the type of guy who is cut out to be with one woman.

Unfortunately for unsuspecting women, there are those types of men out there—men like Telly—but the good news is he's come to terms with his weakness and has admitted his problem. The fact that he did not even attempt the challenge indicates that he knows his weakness well and is making no illusions about it. My only hope is that he retires from this charade and can someday maintain a monogamous relationship. Right now, he can't, and innocent women are falling for him repeatedly.

As far as Rasta is concerned, he is still bald and still trying to impress LaDeisha by going weed free. I still can't believe that boy destroyed all that good weed in the name of LaDeisha; I sure hope she's worth this new Rasta. The man has transformed his life. But soon he has to proof up that they're in a committed relationship, or he's eliminated.

Jarvis is also here tonight, but for the past hour, he has been locked in a text fight. My best guess is he's texting Briana, but he can't admit it. To admit it's Briana would disqualify him from the challenge. Whenever I ask about his twenty-six-year-old lover, he says she's not taking the breakup well—but I think it's Jarvis who is not taking it well.

Last week during Madden Night, he excused himself twice to take a call outside. I let it slide, but that was a dead giveaway. All calls from their wives they take inside, because the background noise is confirmation of location. I cut Jarvis a little slack because I know how young his mistress is, and I consider the sensitivity of his situation with Monica's cancer battle. Then there's Biyell.

*Biyell.*

*Biyell.*

*Biyell.*

He just moved into a studio apartment, and a little over a week ago, he withdrew himself from the bet. That whole dinner with GiGi ordeal was something straight off *The Young and The Restless*. When he shared how it went down between the three of them, you could have heard a rat beating his dick in the corner. Biyell had lived through a player's worst nightmare. On the last night I saw him, he spoke a few personal words to me. He told me how he finally knew what it felt like to be me, and how amazing it was to cook for his wife in that brief hour of transparency.

"I liked being you, Glenn, even if it was just for one dinner. I may have lost out on the bet, and I may have lost GiGi and Tamera, but the feeling I felt when Tamera came home is the feeling

I want for the rest of my life. Save my seat on the sofa because after the challenge, I'm coming back as an honest man." And I believe him, because Tamera and GiGi traumatized his ass.

Then came another disturbance, but this one was peculiar.

"LaDeisha, LaDeisha, listen to me." Rasta gave a gesture to turn the music down as he stepped into the kitchen. "LaDeisha, I know you never changed your position, but can I at least explain?" The phone call ended.

"FUCK!" he yelled.

"Rasta, what was that about?" I asked.

"Somehow LaDeisha came across Shameka."

"What?" we all asked.

"She knows about Shameka. She knows. I knew I should have ended it earlier; I knew she wasn't going to let things die after I returned that truck. That bitch had to track LaDeisha down. I know it was her."

"Did LaDeisha say it was her?"

"No, but she did say someone sent her proof that I was fucking with both of them at the same time. The only person who had the proof was Shameka. When she first heard of LaDeisha, it came from gossip in her nail shop. I'm willing to bet you LaDeisha's mother came back into the shop, and Shameka made the connection. That bitch!"

"Rasta, I need you to calm down for a minute. Let's sort this out."

"Uncle, there's nothing left to sort out. LaDeisha asked me never to contact her again. Our twice-a-week phone calls are over. That's what kept me going—her phone calls. Not sex, not dates, just her voice over the phone. Tonight she ended that."

I sighed. Shameka is that type of girl—the kind that places all her personal feelings on Facebook, the catty kind that loves games and mess, even though every profile post is about how much she *hates games and mess*. In the end, Shameka got the last lick on Rasta, and it was a hard lick—one that knocked the wind out of my nephew. Rasta extended his hand to Jarvis and

Timothy.

"Well, brothers, it looks like I am out. I wish you much success for the rest of the challenge. I took a gamble when I submitted LaDeisha's name—I thought I could fix us in time—but it feels like something or someone is working against me. I bet the house on LaDeisha; I was confident I could win her back. I lost it all. I no longer have a qualifying woman for the challenge."

A very shocked Timothy and Jarvis immediately turned to me with expressions of utter dismay, but the rules had been set. The name that was submitted is the only qualifying woman, and if she decides to leave you, then you're out.

There's a good reason I stand firm on this rule. Men who struggle with commitment jump from woman to woman because of their unwillingness to work things out. At the first sign of trouble, they take off like a jack rabbit in search of another burrow. With this rule in place, I knew they would at least try to work it out with the woman they had named, instead of simply promoting the mistress to full time and then hiring a temp to back her up.

Rasta bolted out the door with Timothy following him. Jarvis's nosey ass bolted to the window and gave me the play by play. In the parking lot, Timothy was trying to console Rasta, which left me alone with Jarvis.

"Are you still in or are you out?" I asked him.

"Uncle Glenn, I plan to win this thing. The way I see it, we started with five, and now there are two—and if Timothy can't proof up, then that only leaves me and eleven months to go."

"Do you honestly think Briana is going away? Let's be realistic here."

"It's not up to Briana," Jarvis said defiantly. "I have made my decision and it's over."

"My only suggestion for you, Jarvis, is to keep her away from your house as much as you can."

"Uncle Glenn, I'm trying, but she still comes to clean on the days when my wife has chemo. I've tried to hire a maid service, but my sister-in-law insists on doing everything my wife is too weak to do. To add to my headache, Briana leaves notes all around the house where only I can find them, like my pockets and socks. She's aggravating the fuck out of me, but I only have eleven months to go."

My cell alerted me of a text. It was from Timothy.

*Rasta is talking crazy, and I don't like the look in his eyes. We're going to shoot pool.*

It was then that Jarvis received another text, one that left him visibly shaken. "This girl is not going to stop until I hurt her."

"What did she do?"

Jarvis turned his phone in my direction. On the screen was a picture of Briana standing at his front door. Under the picture, the text said:

*You have five minutes to call me, or I'm knocking on this fucking door and telling your wife I'm pregnant.*

After reading that, I needed a beer and a seat. "I think you better call her."

Jarvis agreed. After taking a deep breath, he dialed her number. I stood by to listen to his side of the conversation.

"Briana, this is not a game. Do not threaten me. Do you understand?"

*Inaudible.*

"I know you're pregnant, but what do you expect me to do? I've said it a million times already; I will financially support you. What else? Huh?"

*Inaudible.*

"I never said you wanted my money, but we cannot be a family. You decided to keep this baby against my will—"

*Inaudible.*

"Under the circumstances, yes, I wanted you to kill it. You knew I was married."

*"BEING MARRIED DIDN'T STOP YOU FROM FUCKING ME! YOU CAME IN ME KNOWING YOU'RE MARRIED!"* Briana screamed so loud into the phone that I heard her as

if I were on three-way.

Jarvis muted his phone. "Uncle Glenn, do you see the bullshit I have to deal with?"

"Jarvis, get her away from your house before she knocks on the door."

"I'm trying."

"What does she want?"

"For us to raise the baby as a family."

Jarvis didn't end the call, but he kept Briana on mute as she fussed without pause. I heard it all; it was a complete recap of the entire affair. Fire shot out of his cell phone speaker.

"Jarvis, I think you may have to concede to Timothy, because I don't see this ending well for you with Briana. Tell your wife before she learns of this affair in the street. At least give her the opportunity to handle this privately."

He shook his head. "Nope, not doing that, but what I will do is let her know I'm serious. If she comes to my house again, I will call the police." Jarvis left the kitchen and hurried over to his computer bag.

"Jarvis, at the point that Briana is sending you pictures from your front door, it's safe to say the police can't help you."

"She better not be outside of my door when I get there."

"Jarvis, don't do anything stupid. Remember, your wife is in a serious condition and a stressful situation like this could send her spiraling. I strongly suggest that you get Briana to calm down by any means necessary. After that, you may want to con-sider conceding to Timothy because you will need the space to deal with Briana."

"Fuck that, Glenn. I am winning this bet, and fuck Briana."

# CHAPTER 12

Saturday, May 13, 2017
1:15 p.m.

## JARVIS

I'm in Dallas today for a wedding. Monica's youngest sister Latricia is getting married, which means everyone is here. All of them—the entire clan. Monica has five sisters and three brothers, and it seems like a million nieces and nephews. My wife is the second youngest. She has an unbreakable soul tie with Latricia; they were born in the same year but eleven months apart. Monica was going to be here even if we had to roll a hopital bed to the pulpit; there's was no way she was going to miss the wedding of Latricia and Jalen Kurt. Homeboy just happens to start as running back for the Dallas Cowboys, so as you can imagine, this wedding is over the top:

Fifteen bridesmaids
Six junior bridesmaids
Four flower girls

Two sets of parents
Two sets of stepparents
Two ring bearers: one for each ring

Like I said, over the top, excessive, grandiose, and EXTRA.

Latricia offered to fly us up to Dallas, but my wife wanted to drive. It literally took forever to get here. The constant pee stops and puke breaks every fifty miles were punishing, but I smiled through it all—even though it took a total of eleven hours to complete an eight-hour trip.

But who's counting, right?

The good news is, my wife looks amazing.

Stunning!

The weight she's lost with the chemo has taken off thirty pounds. Monica couldn't lose that on her own if I paid her three million dollars. She's back to the weight she was at when we first started dating. If only I could make love to her. It's been hell stalking her around the house with that body, only to get cock-blocked by cancer. And yes, the treatment eventually stole her hair, but I like her short haircut—we even go to the same barber. She looks ten years younger. Nevertheless, we're here. Against all odds, we're here. I have to piss so bad I'm about to cry, but we're also running late.

The Ceremony

The term *megachurch* is tossed around quite often these days, and I think it may have lost some of its accuracy in reference to very large ministries. Such is not the case with the location of this wedding. Latricia's ceremony is being held at Bishop T.D. Jakes's Potter's House Church, which is the size of an NBA arena. All available places to park up front were taken, which meant I had to fit in wherever I could fit in. It felt like I had to walk a mile to get to the church. And it was hot as piss . . . *and* every seat in that big-ass church was taken. Thank God Latricia thought of everything—there was a seat on the end of a pew reserved for me. Thank you, sister-in-law *with your fine-ass self.* Not as fine as Briana, but it's close.

Not only is she superfine, but after today, Latricia will be super rich. Her future husband plays for the Dallas Cowboys. She even offered me free tickets to the games, but I don't fuck with the Cowboys, not even a little bit . . . but I digress. The guy she's marrying is also from Dallas, and from the looks of it he invited half the city to his wedding. But I'm in the reserved seats for the important folk, which is perfect. I will have the best view of my wife and my daughter Symphony as they stroll past on their way to the altar.

The wedding colors are Cowboys silver and blue, and to the delight of family and friends, the first bridesmaid had started her procession toward the altar. Her form-fitting gown glittered like mercury as she strolled by holding a beautiful bouquet of blue and white flowers.

Next in line was my daughter Symphony, and I know that look—something is wrong. I wonder if it's over the boy who's escorting her? Monica chewed her out about last night because Lyric snitched on her about video-chatting with him after eight o'clock. Lyric and Symphony flew up here two days ago, and I knew we were going to have an issue when Symphony was paired up with that lil' Negro at the rehearsal. My daughter's eyes are watery, but she's still managed a smile.

Suddenly, her smile mutated downward the closer she came to the my pew. The hand-in-hand, step-by-step rhythm of their procession was disrupted after she digressed in order to square up in front of me and stomp. Then, she continued toward the altar.

*Hold up, Symphony is angry with me?* But I wasn't the one who repossessed her cell phone—I stayed out of it completely. *Why does she have an attitude with me?*

Out of a few bridesmaids, I recognized Connie's daughter Jodie. She walked toward the altar like a royal princess with a smile that was radiant and luminous—until she noticed me. Her entire aura instantly descended into disgust.

I shot her a baffled look.

She shot me a silent *fuck you*.

Once Jodie strolled by my pew, her smile returned. *I don't understand.* She was just at the house yesterday and gave me a big hug.

Several bridesmaids later, Connie's other daughter Bethany made it a point to look down in my direction. Like her sister, she wore the same *fuck you* expression when we made eye contact. Then came another bridesmaid named Courtney, and with her eyes, she called me everything but a child of God. I even heard her mumble:

*"You're dead after this wedding."*

*Why would you want to hurt me?* I wondered.

My wife was with the bride, so I had no way of knowing why five of the women in her family just spat on me with their eyes, but I needed to find out.

*Crap, I left my phone in the car.*

Suddenly, Monica appeared at the top of the aisle—she was the matron of honor. My beautiful wife appeared as Nefertiti at the entrance of a grand palace in Egypt. In the entrance to the sanctuary, at the top of the aisle, Monica showed no signs of sickness. And that gown . . . my Lord, that gown.

That booty hugging, full-length sapphire gown with metallic lace trimmings. Monica accented the ensemble with flawless makeup. Upon seeing her, several family members who knew her struggle with cervical cancer couldn't hold their cheers as she held her stance for the photographer. Then, with one foot in front the other, she entered the sanctuary on a cloud.

I stood as Monica passed me, but she never looked in my direction. The air between us was thick. Her face was stiff as cement. Her neck was locked like whiplash. The only parts of her body that moved were her legs and her nostrils, which flared. She continued toward the altar and never acknowledged me— not even a blink in my direction.

*What the fuck is going on?*

*Where's Briana?*

*Why didn't she enter with the other bridesmaids?*

Suddenly the entire sanctuary stood in honor of the bride. The bride was then handed off by a dad and a stepdad. Then Jalen escorted Latricia to the alter. On the pew directly across from me sat Connie, the mother of Briana. Only the aisle separated us, but I could feel her eyes stabbing me in the torso over and over, deep and deadly. Something was wrong. I needed my phone, but I was seated directly at the end of the pew. To my right were at least twenty people, and to my left was the center aisle. I couldn't step into the center aisle, not now that the bride was at the altar.

I was trapped by the unknown, confined by the uncertain, and tormented by a nightmarish probability that something had transpired in the bridal dressing area. But what? Connie's head was honed in my direction the entire time the pastor spoke, as if I were a jilted lover who came to object during the wedding vows. Her eyes were bloodshot red and flooded with tears. I knew then that she knew. They knew.

*And if they know, then my wife knows.*

Then again, I've always known that Briana is a short-tempered hot-head, but there is no way she would confess our affair at her aunt's wedding. Sure, she's threated many times to knock on my door, but those were empty threats.

Recently, the tone of her texts has changed from scattered thunderstorms to partly cloudy. She's been less argumentative and more inquisitive. Now that I think about it, last week she sent me an apology for all her temper tantrums. Whatever is going on with Connie, her sisters, and my daughter . . . I doubt Briana said a word.

And no one in her circle knows about us. Maybe I'm just paranoid? But why is Connie staring at me like that?

What the fuck is her problem?

Why didn't I piss before the wedding started?

# CHAPTER 13

One hour earlier

## MONICA

My sister hated the colors for the wedding, but the colors were Jalen's only must-have on their wish list. Latricia fought against them for months before I was able to convince her to concede. *It's only silver and blue for day, and then a lifetime as his wife*, I said. Everywhere my eyes come to rest are the colors silver and blue; they are the colors I have worn for nearly six months. The silvers and the blues; some days are sunny, whiles others are a grayish hue. Then on days like today, when everyone is jovial and it's sunny all around me, the innermost parts of my soul, mind, and body feel like the clouds in a tropical depression—the type of gray that chases away the blue.

I'm tired, and even worse than being tired is the mental exhaustion of feeling tired all the time. I want to enjoy this special day with my sister. I want to be the life of the reception, and I want to dance until the DJ unplugs the speakers, but I can't—

because I'm tired. If my mom were here, she would tell me in her firm but loving voice, *Monica sit your ass down somewhere, you're doing too much.* But I'm tired of sitting and resting, and tired of the overly concerned gawks from those who knew me before and are seeing me now. *Momma, I want to enjoy just a day without cancer and forget this horrible fatigue.*

*I'm too tired to cry, but I feel myself crying. My ration of tears has dried.*

In the end, I think that is what kills you.

You get so tired of being tired that you give in to whatever your body is feeling, even if that feeling is death. But I don't want to die—not now with a fourteen-year-old daughter who is already boy crazy and another daughter who's twelve going on twenty-two. They need me. I need me. I need to be the woman I was before the gray clouds blew in from south of Plaquemines Parish. Isn't that where all storms come from? From somewhere way down yonder, as Momma would say; a place you least expect something to blow in from on the sunny days, but are quickly reminded. I want to see my girls graduate from college and walk down the aisle on their wedding days; it's the least that I hope for on the days I have the strength to hope.

I'm so tired, but my little sister needs me, and I need to be needed right now . . . but first I need to get this off my chest.

*Fuck this shit.*

*Fuck you, cancer!*

Fuck who you are and fuck where you came from. I don't even care what lead to you—the carcinogens, the chemo, carcinoma, clinical trials, case manager and any word that starts with C—fuck all of you. We're spending money going to the fucking moon and financing the military to fight these bullshit wars when the greatest threat to mankind is a malignant tumor. It doesn't make sense. It's not fucking fair. You're killing the women in this family one by one, and we can't stop you, because you're coming no matter what we do, or how long we pray, or how much money we donate to church. Death is never rescheduled, you appointments are irrevocable, because you are a fucked-up, sadistic coward who hides in blood and bones and just beneath the skin like the pussy you are. If no one else has said it, then I'll be the first—*Fuck you, cancer. With the last breath in me, fuck you.*

If I'm pardoned into Heaven, you will hear me in the thunder. Or, from Hell, I will look upwards and yell—*FUCK YOU, CANCER*.

And Lord, I don't get you.

And I don't understand you.

And I'm owed an explanation.

Why me?

I know I'm not perfect, I know I've made mistakes, but I'm surrounded by morally bankrupt people who still have fullness of life. Why are you doing this to me? What have I done that was so vile in your eyes that you sentenced me to *death by lethal hope?* I need to know right now. Shine a light through the ceiling, send a raven, talk through the toilet, it doesn't matter. Before I leave this stall, I demand to know, Lord—why me? Answer me!

"Momma, are you still in here?" my daughter Lyric called out.

"Yes, Tulip."

"Aunt Connie sent me to check on you, arc you okay?"

"Yes tulip, I'm fine." When my mother passed away, Connie became the mother of all of us, but worries ten times worse than my momma did. "I'll be out in a second. Where's your sister?" My words traipsed across the stalls.

"All up in the face of that boy. Again . . ."

"The one who's escorting her down the aisle? The same boy she was on the phone with late last night?"

"You're correct, Mommy."

"The one she sent the pictures and video chat to at eleven p.m.?"

"You're correct, Mommy."

"Where is she?"

"In the front of the church by the limo."

"Tell Symphony she has ten seconds before I drag her by the crown of her head."

Lyric was more than happy to deliver my threat. She's my honorable tattletale, my twenty-four-hour drone, and few things give her more joy than watching her sister get in trouble for being sneaky; but she gets it honestly.

"Mommy, one more thing . . ."

"What is it, Tulip?"

"Symphony has another cell phone."

"What? Did she go in my purse and steal her phone?"

"No, Mama, she has an iPhone—like the kind Jodie has."

"And where did she get that phone?"

"I don't know, probably from . . . *that boy.*"

I'd better get back out there and deal with sneaky Symphony—and make sure things are progressing on schedule with the bridesmaids.

At the sink, I catch a glimpse of myself in the mirror. I look prettier than I feel. I miss my hair. My hair was always shoulder length; it was my signature. My hair was my business card. This low cut is cute but it's not my crown, and I'm too thin. I look sickly. Fuck you, cancer! Fuck you, fuck you, fuck you. There, I feel a little bit better now.

Today I must pull myself together.

Today is not about me.

Today is about my sister—not my nausea, not my fatigue, my hair, or my weight. It's definitely not about the results of my CT scan, or the possibility of my cancer spreading down my leg, or how much time I might have to live. Nor is today about any of my regrets or how I could have been a better wife. On the contrary—today is a celebration of happiness and commitment, that's it and that's all. I will find the strength to smile, enjoy my family, and watch my little sister make a vow of matrimony.

What a beautiful day it is for a white wedding.

When your future husband is fresh off a twenty-million-dollar signing bonus, you can have the wedding of your dreams—and my sister deserves the wedding of her dreams. She did everything the right way; finished law school, became an attorney for the Dallas Cowboys front office, and forced Jalen to chase after her like she was a fumbled football. *Bravo, little Latricia.*

With my daily rant out of my system and my noonday regiment of meds in my bloodstream, I rejoined the pre-wedding madness, aka the bridesmaids' dressing area. We've converted one of the reception rooms in the Potter's House Church into a bridal party dressing room, with our own backup supply of everything. At first glance, the floor looked like a clearance sale at Macy's on Black Friday—I couldn't see the floor with all the strewn carry-on bags and makeup cases. And what bridesmaids' prep area would be complete if someone hadn't forgotten pantyhose, contact lenses, or their decorative pearls? One even forgot her shoes. Thankfully, we planned for everything; we had our own little bridal depot overstocked with one of everything.

For all of us family members who wanted to be part of her wedding, Latricia bought us the dresses. This elevated this wedding to family reunion status. I have a total of seven of my nieces and one daughter in this wedding, while all of Connie's daughters are bridesmaids. The oldest is Jodie, then Bethany, and finally my godchild, Briana. She has been my angel, that Briana—I thank God for her every day. It's because of Briana that I can boldly accept my reality—that I may not see another Zulu Ball. I have already worked the details and just have to clear it with Jarvis, but if anything happens to me, I would like Briana to mentor my girls full time. Lyric and Symphony see her as a big sister, and I trust her unconditionally.

What Briana is to my girls, Latricia is to Briana. This is the system that my mother put in place: we're all responsible for each other. Before Latricia moved to Dallas, she hosted girls' nights out with all her nieces, including my daughters, and it was during those girls' nights that all of them bonded. Since I don't trust Jarvis to marry the right woman after me, I would rest better knowing they spend most of their time with Briana.

Here comes the wedding planner. Oh my, would you look at the time?

"All right, ladies, let's pull it all together. We have less than thirty minutes before the sanctuary doors open!" she yelled.

That's when I heard a commotion. We were ready for whatever, but no one could have planned for Briana.

# CHAPTER 14

Bridesmaids' Dressing Room

## MONICA

In the furthest corner of the dressing room, I saw three women gathered around Briana: her mother, the wedding planner, and a very pissed off seamstress. While being mindful not to overexert myself, I finally made it back there and joined their frantic huddle. As you would imagine, the seamstress held three bobby pins in the corner of her mouth and stitching tools in her hands. Her name was Mrs. Evelyn Chevelle, and she was from Haiti. Half of her bitching was in English, while the other half was in French.

"*Ce n'est pas ma faute,* I measure correctly. You are pregnant."

"I'm not pregnant," Briana objected.

"Yes, you are."

"Stop yelling at me!" Briana snapped back. "There has to be something you can do to fix it! Please!" Brianna's voice was filled with emotion.

"*TU ES ENCEINTE,* and you know it." A hush moved across the dressing room.

Latricia had flown Mrs. Chevelle in from Haiti because she was one of the most talked-about designers at all the bridal shows. When the cases of dresses arrived two weeks ago, I understood fully why my sister would import a designer from Haiti—the gowns were flawless.

But there was no way we could have prepared for Briana.

Her zipper ripped away from the fabric, and the only option was to tie a scarf around her waist. It was time to have a one on one with Connie and face the music—she's about to be a grandmother. I hooked my arm inside of her arm, and we strolled to a discreet corner.

"Connie, I'm on Team Chevelle. Briana has gotten knocked up."

"Monica, she says she's not pregnant, but she looks pregnant to me."

"That's because she's too scared to tell us, as if you're going to beat her ass with a belt."

Connie pinched my arm. "Girl, watch your mouth in the Lord's house."

I'm thinking, *the word ass is a misdemeanor compared to what I said in the restroom ten minutes ago.*

"Connie it's not like she's Symphony—by the way, remind me to tell you the latest with Ms. Hormones later—but Briana turned twenty-seven last week. Why hasn't she come to one of us to talk about this pregnancy?

"Girl, your guess is as good as mine. Why she feels the need to hide this has me at a loss. If you're pregnant, you're pregnant. She's still my daughter, no matter what."

"And she's still my angel no matter what."

"Something is truly strange about her behavior because Bri is like your Lyric; she tells me everything. I hurt that my daughter is afraid and not asking me for help. Why lie about something so obvious?"

"Because she looks up to Latricia and didn't want to disappoint her by dropping out. That's why. But we have to pull her out."

"And who's going to walk with Jalen's friend?"

"I'll have that young man escort one of our great aunts and no one will notice the difference until we get to the reception. By that point, *Ms. Fertile Myrtle* can rejoin the bridal party for group photos, and Latricia will not notice the difference. Later on tonight we'll get to the bottom of this. As for now, you have to break the news to her."

"She's going to lose it. You know Bri is a drama momma."

"After you break the news, I'll tag in Jodie to calm her down."

"Jodie?"

"Yes, Jodie."

"My child, Jodie? The one who with the bad attitude who bullied our house for over twenty-three years, that Jodie?"

"Yes, that Jodie."

"Good luck with that." Connie said. "I'll go break the news to Bri, then pass it off to you." Connie threw her hands in the air as she walked over to the huddle and yanked Briana out of the wedding.

It didn't go over well. Bri cried like a three-year-old when her mother broke the news, but we couldn't have a jacked-up dress in the midst of all of this perfection. Connie explained that she could still take pictures at the reception, but not in the sanctuary—not with a dress that looked like a rat ate the lower part of her back. Briana was not at all understanding, and we were losing control of the situation. All the months of planning for this perfect day, and it was in jeopardy. *Jodie, I need you.*

I located her over by one of the makeup stations, where the makeup artist was spraying a sealant mist across her face.

"Jodie, I have a mission for you."

"Whatever you need, Teedie."

"Find out what's going on with Briana. It's obvious that she's pregnant, but for some crazy reason, she's too afraid to tell us."

"I said it this morning at breakfast—she denied it."

"That's just crazy, but I need you to go over there and calm her down. I don't need her making a scene in the church, and you're the only one she listens too."

"Used to."

"You're our only hope."

"But I don't know what to say to her—sorry dude's pull-out game was weak, better luck next time?"

That's Jodie—either she's insensitive or abrasive. There is no cordial middle area. Maybe it was the childhood of mandatory church attendance that made her nerves bad; in many ways she rejects and resents her mother and takes pride in being her polar opposite. It's a miracle Latricia convinced her into a gown and heels—her daily uniform is a new pair of Jordans and jean ordered from the Thuggish Ruggish Outlet. I guess denial runs in the family: Connie has two daughters and a son whether she admits it or not. The positive side of Jodie that I find refreshing is I never have to wonder how she feels about me or anyone else. if I stick around her long enough, it's coming out.

"I told Momma she spoils Bri too much—still treating her like she's a baby. Back in January when Bri told her she was moving out into that apartment, I thought my momma was going to have a nervous breakdown. All of this is connected to that— she has to have attention or she creates a scene. I don't have the patience for Briana."

"Jodie, I agree with you and Connie has held onto her longer than you and Bethany—no argument from here—but right now we have a crisis, and that big baby you just described will throw a tantrum if we don't pull together. Please, for me, because I don't have the strength."

"Teedie, I don't know what to say to her."

"Be creative—come up with anything—but we can't risk Briana causing a scene and ruining this day for Latricia."

I watched as Jodie reasoned internally then nodded about four times.

"Teedie, you know what? I lost my new iPhone; it's around her somewhere. I'll ask Briana to use her phone to call my phone, and then I'll try to calm her down."

"Great, we have twenty minutes before it's showtime. Let Bri know we still need her even though she's not a part of the church photos. At the reception, no one will care about the back of her dress."

"I'm on it, Teedie."

"And by the way, Symphony has your phone. When you call it, she'll be the who answers." Jodie was relieved.

As Jodie headed in the direction of Connie and Bri, a very agitated Mrs. Chevelle moved like a windstorm in my direction. The panic of the damaged gown situation had left the seamstress drenched in sweat and near hyperventilation, but it wasn't her fault.

"Mrs. Chevelle, it's not you're craftsmanship, it's my niece."

"I have six daughters," she plucked six fingers inches from my nose. "Two in New York, one in France, one in London, one in New Orleans, and the other one is over there." With a single finger on her right hand, Mrs. Chevelle pointed in the direction of a young lady who was her spitting image. Both had the Angela Basset eyes and skin tone. "Half of my daughters tried that same lie—talking 'bout them not pregnant. Briana is a lying wonder. She's pregnant, I tell you, no less than *trois a quatre mois*."

I failed French in school, and I guess she read the confusion on my face.

"She's three to four months."

"That explains why the dress tore in the back."

"Oui!" Mrs. Chevelle started to cry. "I wanted everything perfect for Latricia. If it wasn't good enough for one of my daughters, it wasn't good enough for her. We worked through the night to double-stitch these gowns. If Briana would have said something earlier, we could have altered it before we left Haiti."

"Mrs. Chevelle, today is perfect, and a pregnant bridesmaid doesn't stop no show. We have pulled her out the wedding and she will rejoin the wedding party at the reception. Job well done, my sister, your work here is finished."

Mrs. Chevelle smiled at me, then joined her daughter, who was rolling a lint brush up and down one of the bridesmaids in the corner. Then, out of nowhere, the wedding planner appeared again.

"Less than fifteen minutes! Wrap it up now and get into formation."

Just then came sound of a scuffle.

Instinctively, I turned.

*A fight?*

By the neck, with both hands, Jodie was choking her sister against the back wall. In an angry monotone, she spoke into the side of Briana's ear—low enough to maintain a level of privacy but loud enough for her sister to hear her every threat. Surprisingly, there was no reaction from Briana. Whatever was said she accepted, like a child in possession of stolen cookies. Their mother was near the scene—less than three feet—but she seemed trapped in a land far, far away, transfixed by something she held in her hand: a cell phone.

As fast as I could, I hurried to be by her side, but this was one of those bad dreams where the floor became a treadmill and your loved one drifted away.

Helplessly, I watched my sister scroll and scroll through the phone with her thumb while her other hand covered her mouth— neither hand wiped her tears. There appeared to be a fork in the road: on the left was my sister and a cell phone, on the right was my niece, whose life was in danger. I decided to save Briana.

I pulled and pleaded, pried and weeded at Jodie's arms, but I wasn't strong enough. In my ear was my mother's voice: *Monica, you need to sit your ass down and rest.* The voice continued to repeat itself while Jodie continued to spit fire and fury into

Briana's ear, burning the sides of her face. As I struggled to pull Jodie off Briana, I got close enough to hear what I thought I heard.

*"How could you fuck our uncle? All the dudes out here and you fuck our uncle? Momma didn't raise no hoes. You hear me? If you weren't pregnant I would fuck you up in this church. You hear me? Briana, I swear on Grandma's grave—I'm done with you! You hear me?"*

After my failed rescue attempt, Jodie finally released Briana's neck and started to back away. "Just remember, you brought this on yourself and you deserve everything that's about to happen." Briana slid down the wall like a fallen portrait and crumbled out of her frame.

*Which uncle did Briana fuck?* It took me a minute to process Jodie's statement. Not Uncle Charlie—he's sixty-eight years old. It couldn't be Uncle Buck, he's seventy years old, and our Uncle Paul is bedridden from a massive stroke. It's Uncle Charlie—I bet a nickel to a nail it's Uncle Charlie. *Briana is pregnant for wrinkled-ass Uncle Charlie? How fucking gross! Look at her—if I had that face and that body, I would be starring in the next Tyler Perry movie. She's gorgeous    too gorgeous to give her body to a man old enough to be her grandpa.* But I was thinking in terms of my uncles.

"I'm so sorry, Teedie. Don't take this out on us. We love you."

Before I could gain clarity, Jodie wrapped her arms around me and squeezed me so tight I felt the wind leave my lungs. Then she left a teary kiss on my cheek and ran off to join the other bridesmaids. I turned left to face my sister. Connie was as stiff as a pine tree, with Briana's cell phone cradled in her twigs.

"Is there something on that phone I should know about?"

"Yes." Connie answered in a grief-stricken voice.

"What is it?"

"Monica, I don't have the words to describe what's on this phone. I ask that you wait until after the wedding to view it."

"Connie . . . does it involve my husband?"

A sorrowful nod.

"Hand it to me."

"Monica, no. I promise you will see it, but can it wait."

"Connie . . ."

I held out my hand, and Connie conceded the phone. It was all there—gift-wrapped like a present from Satan. Starting with my eyelids, my skin peeled away with each text I read between my godchild and my husband.

1st picture: My husband's dick.

2nd picture: My husband after ejaculating on his stomach. My back was in the picture.

3rd picture: An over-the-shoulder view of my husband fucking my niece from the back.

4th picture: A photo of her waxed pussy she sent to my husband's phone.

5th picture: My husband's dick in Briana's mouth.

6th picture: A text from my husband: *I love you.*

7th picture: A text from my husband: *When this is over let's get married and move to New York.*

8th picture: A text from my husband: *Seriously, you have the best pussy I've ever had. The best.*

9th picture: A picture of a pregnancy test in a gift bag—the same gift bag I found in the trash.

10th picture: A picture of Briana's belly, taken two days ago with a caption that read: *It's a boy—I can feel it.*

But it was the next picture that was far more painful than the previous batch; a picture so traumatic it left me critically wounded. Standing right where I stood, I blacked out. I didn't stumble or faint—in my mind, I ran away.

From near the formation of bridesmaids, the wedding planner tried to get my attention, but my ears powered off when my nervous system re-booted. I drifted away. I left that room. I went back to a time when I was a child and Grandma had that huge fan in the middle of the floor; my favorite place was directly in front of that artificial breeze. I felt the joy of humid air tickling the pores of my skin as I slept under the therapeutic swooping of the large blades. Then I drifted off into magical wonderlands.

Suddenly, a flash of fluorescent light surrounded me. It glowed soft and white. Through the light, I saw my momma in her kitchen, standing over her large cast iron pot. She was pouring even circles of hot pralines on a long sheet of aluminum foil; four across the top and eight straight down. Oh, how I hated the game she would play, but I couldn't eat a crumb unless I answered correctly.

"What's three rows down times five across?"

"Fifteen."

"Aren't you a little smarty?! You will be Math Teacher of the Year one day."

My mother always used to say that, but I majored in finance instead. *I feel dizzy.* I felt my heart beating in my chest. The wonderful memories of cooking in the kitchen with Momma were replace by the urge to find something long and sharp with a decent grip. I became possessed with Jodie's spirit. My eyes waxed into different shades of rouge, but I could do what I wanted to do because I was obligated to something more meaningful. It was time to line up for Latricia—I was her matron of honor—but first I needed to bid farewell to my niece.

I looked down at Briana crumbled on the floor as if I were looking down into a coffin. She was dead to me, and all that was left was to pronounce her dead. First, I lowered myself to within earshot.

"I trusted you in my home, with my family, and around my husband. I loved you so much and would have given you my last. I pray that as long as you live, you never feel the pain you have caused me. I battle cancer every day, but make no mistake about it, on the day I close my eyes, know that it was my husband and my niece who killed me."

I turned away from the greatest pain I have ever felt and lined up for my Latricia, because that's how my mother raised us. *Men come and men go, but y'all sisters have to take care of each other.* With one arm, Connie pulled me to her hip and guided me back to the bridal party.

*The matron of honor.*

# CHAPTER 15

The Reception

## JARVIS

It was a Royal Wedding in Dallas, both in ambiance and pageantry; a transforming moment to behold when two individuals agree to do life together. The deal was sealed with a kiss. A common, everyday pressing of lips, but in this setting, in front of these witnesses, that kiss is was notarized by God. As for me? I was just spectator, a blurred face in the crowd, but after hearing Latricia and Jalen's vows, my heart became weighted down by sinkers which pulled me down to floor of the sea, where I sat for an eternity.

Woe is me.

Somewhere along the way, I forgot my vows and every promise I made to my wife. *To have and to hold until death.* But I'm still here—that should count for something? No?

At MD Anderson in Houston; I was there.

For every chemo treatment; I was there.

Funeral pre-arrangements; I was there.

I know it's the responsible thing to do, but fuck that—fuck funeral arrangements. Sitting at my kitchen table in front of a brochure of funeral packages feels like quitting. I want to fight and believe at this very moment that we can beat this thing . . . but not Monica. She lost her faith on the way home from Houston, but I still believe she will beat it; I still have faith. I haven't thrown her away the way Timothy threw away Kayla. He's such a fool, I wish my issues were as simple as a few extra pounds. Sometime in life, losing weight is greeted with sorrow. Although she looks great, I had to take Monica's pictures off the wall because when I stood there looking at them and really thought about it, each one reminded of how far she was from life and how close she was to goodbye. But I'm there, right by her side, watching pound after pound fall off like leaves in November, and I will stay until death do us part.

*If staying is still an option.*

*Something is wrong.*

From the foyer of the church, I watched the door close on a white Rolls Royce, sealing the newlyweds inside. Then, it slowly drove away. All around me, people raced to their cars and merged into the reception caravan, but I had parked so far away it I couldn't even see my car. After a mile jog through the parking lot, I'd never been more relieved to press the unlock button on my Denali. There was my cell phone.

Left for dead in a hot vehicle.

Unconscious.

Shame on me.

*I have to piss.*

After pressing the ignition button, I dialed up the AC to winter storm and placed my cell phone on the charger. Large beads of sweat were racing down both sides of my face like ski jumpers, in part due to the heat and in part due to high anxiety. Something was wrong; I felt it in my gut.

I waited anxiously for the battery meter on my cell to increase from zero to one percent—all in all that short span of time felt like an hour. I didn't have the patience for two percent, so I powered it on.

The slow-moving traffic snaked out of the church parking lot and onto the street. Motorcycle cops halted traffic to allow the wedding party to pass. It was cool feeling this important, having a brother-in-law who plays for the Dallas Cowboys. That carries zero prestige back home in New Orleans. My cell phone battery icon had risen and was ready to reconnect me with the my world—which was about to collide with a giant asteroid.

The first text message wasn't from my wife. It was from Briana's phone, but it didn't take me long to realize Briana hadn't sent it.

*Bruh this Jodie, you fucked my sister? For real, you have been fucking my sister? When my daddy hears of this, he will shoot your ass in the face.*

Less than ten minutes later, we arrived at the reception venue. I sat in the car and watched the wedding guests enter the building, wondering how many people other than Jodie knew. I called Monica's phone, but it went right to voicemail. Symphony's phone was in Monica's purse. *What do I do? Do I sit here for the entire reception, then grab Monica and head home?* Then I remembered their faces as they walked past my pew. I remembered Connie on the side of the aisle. I remembered Symphony stomping in front of me. I remember how Monica never acknowledged me even though she was so close I could see her freckles under her makeup. They all knew.

In great sorrow and devastating grief, they pulled it off—the entire wedding.

Latricia's special day isn't ruined, though I've ruined life for my wife. Internally, in the time it takes a runny nose to sniff, I was the antagonist; the bad guy, the evil villain. Each minute I sat there thinking about what they could be talking about inside the reception hall was excruciating. It's true, *the anticipation of death is far worse than death.* I have to go in, even if it's just to notify Monica that I'll wait for her outside. I have to go in. If she knows about my affair with Briana, we're leaving right after she takes pictures. The girls are flying back to New Orleans with the rest of the family, so it will just be the two of us and eight hours to talk about how I fucked up.

I have to go in.

I have to piss.

I'm going in.

There are ironies in life that you that you can bet a kidney will occur now and then to add to your misfortune. Ironies like catching every red light when you're running late for work, your child wanting that must-have toy for Christmas and another customer grabbing the last one on the shelf, and, last but not least, taking the long way to avoid a bully only to run into the bully far away from home.

There she was, in the narrow hallway that led to the men's restroom. There was no avoiding Connie; the hall was only four feet wide. Connie was only 120 pounds soaking wet, but she appeared huge like Shaquille O'Neil—no bullshit. Her shoulders scraped the wall on both sides. My path to the restroom was blocked by an immovable object; a pissed-off brick wall.

Before this moment, I had never been slapped in the face in my forty years on Earth, nor had I ever been punched in the face. Nor had anyone ever made any violent threat to my face . . . but there's a first time for everything. I didn't see her hand connect with the smooth skin on my face, but I did hear the approaching gust that whistled toward my left ear. I knew then what it meant to have the taste slapped out of your mouth—that cliché was accurate. Not only did the taste leave my mouth, but I felt every bone in her veiny little hand. After the slap, she holstered that veiny little hand on the left side of her body. My eyes fell out of focus. I saw a soft, white glow and for a second, I thought Connie had slapped me into heaven. In my ear was a pinging, but it couldn't mute away the revulsion in her voice.

*"If I had a knife I would stab your ass in the neck."*

Connie was a woman who never spoke above a whisper, let alone spewed threats laced with profanity. Her husband was the pastor of a growing congregation in Slidell, Louisiana, and she was the prototypical First Lady of the Church—but not tonight.

"How dare *you, you, you* filthy son of a bitch?" Her words were low in volume but blared like stadium speakers. "I will deal with my daughter for what she has done, but you are the lowest piece of shit I have ever known. My sister has been fighting for her life, and you're having sex with her niece? My daughter? My husband and his brothers are looking for you as we speak, and I hope they drag your ass in a month from now stinking from the woods."

"Connie, I'm sorry . . ."

*"Fuck your apology.* I would tell you to stay away from my sister, but she's married to your pitiful ass."

Briana's threats had been empty, but her mother's threats were playing out in real time. Her husband, his brother, and two other cousins were looking for me. I looked forward into the hall and saw them shuffling through the reception. With my head down, I skulked past Connie into the restroom.

In the restroom stall, I continued to dial Monica's phone. She finally answered, and I quickly gave her my location.

"I saw you when you entered the reception, I'm waiting for you in the truck," she told me.

Those words made me very happy, because I needed to get the hell out of Dallas as quickly as possible. I managed to walk thin and low clean out the door without encountering my brother-in-law the pastor and his brothers, but this was far from over. Once outside the reception hall, I ran the rest of the way back to my truck to find Monica in the driver's seat.

"Do you want me to drive?" I asked. She didn't reply, so I took that as a no and got in on the passenger side.

Driving east on Interstate 20 was quiet. I wanted to break the silence, but I yielded the floor to Monica. She, however, kept her eyes on the road like an Uber driver. Only an occasional deep sigh and a grunt—that was basically it from Dallas clean through Tyler, Texas, but at least I had escaped Dallas and that gangster pack of pastors who wanted to shoot me in the face.

The sign outside my window read ten miles to Shreveport. The solitary confinement of the passenger seat was torture; I'd much rather her scream and yell than hear her sighs, which only seemed to sink deeper with each passing mile. *Just say it got-damit, curse me out already.* Not a peep. Not even a song on the radio, only the hum of soft rubber rolling across a tar-paved interstate.

*Welcome to Shreveport.*

I can't take it another minute, we have to talk. The only way I can begin to fix this mess is if we talk. So here it goes.

"Monica, I just want to say that—"

She silenced me with an sharp finger and cleared her throat.

"Here's the part that hurt the most." I could tell from those seven words how the rest of the conversation was going to go. She knew everything, so it was no use to make a fuss. *Hear her out, then counter with an apology.*

"Here's what stings far greater than the affair you had with Briana. It's the picture of her in the maroon bra and panties. I recognized those panties. One night I wanted to do something special for you, but I couldn't find that maroon set. I remembered how much it turned you on, but I couldn't finish out that evening. In that picture of Briana, I not only recognized the panties and bra, but I also recognized the room where the picture was taken. She took those pictures in the *TempStay Habitat for Patients.*

Her voice was empty.

Her words were gelid.

Her tone was scratchy.

"While I was getting pumped full of toxic drugs to flush out this cancer, you and Briana were in the room provided as a courtesy by MD Anderson? Jarvis, directly across the street from the hospital? That photo right there was the one that cracked open my chest plate."

"*Monica I am so—*" Her finger cut me off again.

"I knew I could not perform my duties as a wife, I knew my illness was a heavy burden on our marriage, but I offered you a way out. Do you remember?" That wasn't really a question for me to answer. "I offered you a divorce on the grounds that I no longer felt sexy, I no longer felt like a woman, I no longer felt like I was alive, and it wasn't fair to you. I tried to set you free. In my twisted mind, I wanted you to find someone who could please you, and make you happy, and give you the pleasures I couldn't. I cared for you that much. Didn't I offer you that?"

"Yes." She allowed me to speak a word, just a single word.

"And what did you say?"

"I said no, because—" The finger was back.

"That's right, you said no." A superficial smile appeared as if she were having a eureka moment. "Back when I woke up in the morning and half of my hair continued to sleep on my pillow, I even offered to hire a call girl for your birthday. Didn't I? I selected five girls for you, printed out their pictures, and made a little menu for you. Even hung a banner that read, *Welcome to Fantasy Week*. I did that, sure did. For my husband. But you said . . ."

"I said no." Her finger lowered long enough for my reply, then it silenced me again.

"If I was willing to do all of that for you, why would you do this to me?" Her finger rested in her lap.

Monica wasn't lying. She offered me all of those things, but I wanted the Husband of the Year award, so I declined each one. In the back of my mind, I didn't think she was serious. It felt more like a trap. Even the guys said, *Boy, you better not take that offer—she's baiting your dumb ass*, but it wasn't a trap. Monica was serious; she was willing to make those sacrifices for me.

"Monica, it's like this . . . it happened so fast. Once it started, I tried to stop it, but—"

"So you couldn't stop?"

"I tried, but—"

"Was it that good to you?"

*"Monica, that's not what I'm trying to say—"*

"Then what are you saying, my dear hubby? What are you saying?"

"I'm trying to say I love you, and I love our family, and I fucked up, Monica. But I'm taking full responsibility for all of this, for everything that's happened. Baby, I'm sorry. I'm begging for your forgiveness. No matter how long it takes, I will work to earn your trust again; I will make this right. Please forgive me, please Monica."

The first exit in Shreveport is one mile ahead. The gas light has been on since Tyler, Texas. I'm hoping she takes this exit.

"Do you love me?"

"Yes, I love you."

"And you love your family?"

"Yes, I do. I'm trying to save my family right now. This was my first time ever cheating on you. Please don't leave me."

"I just want to make sure I have all the facts and that I know your position. So, you're saying you love me and you love your family. You love me, and you love your family." Her hands moved up and down like a scale as she weighed each sentence. Then, she excluded me out of the conversation altogether.

"He says he loves you and he loves his family . . . ain't that some shit? Ain't it, though? This has to be a new kind of love where your man says one thing, then turns around and fucks your niece. *Dude's actions are bizarre*." Monica continued to converse with herself about me as if I weren't in the car.

"Monica, I know how this looks, but baby, please hear me out . . ."

"Honeybun, I have one more question, then I will hear you out all the way back to New Orleans."

"Okay, that's fair."

"Here's the part I'm struggling with." Her voice was calm and soft like that of a kindergarten teacher. "If you love our family, why did you fuck my niece?"

Before I could answer, that single finger which controlled our conversation slowly balled into the other fingers beside it. Just as I was about to answer her question, her fist landed just below my ear, causing pain to shoot down my neck like a lightning bolt.

"If you love me, then why did you fuck my niece?!" I tried to shield my head from a storm of slaps and punches. "I find out from my sister that my husband is cheating on me with my niece. You think sorry is going to fix this shit? You humiliated me . . . in front of my entire family! And you think sorry with fix this?!" My Denali swerved like a drunk driver was behind the wheel.

Suddenly, Monica released the steering wheel, bar-stooled her body in my direction, then started kicking me with her stilettos. Our vehicle wasn't a driverless vehicle, but it quickly became one as she kicked my ass. The tires bounced along the beveled warning strip as we veered toward a deep center median. I reached through those stabbing heels to grab the wheel, and that's when she raised herself to her knees in the driver's seat and started boxing me in the face. I tried my best to keep us on the road, but I was failing miserably. We were headed for the deepest part of the center median.

"While you were fucking her in Houston, I died. I coded. Twice. I made you promise me when we were in driving to Houston that you wouldn't resuscitate me. And you had them resuscitate me. You brought me back to life. For this? Why didn't you let me go?! Why didn't you let me die?! You cruel mother-fucker. You brought me back to life to rip out my heart?"

I caught a quick glance in the side-view mirror and saw that the traffic had fallen back. No one tried to pass us, as if we were in a white Bronco. Bleeding from several places, I managed to gain control of the truck. That's when the licks ceased. That's when I managed to swerve right across three lanes, shift into neutral, and coast off an exit ramp.

We came to a rolling stop on the shoulder of the exit.

It was there that I heard a cry like none I had ever heard during our marriage. Not even during childbirth, or at the funeral for her mother, did I hear her in so much pain—pain in the highest human decibel. It wasn't my life that flashed before my eyes, but every night I snuck away to be with Briana. Every lie I told to see Briana, and every time I released in Briana. It was there, at Exit 17B, with the interstate to my left and an Exxon gas station to my right, that I came face to face with the full measure of emotional trauma I had inflicted on my wife.

The sun overhead was just about ready to clock out for the day.

"Why didn't you let me die? My entire family knows, our daughters know, and my poor sister. My poor sister. Her daughter is pregnant for my husband. I married this monster into our family. You impregnated my godchild. You never loved me."

With those words, Monica fell silent, as if she had fallen asleep with her eyes open. I sat there and allowed every word to cut through me. This is what I deserved. There we sat for another ten minutes, with a bright orange low fuel light on the dash.

When Monica lifted her head from her waking nap, she shifted the Denali back into drive and followed the curved road into the Exxon gas station. I got out to started to pump. Standing there, I saw my battered reflection in the window of my truck. I also saw the blood on my shirt. I was still bleeding from the side of my neck—I needed something to stop the bleeding. Once the truck filled up completely, I asked Monica if she needed anything from the store.

"I need a Sprite to settle my stomach and some Goodie Headache Powder."

"Is that all you need? Do you need to use the restroom while we're here?" The conversation was normal, which made it abnormal.

"No, that's all I need."

"I'll be right back."

I stumbled into the Exxon feeling like I had left a dog fight in which I was one of the unlucky pitbulls. In the restroom, I tried to cool my flaming injuries by pressing a cool stack of paper towels to my neck. I looked in the mirror again. My face was covered with flaming-hot red lines, all of which leaked blood. I tried to wipe and clean as best I could, but a few of the cuts were deep. I was going to need a few stitches.

I stumbled my way to the front counter with a sixteen-ounce Sprite, a thirty-two-ounce orange Gatorade, and two Snickers bars. At the counter, I asked the lady for a pack of Goodie Headache Powder. When she turned back to me with the headache powder, she also handed me a couple things I didn't expect.

"When you were in the restroom, the woman in that fancy SUV handed me these and asked that I give them to you." The elderly blonde-haired clerk placed my cell phone on the counter, then sat a ring on top of it.

It was Monica's wedding ring. When I looked through the large, glass convenience store wall, I didn't see our cherry-red Denali. It was gone. Monica was gone. Every call went to voicemail on the first ring. On some attempts, there wasn't a ring at all.

On May 13, 2017, at 7:24 p.m., Monica left me at an Exxon gas station off I-20 in Shreveport.

The next call I placed was to Uncle Glenn, who answered on

the first ring.

"What's up, Jarvis?"

"She left me, Unc, she left me!" I cried into the phone.

"Where are you?"

I couldn't compose myself long enough to give my location.

"Jarvis, where are you?" he asked in the tone of a concerned father. "I'm coming get you."

"I'm on I-20 and 1-49, Exit 17B."

"Go catch an Uber to a hotel and make yourself comfortable. We're on our way."

He never even asked what happened. It was as if he knew this day would come and he would get this call. He tried to warn me, but I didn't listen—I didn't want to hear it. Even though my truck is probably on I-49 South by now, I can still hear that cry. Even on the phone with Uncle Glenn, I still hear her pain. It was best she put me out—I couldn't bear to hear the pain I've caused.

"I have Biyell here, we're on our way."

"One more thing, Uncle Glenn . . ."

"What is it, Jarvis?"

"Crown Timothy the winner; my marriage is over."

# CHAPTER 16

7:30 p.m.

**JARVIS**

A text from Briana:
*You're all the family I have left.*
*I love you.*

# CHAPTER 17

Madden Night
Thursday, May 25, 2017
6:45 p.m.

I can still feel the silkiness of Diana's lips on mine. I can still inhale her seductive redolence, even though she departed an hour ago. Her femininity, her soothing vibrations, and her touch all make me possessive and territorial when I have no reason to be concerned. The thought of her loving another the way she loves me drives me mad, but there isn't anything wrong with that—how I feel is a byproduct of a good woman, and evidence that I have one—as long as I don't act crazy or deranged.

Earlier today, Diana mentioned that she wanted to hang out with her girlfriends, and I was okay with it. I like the fact that she has a circle outside of our marriage. Her friends don't have to be my friends. Our marriage is not a cult in which we're threatened by extended relationships. My wife is married, but free to learn from others and grow healthy bonds, and I am free to do the same. But I'm sad. Not because she's out with her friends, but because it's Thursday night and I'm home alone.

But this is self-infected loneness.

In the center of the coffee table are two black PlayStation controllers who appear as puzzled as I am. Where are my friends? How could I gain so much and yet lose something far more valuable? This is self-inflected isolation that was self-imposed, all because I tried to change five men. I enjoyed them much more in their original states, as they were—yeah, I said it. But I had to open my big mouth. I had to try to change them, and what do I have to show for it? Only two lonely controllers and a wife who is out living her best life.

It wasn't worth it.

It's been about two weeks since I picked Jarvis up off the side of the road; he looked like he'd lost a fight with weed-eater. In trying to change him, I may have destroyed his life, and I have to live with this new reality. In this short period of time, Monica Napoleon has already filed for divorce from Jarvis Napoleon. The dude did make a hard effort to apologize—in fact he begged every day—but in the aftermath of *I'm sorry,* there was nothing left to say, reconcile, or salvage.

During a recent conversation with Jarvis, he told me that he moved into an apartment complex in Carrolton. Briana also lives in that complex, but that's neither here nor there at this point. Jarvis has crawled under a rock, and everyone he called friend or family has ostracized him—even his mother has refused to accept his phone calls. But if he ever needs me, I will drop what I'm doing and help him. He would do the same for me.

Excuse me one second, there's someone at the door. Crowd Noise Telly.

"I know you kicked me out the group and all, but it is Thursday—can a brother get a game?"

"Then come on in with those garbage-ass Falcons, let's get it on." I've never been happier to see the dude.

"Lock the door!" Telly yelled in the big, booming voice that always rattled the picture frames. "Uncle Glenn, I'm about to lay down a Mike Tyson ass-whipping on you and there's no one to save you."

We embraced in a hug. I've missed him.

I hopped my way back to the living room. "Crowd Noise, what are you drinking?"

"Whatever you got, Unc."

From the inside of his tired suit, a bag of weed flopped onto the coffee table. Call me crazy, but I swore I saw the two Play-Station controllers smile at each other when they saw the weed.

"So who's your new connect now that Rasta has retired?"

"I don't have one; this is the last of the *good shit!*"

I placed a Heineken next to the bag and popped the top off my bottle. "You sure that weed is still good? It's been a few months, it could be molded . . ."

"Glenn, how I'm feeling right now it could have dog shit on it . . . pass me the lighter, *ya heard me?*" We shared a laugh.

"I missed you, brother." I slapped his back then reached for my controller. "What's been up with you?"

"Missing the fuck out of you guys, and trying to keep these women from driving me crazy."

"Don't tell me you still have the dual thing going with the lawyer chick and Erica?"

"Erica and who?"

"Boy, don't tell me Yolanda busted you?"

"No, it was the other way around. Uncle Glenn, that bitch played me like a bass guitar."

"Come on, man?"

"Yeah, she got me, but that's the last time I ever feel that sting. After her, I looked down my bench and put another starter in the game."

"What about Erica? She can't hold down the starting job?"

"Yes and no." On the TV screen stand my Packers versus Telly's Falcons, but the game can wait until after he rolls these last two blunts. "Here's the deal with Erica: She can pass, and she can play good defense, but she can't shoot to save her life. She's

Shaquille O'Neil at the free throw line."

"Why not commit to the process and practice with her?"

"I am, but in the meantime, I've put in a freak with a hot hand. The freak is under no pressure to win the game for me—just shoot all three nets."

"Let me guess . . . the pussy is good?"

Telly leaped to his feet and gave a salute. "Uncle Glenn, that pussy is like hitting all four quarters on a Super Bowl pool!" He saluted again.

"That good, huh?"

"Uncle Glenn. Uncle Glenn. Uncle Glenn."

"So the pussy fire-hot?"

"Uncle Glenn, that pussy is like some gumbo that's been in the freezer for five days, ya heard me?"

Telly started down the robot dance, then the running man, then the cabbage patch. I'm thinking *here we go again*, but this time I'm minding my fucking business. He can run from silk panties to lace panties until his dick catches an asthma attack. Telly is the last of my crew, and I'm minding my fucking business.

"And don't get me wrong, I love Erica, I love her kids, and we have managed to build a little family." After a hard drag on the blunt, his jaws swelled like Dizzy Gillespie, then he released the cloud.

Oh, how I missed the cloud, and the puff, and the fluff. It hasn't been the same in the worst way—*there's no sunshine when it's gone*. Euphoric fog is the evidence of good will and freedom, laughter and fellowship. Not the church kind of fellowship, but the free indeed type, where all things are shared, where no one goes without, where we matter. All of that was contained in the space just below my ceiling, and I thank God our cloud is back.

"Don't get me wrong Uncle Glenn, I'm happy with Erica—happier than Bill Cosby at a slumber party—but gooooood pussy is my drug of choice."

"But I thought Erica was good?"

"She is."

"But?"

"My new bitch . . . *did I mention she was white?*"

"No, you left that part out . . . but continue."

"Well, she's white. Not fake white like those Kardashian girls: she's like, real white."

"Telly, what the fuck are you talking about, real white?"

"You know . . . like Megyn Kelly white. Like she's comfortable being her white self, and I like that."

"So in other words, this is your first interracial relationship, and now you're sprung?

"Who? Me? Sprung? Uncle Glenn, I'm a lawyer during the day and a plumber at night. Nigga, I lay pipe!"

"*Shiiiiid*, Telly, you sound sprung to me. It also sounds like Erica is in trouble?"

"Erica is safe for now, but Megyn Kelly is forty-three years old, her ass feels like a new sofa, she has jet-black hair like a vampire, and can she suck the life out of a dick. But wait, there's more! Megyn is financially secure—dick and dinner is all she needs. Oh . . . and did I mention the pussy was good?"

"Yes, that's all you've talked about is the pussy."

"Uncle Glenn, that pussy feels like you've climbed to the top of the Super Dome, then jumped off that bitch into a tub of pudding. *Banana pudding, nigga.* Did I mention her pussy is pretty?"

"What? Telly put the weed down, you need to walk off this high." I chuckled.

"Uncle Glenn, Megyn's pussy, it's not really pinkish like you would think, it's more like the color of salami. Yum, yum, nigga!" We both choked on the blunts and shared another hard laugh.

Suddenly there was another knock at the door. Crowd Noise

headed up the hall to answer it, then came the sound of a brotherly reunion.

"Come on in here with those *jinky-ass* Steelers! I got something for you." It was Biyell.

Once he entered the living room, he yelled, "*Uncle Glenn, you sum-bitch you!*"

Biyell dapped me off where I sat and settled in on the other side of Telly. It was starting to feel like us again minus three, but I'll take it. Sadly, I report that Biyell's eye has healed poorly. Dude will need cosmetic surgery to fix that shit. It looks like he tried to draw an eyebrow with his foot. But broke eye and all, I missed him.

"You two *niggas* trying to practice, huh? Sorry asses. . ."

"Practice? To play your sorry ass? The last time you beat me, Destiny's Child was five girls," Telly reminded him as he offered a blunt. "I missed you, brother."

"Man, I missed you guys. Shit ain't the same no more. Uncle, I was coming here tonight even if I had to break in this bitch, I needed to be here," Biyell said in a relieved voice.

"I needed you to be here too, Big B." I offered him a drink. "Thursdays haven't been the same."

"Not at all," Telly agreed.

"What's going on with that situation, Biyell?" I asked, but I already knew.

Biyell shook his head forever and slumped. "It's over with Tamera and GiGi, but at least Gigi is allowing me to see my baby. Tamera, that bitch, she on some bullshit. Even got a restraining order, as if I were beating on her."

Telly caught his laughter just in time. "Wait, you got busted in the head with a brick, and one of them filed a protective order against you?"

"And it was granted, without a hearing! The cops have never been to my home for a domestic incident, yet I have to stay five-hundred feet away from my house. I haven't seen Braylyn in nearly a month." His lips fluttered. "It's so fucked up how they do us."

As for me, my guilt felt like someone just threw a cup of water in some hot fish grease. This is all my fault; I encouraged Biyell to decide between the two—Gigi and Tamera. And yes, he would have eventually gotten busted, but it wouldn't have been on me. I simply wanted these brothers to have what I have, and to get their lives to the point where they could take their ladies to dinner and not have to scan the room like Facebook looking for mutual friends.

"So why not try to make things work with GiGi?" I wondered.

"I don't know. I guess I'm still pissed at her for setting me up like that."

Telly erupted in laughter. "*You cheeky fucka*. You got busted, and you're mad at GiGi? That's why I love this house on Thursday nights—you narcissistic niggas have convinced me that I'm as fucked up as I thought."

"For real dude, that shit pissed me off. And my forehead is still jacked up. Every time I look at my face in the mirror, I see that bitch pitching that brick at me. I can't brush my teeth without thinking about that brick."

"Then try to make it work, Biyell," I urged him. "At least you will be with two of your kids and raise your boy. Speaking of which, she should be big pregnant about now?"

"I wouldn't know, her mean-ass mother is the mediator. That bitch can't stand me, and I can't stand her."

"Wait, you're having a boy?" Telly offered Biyell a congratulatory shake. I reached across Telly to offer the same.

"Biyell, you know as well as I do that you're not going to like another dude being around your kids. The first time you see Joe Blow at the park with your kids, you're not going to like it."

"Do you think if you chilled with the hoe shit and put forth a real effort, GiGi would take you back?" Telly asked.

"I do, because raising two kids without their father under the same roof breaks a long winning streak in her family. She would be the only one with a baby daddy. Baker women don't play that shit; they're in it for life."

Suddenly there was another knock at the door—this time Biyell answered it while the two PlayStation controllers waited patiently. It was another brotherly reunion.

"Smells like you niggas smoking a rose bush in here!" It was Rasta.

"If you hadn't dropped us for LaDaaaaaisha we would have something to smoke. So fuck it, rose bushes it is," Telly said as the room burst into laughter. "I don't like this new *Jehovah's Witness Rasta*; you haven't caught a bullshit charge in six months— not even a traffic warrant. LaDeisha put you out of business."

"What? Jehovah's Witness? *Maaaan, fuck you.*" It's been a while since I've seen Rasta laugh that hard.

"What are you drinking, Rasta?" I yelled from the kitchen.

"Lemonade or water."

"What?" Biyell leaned forward. "Bruh, you gave up weed and Heinekens? I don't know what kind of pussy LaDeisha put on you, but I don't want none. Fuck that . . . no thank you."

"Dude, you must be a Mormon now! You rode over here on a ten-speed bike with two white boys from Utah, huh?" Telly asked.

"Just detoxing my life and—"

"Detoxing my ass," Biyell cut him short. "That bitch really, really hurt you! You can't fake the funk with me. I know you. We used to smoke weed in junior high, after Sunday School, during Sunday School . . . even our grandmothers smoked weed together. That LaDeisha chick zapped your motherboard."

"Bruh, it's not her. I just gave it up, that's all."

"Time out." Telly gave the signal. "Seriously, all jokes aside. For real bruh, you really expect us to believe that?"

"It wasn't just LaDeisha, it was everything. It felt like life was crashing down on me. Believe it or not, it was Timothy who walked with me day and night until I felt like living again."

That was news to all of us, because Timothy is the last person I would think of to help someone through a difficult situation.

"Speaking of Timothy, did he ever proof up on Toostie?" Biyell asked. "It's not that it makes a difference to me, because I went down in flames, but I would like to know. I was betting on Jarvis, but after Glenn asked me to ride with him to Shreveport, I knew then Timothy was the last man standing."

"It's interesting that we're talking about this," I said, "because he called earlier and said he had a surprise for me, and that I would find out around nine o'clock. The surprise could only mean he's about to propose, or he has proposed, and Tootsie said yes. Tonight is the first Madden Night after the forty-fifth day. If he stays with Tootsie until April 6th of next year, he takes the pot."

Biyell slapped his leg. "That fucking GiGI . . . bitch."

Rasta's face wrinkled. "Uncle Glenn, did you just say Timothy called you today?"

"Yeah, around noon."

"He hit me up too, around noon," Telly said.

"That's how I knew you guys were playing tonight, he called me," Rasta said.

From down the hall came another knock high on the door—a very familiar knock. Rasta opened the door and we heard another brotherly reunion. Seconds later, he entered the living room carrying a box.

"Got-damn, look who we have here . . . Tina Turner!" Telly's annoying ass yelled out. "Ike know you over here?" The room huddled around him in laughter as he sat the box on the table.

"Tina you better eat that cake—eat the cake before *I kick yo' ass!*" Biyell said in his Ike Turner's voice.

"Oh, oh, Frankenstein's got jokes? You *brokeback-eye moth-*

*erfucka!*" Jarvis shot back.

I peeked in through the top of the box. "Jesus Jaquan Christ!" I yelled in excitement. "You finally finished the damn thing?"

"Yes, here it is, fellas."

Jarvis handed everyone a glossy, hardcover book with his name written in bold letters at the bottom. In the center of the book was a drawing of a black hole with five men in a single-file line. The first man was in the act of falling into the hole. On the other side of the hole was a man in a construction worker uniform who held a sign that read, *Caution: Make U-Turn*. At the bottom of the hole were seductive caricatures of women with exaggerated breasts, hips, and lips. Then I read the title of the book and the hairs on my arms shot up like St. Augustine grass.

*Stop Falling Into Hoes.*

"Yes, it's about us," Jarvis said as the room fell silent.

Suddenly the weed didn't matter. John Madden Football didn't matter. The beer didn't matter, nor did anything else. In that instant, we settled in like members of Oprah's Book Club. When I flipped the book over, I saw that there was only one guy who didn't fall in the hole full of hoes.

"Dude, all I want to know is, which one of these characters is me?" Telly asked.

"Read the book, and you will know." He said in a somber voice.

"Jarvis, brother, *I'm so proud of you*," Rasta said.

"For real, bro, I never knew what you were writing, but if this is about how I fucked up my marriage, then I'm honored. Hopefully, someone will read it and make the right decision," Biyell affirmed.

"Uncle Glenn, I wrote this book as a tribute to you—for being the only man who has ever called me out on my bullshit and challenged me to be a better man. I had a good woman, and if I'd listened to you when I was on the edge, I wouldn't have fallen in that hole. But I fell, and I couldn't get out. Even though I didn't listen to you, I heard you. I wrote it down like John, Matthew, and Luke—every word you said, I heard you. Hopefully, someone else will hear you and make that U-turn."

I don't remember when the tears started to fall, but they landed on my book.

"So I must be this guy Byron?" Telly asked.

# CHAPTER 18

One hour later

I concluded that this little get-together was a brain child of Timothy; he wanted us all here for his big announcement. The only problem was, the guys couldn't care less. The star of the show for now is this book, *Stop Falling Into Hoes*. The only sound in the room came from the turning of the pages, and the occasional, *I can't believe you put that in the book* and, *Bruh, you giving away the game.*

It's all here. Everything that's been said, done, heard, and felt—it's all in the book. Every fistfight, every roast, every drama-filled moment is in the book. I've only made it to Chapter Two, but he nailed it. All our mannerisms, all our inside stories—like how Telly got the nickname *Crowd Noise,* and how every time I would get up off the sofa there would be a roll of toilet paper in that spot when I returned—it's here. As if getting rolled over in a porta potty was my fault. It's all in the book—even her.

"Nooooo! You put Spider-Bitch in the book?!" Biyell fell out in laughter.

There she was, in Chapter Three: *Spider-Bitch versus Biyell.* Her real name was Felicia; she was the woman Biyell was with the day he gave GiGi his phone number. That Felicia; the one who settled all arguments with a fistfight. Her apartment was two floors above my unit, and I knew once he stepped to her that it wasn't going to last.

I said, "Biyell, I have been living here for twelve years and I haven't seen that girl smile—not one time."

"That's because she needs a real man in her life. Real dick in her life. Give me a week and I'll have her smiling like Elmo."

In the beginning, it all started out like the typical relationship. Then it got serious, and then Biyell was formally introduced to the reason Felicia was single. She took zero shit. During Madden Nights a few years ago, Biyell had to wait for his turns in her apartment or it was going to be some shit—from what he shared with us, she hated our Madden Nights.

One such Madden Night, Jarvis went to his car to get his car charger when he heard what sounded like two people fighting. Jarvis said when he looked up, Felicia had a fistful of Biyell's nuts in one hand and his cell phone in the other.

"Hey what's going on up there?" Jarvis called up to them. "Come on you guys, chill out."

"Felicia, let go of my phone."

*"Who the Tamera bitch?"*

"Felicia, I'm not fucking playing with you. Let go of my nuts and my phone."

"You think this is a game? Who's the bitch? Huh? Who's the bitch calling you this late at night?"

"Felicia, it's seven-thirty . . . the sun just went down. The-fuck are you talking about? My phone, let go of my phone!"

"Who in the fuck is Tamera?"

"Nobody!"

"Nobody, huh? Then I'm about to call Ms. Nobody, because Mr. Somebody thinks I'm fuckin' stupid."

Even with all that pushing and pulling, Felicia managed to

press call, and that's when Biyell shifted into sheer panic mood to free his phone. The obstacle was, his phone was gripped behind five acrylic fingernails. Once he saw his phone in dial mode calling his wife, Felicia left him no other choice.

*Snap!*

*"Ouch!"*

*Snap!*

*"Ouch,* stop it!" Jarvis heard Felicia scream from the top upper balcony. "You're willing to break my fingernails to stop me from calling this bitch?! Ouch!"

After the third nail, Jarvis reported that the phone slipped out of Felicia's hand. The phone slid off the third-floor balcony and came to rest in the shrubs. Biyell later told us that he bolted for the stairs as fast as he could, but was surprised when Felicia didn't follow him.

When I finally made it outside that night, I couldn't believe my eyes—it was the craziest damn thing ever. Felicia was sliding down the balcony pole from the third floor. Once she reached the midway point of the pole that supported the second-floor balcony, she jumped down and tumbled onto the grassy area near the shrubs. Before Felicia could stand, Biyell made it downstairs and dove into the bushes for his phone. She dove in after him, and they tussled while the five of us stood there laughing our asses off. Finally, Jarvis and Rasta separated them. Yes, Spider-Bitch made the book. Even the song we made for her was in the book.

*Spider-Bitch*
*Spider-Bitch*
*Give me that phone*
*I'm Spider Bitch.*

After that situation, Biyell eventually promoted GiGi, but he didn't learn his lesson from Spider-Bitch.

"Bruh, why did you have to put in the story of the old lady and me? That story provides no literary value to the book. You got all my shit in here," Biyell complained.

"If he put every grandmother you fucked in this book, it would be the size of *Harry Potter*," Telly laughed.

On the kitchen counter is my cell phone, and I just received a text. So too did Jarvis, then Biyell, then Telly, then Rasta. I hopped over to the kitchen counter. It was a text from Timothy with two YouTube links attached:

*Uncle Glenn, here it is—the proof you wanted. It also appears that I will be the winner of this challenge, and I look forward to receiving the prize money on March 30, 2018. Enjoy the videos.*

Simultaneously, the fellas clicked the link to the first YouTube video. Timothy's face appeared—he was in a hotel. Behind him? A sandy beach and crystal blue water.

*Hi, guys, it looks like I have you all together. I wanted to be with you tonight, but I just woke up in beautiful Miami Beach. First of all, Uncle Glenn, I want to thank you for this challenge. Even without the generous prize money, this was just what I needed to make a grown man's decision.*

I gathered that Timothy had filmed the video this morning, because he was wearing a bathrobe and held a cup of coffee in one hand.

"I wish he'd stop all the talking and shit—let us see this Tootsie chick. This better be a bad bitch after the way he trashed Kayla," Biyell said.

"Nah, Tootsie didn't make him divorce Kayla, he did it on his own," Telly countered.

"*Shhhh*, I can't hear," nosey-ass Jarvis complained.

"All I know is, this Tootsie bitch better make Beyoncé look like Precious. That's all I'm saying."

"Biyell, *shhh*," I said.

On our screens, Timothy appeared winded in his speech.

*I know you guys didn't agree with the reason I left Kayla, but knew I had found the one from the first snap of my camera. I now know how Berry Gordy felt about Diana Ross, and how Lenny Williams felt about that bitch he cried about, how Daryl Hall felt about Sara—*

"Dude, fuck the songs and let's see this super-bad bitch!" Biyell had lost all patience.

"Biyell!" Like kindergarten teachers, we placed our fingers over our lips.

*And it was by accident that I fell in love with her. I wasn't looking for a love affair. Then she entered my studio with her mother—her mother was running late because her nail appointment was canceled, so I referred her to a friend of a friend. When she walked into my life, what started out as a photo shoot for a state representative campaign became a photo shoot of my future wife. Uncle Glenn, you asked me to text you the name of the woman that I could commit my heart to without a second thought, and I replied 'Tootsie'. Uncle Glenn, meet Tootsie.*

The first video ended, so we immediately clicked the second link. This time, we could hear a woman's voice in the background. She seemed to be in an elated conversation with someone else. Her face soon appeared on-screen, and the one good leg I have failed me for the first time.

*Uncle Glenn? Hi, Uncle Glenn, I remember you from that Christmas party.* She turned and smiled at Timothy. *Uncle*

*Glenn, it is official. I am going to be Mrs. Feltus. We're getting married!*

LaDeisha giggled, then buried her lips in Timothy's dimpled cheek. Then, she ran away to the back of the hotel room to finish her phone conversation. We could hear her say, *Girl, he proposed this morning, the ring was in my makeup bag.*

Do you hear that?

. . .

. . .

. . .

. . .

. . .

That's just how quiet it was in my house.

That's why Timothy never referred to Tootsie by her real name.

It was LaDeisha.

All this time.

Tootsie was LaDeisha.

And Timothy was Judas.

# CHAPTER 19

Madden Night
9:12 p.m.

Is this how Peter felt when he received word of the thirty pieces of silver? Is this the same discomposed feeling Caesar felt as Brutus approached with a pointed sword? Is this the sting that Coretta Scott King felt when she discovered that an African American photographer she had welcomed into her home and granted exclusive access to her husband's funeral was a registered agent for the FBI? Perhaps, but if I didn't know before, I know now—Timothy would slit your throat, then wipe the knife on your white, silk shirt.

The turquoise numbers on the microwave display 9:12 p.m., and I just managed to take my first breath. The surface of my tongue was covered in Velcro. There was so much I wanted to say, but the words scattered like migrating birds. It felt like every tendon in my body had snapped, leaving me unable to move an inch, or close my mouth, or blink. The circuitry that connects my brain to my mouth was severed. My words back-piled in my throat.

We were more than just a group of guys who connected once a week to play *Madden Football*; we were a band of brothers. The same blade used to stab Rasta in the back punctured every man in my living room. In that painful instant, I could hear their thoughts, and they could hear mine.

*How could you do that to Rasta?*

*How could you do that to us?*

*How could you do it to me?*

And I have to take my lick in all of this because I never paid attention to her name; all of the mistresses have two names. Her name was simply Tootsie, and I never gave it a second thought . . . but now that I think about it, Rasta was doomed from day one. How could you submit LaDeisha when she was romantically involved with Rasta? Who does that?

Timothy.

LaDeisha was Rasta's woman. She was the woman who inspired Rasta to change and rearrange every aspect of his life—even compromise his religion—as he attempted to assimilate into her world. Unfortunately, Rasta never stood a chance, and every strand of his dreadlocks had died in vain. Timothy, that greasy snake, slithered through our lives undetected and unsuspected until he found the weakest among us—then out came the fangs.

To my left stood Biyell, who covered his eyes—the vicarious humiliation was too much to bear. Even I looked away from Rasta; I wasn't ready for the aftermath. We needed a little more time. On the sofa, Jarvis sat with his head in his hands as he replayed LaDeisha's portion of the video, hoping the same video would have a different ending. It didn't.

"Looks like I finished my book too soon."

"No worries, it's going down in the sequel," Biyell said.

Next to Jarvis sat Telly, who gazed off into space as he searched the files in his mind for a clue or hint of Timothy's motives, but there was none. His plan to win LaDeisha had been executed to perfection, and when a plan is flawless, dumbfounded reactions are the spoils of war.

Directly in front of my television sat Rasta. He was motion-less, stiffened by the realization that two individuals he had al-lowed into the most private compartments of his life had just announced their engagement. His face bore the look of someone who had just lost his wallet and paused for a second to backtrack.

Biyell was first to break the silence.

"My only question is, are we kicking his ass at the airport or outside?" Biyell's hands still covered his eyes.

"Man, I'm all in," Telly replied.

"Who else?" Biyell wanted to know.

"In the name of Rasta, I need to kick his ass. I need to stump his head a few times." Jarvis was pissed.

Biyell recited out a text. "Congratulations Timothy . . . when . . . are . . . you . . . coming . . . back?"

"This shit all makes sense now," Rasta finally thawed. "The constant requests for updates, asking if I spoke with LaDeisha . . . dude even came to the flea market a few times and made a few suggestions. I took his advice—"

Telly cut him off. "And all the while he was doubling back to LaDeisha . . . like a spy, seeming like a genius to her because he knew your next move."

"That was straight hoe shit," Jarvis interjected.

"Timothy knew my every move. Over these past few weeks, we hung tight and all the while—"

"He was using that information to get to LaDeisha." Biyell was agitated. "There are two things we don't touch . . ."

"The main lady and your sister," Telly recited.

"Fucking right! We keep our hands off the wife or the main lady, and I don't care how fine she is, I will never fuck with your sister. I know we have our *personal shit* we deal with, but none of us have ever broken that code—"

"Until now," Telly said.

"Fucking right, until now. Timothy broke the code. He's in violation. I have to put some hands on him. That's in the rule book," Biyell said as he sent another text to Timothy.

"No, we're not going down that road. Timothy asked LaDeisha to marry him, and she said yes." Rasta paced. "I watched the same video, and I've never seen her that happy. The smile I saw tonight was something I could never accomplish. I don't like it, but in the end, there's no way she could have loved me and accepted that proposal."

"Rasta, I feel you on that, but hear me out," Biyell shook his head in protest. "To submit another man's woman as the woman you plan to commit to for a year is the dirtiest shit I have ever seen. We have to kick his ass, so all the other pussy-ass niggas will have an example."

"No, because that's what he's expecting. At the end of the day, he was never my friend and she was never my woman. I have to eat that."

"The planning that went into stealing LaDeisha is what has me tripping out," Telly said.

"And you didn't see any sign of this when you handled his divorce?" I asked.

"Hell no."

"But would you tell us if he did confess? Aren't your lips sealed by attorney-client privilege?" Biyell asked.

"Fuck no, and even if they were, I would have notified Rasta to his face." Telly stood over Rasta. "If I would have known that he was pursuing LaDeisha, I would have told you. I don't rock like that. There's too much pussy out here to cutthroat over a woman." Telly was offended.

Biyell met him nose to nose. "I just find it strange that he never mentioned who Tootsie was to you."

"So you have a cable degree and a law degree too?"

I hopped in their direction.

"Nigga, I don't fuck with Timothy like that," Telly continued. "I handled the divorce for his bitch-ass—it was non-contested, they didn't have any kids, she never caught him with a bitch. There wasn't shit to discuss. And quiet as kept, I thought the nigga was gay. Especially when his wife walked into the court looking like *Queen of all the Bad Bitches*! I figured if he'd lost his appetite for Kayla, with her tall, delicious-ass self, then maybe he'd developed an appetite for dick. But I held my peace."

Truth be told, all of us shared that thought, because Timothy loved the nail shop a little too much. It even came up once in a conversation with this same group, but we dropped it. Then Timothy divorced Kayla.

"I don't know who could leave a woman like Kayla," Telly shook his head.

Well anyway, more about Kayla later. Biyell and Telly are about to start swinging in my living room, and I'm not for it tonight.

I hopped between them. "Fellas let's calm down. We're all dealing with the shock from the video. No one is to blame for this but Timothy and LaDeisha, so chill the fuck out."

Rasta and Jarvis helped me separate the two.

"He never mentioned LaDeisha or Tootsie to me." Telly was still pissed at the accusation. "The only thing that felt off about it was Timothy wanted to be the plaintiff. That was important to him; that the record state he was the one who divorced Kayla. He was in a hurry—"

"Because she ended it with me, which presented a very small window. He knew from inside information that I wanted her and was going all out to get her back. He used me against me," Rasta sighed.

"But how did he come in contact with LaDeisha?" I asked. "Timothy wasn't at our Christmas party."

"Because I referred her to his business. LaDeisha needed a good photographer. I wanted to show him some love—"

"You did; he fell in love with your lady," I added.

"Uncle Glenn, that's savage, bruh," Jarvis said.

"For lack of a better description, that's what happened."

"Jarvis, he's right—I can't argue the facts. I was trying to help him out, shoot him over some business. I would never have thought—"

I interjected. "None of us *ever would have thought* Timothy was this low, but I agree with the point you made earlier—he's expecting a confrontation, so let's not give him one. I say we respond like gentlemen—not because Timothy is one, but because we are."

"Fuck that, Uncle Glenn." Biyell's patience with nonviolent suggestions soured like a gallon of milk. "We have to kick his ass; it's our duty. We don't have a hoe in this room. So why are we letting Timothy play us like hoes? An action comes with a reaction."

"So now you're Confucius? A minute ago you were OJ Lawyer," Telly barked at Biyell. "If Rasta said let the shit go, then let it go."

"You let it go, *imma bust* his ass when I catch up to him."

"*Nah*, brother, I love you for that, but I'm good." Rasta walked over and extended his hand, then pulled Biyell into a chest bump. "I'm good, bruh, I am. She stung me, I ain't gone lie, but I'll be all right."

"Rasta, trust me on this, you will feel much better when we kick his ass for pretending to be your friend while going behind your back to steal your girl."

"Biyell, he didn't steal her," Rasta said.

"I hear you but, if he wouldn't have interfered, then—"

"Can any of us take Diana from Uncle Glenn?" Rasta made eye contact with every man in the room, then turned back to Biyell. "Fuck no, because what you see between those two is real; it's as sure as steel. What I had with LaDeisha was plastic, and the moment it got too hot, it melted. If someone comes in between Glenn and Diana, that's the nigga you deal with. That marriage is sacred."

"The way I see it, Timothy should be disqualified from the competition because of the underhanded shit he pulled," Telly protested.

"That much we agree on," Biyell said.

"Not one copper nickel," Jarvis agreed.

"Fellas, I can't think about a contest right now; let's have this part of the conversation later in the week," I said.

Rasta moved around the room and embraced the crew on his way out.

"That shit ain't right Unc; we can't let Timothy walk away with the prize money on some underhanded shit," Biyell fussed.

"Uncle Glenn, I agree, this is some bullshit," Telly affirmed.

"Guys, I will address that later. Right now, my main concern is Rasta."

"Uncle Glenn, this cannot end on an act of betrayal. You can't allow that to happen."

"Biyell, give me few days to process this."

"But I don't see what there is to process?" Biyell made it to the kitchen in two strides. "Basically, he sabotaged Rasta. There's no way a cheater should win after all the shit we've gone through. Look at my eye, Unc." Biyell pointed at his scar.

"Yeah, I agree. It was an act of lowdown betrayal," Jarvis added.

"Gentlemen, I understand your beef, but this entire challenge started because of betrayal, and lies, and hurting those we say we love. What you're feeling right now is only a teaspoon of the pain you have caused. The only difference—Timothy cheated you." They listened, but none of them heard me. "I will have a conversation with Timothy when he gets back, but before I pass judgment, I would like to at least hear his side of the story. Can you at least allow me a few days to speak with him?"

Not one of them verbally agreed. Instead, they packed up, shot me a nod of the head, and filed out.

In the solitude of the kitchen, I sent Timothy a text.

*First of all, congratulations. When you get back, can you swing by?*

After about ten minutes, he replied.

*I'll bring her by on Saturday to see you, and I would like for you to be in my wedding.*

# CHAPTER 20

Friday, May 26, 2017
11:35 p.m.

## RASTA

I've always ignored my own subconscious voice, but not this time—for the first time in my life, I'm glad I listened to the inner me and obeyed. I'm so happy I obeyed, and it felt wonderful. It was cool, like an effervescent tingle from my neck all the way down my spine. I should have listened to that voice sooner; maybe some of the things that mattered so much yesterday wouldn't have mattered today. Nevertheless, I obeyed, and everything wrong became right, and everything jagged became smooth. That's where I was just moments ago—in a comforting state of smooth.

It was the like the greatest blunt I never smoked, and that vice grip feeling in my chest was gone, my mind was clear, and the air was a joy to inhale. The air was so thin it tingled the membranes in my nostrils, like the warm water that whisked across my bald scalp the night I cut my locks.

Then came her voice.

Not LaDeisha's voice, but a cruel, scratchy voice that carried no compassion for me. The voice has me confused. Where did she come from? Why is she in my bedroom? Who is this bitch and why does she have to scream in my face? Maybe she's a weed-head trying to rob me? If I wasn't so tired, I would chase her ass out of my house. Don't you just hate when you're in a good sleep and someone enters the room, clicks on the light, and start asking you questions? Fuck, I hate when I'm in a good sleep and someone wakes me up. Now I can't reconnect with that cool feeling. Damn, that light is bright.

"Drink it, Roderick; if you spit it out again we're going to fight."

My eyes cracked open a third of the way.

*How did this white woman get in my house?*

I think I'm stuck halfway in a dream—this isn't my house.

*But . . .*

*But . . .*

I don't remember how I got here.

At the foot of my bed I can see a man who looks like Uncle Glenn. To my right is a woman with the same voice as my mother, and on my left I think that's Aunt Diana. My mother—yes, that's my mother—has that sound in her voice like she's been crying. I haven't heard her cry in years. Everything else is a blur. I'm so weak. My throat feels like I have thrown up all night. In a curved plastic pan on the bed tray is my vomit—black as tar. My mouth tastes like tar. Where in the fuck am I? Next to Glenn is a woman I don't recognize; she's the one who turned the lights on and yelled in my face.

"*Roderick, you have to drink this and keep it down, or we will be here all night.*" She sounds like Marge Simpson.

The mean bitch handed me another cup filled halfway with the black liquid. It was clumpy like sour milk, and gritty. She can yell at me all day, I'm not drinking that shit.

"Roderick, either you drink it, or I will have you strapped down and push a tube down your throat. The choice is yours, but you will drink it."

"Rodie, please drink it, you're not going to like that tube down your throat." My mother has always called me Rodie.

"Momma, where am I?"

"Shhhhh, please drink. We'll discuss that later."

Like a reluctant four-year-old, I forced myself to swallow the cup of what I could only imagine was black motor oil. Why is my mother forcing me to drink this? Why isn't Uncle Glenn trying to stop this? Where did Aunt Diana go? Every question I asked was greeted with the same answer.

"Drink up, and try to keep it down."

In the back of my throat, I felt my esophagus contracting and releasing, so I asked Uncle Glenn to incline the bed. That did the trick. Once I sat up, my eyes came into better focus. I was in what appeared to be a hospital bed. The emergency room.

Fuck, I failed.

At something so easy even a teenager could do it.

The plan was so simple, how could I have failed it? Where did I go wrong?

The last thing I remember was swallowing a handful of Tylenol PMs. Then I wrote a letter, then I dressed in the best suit I had in the closet, then I placed the letter next to my head with my expired driver's license, then I drifted off to sleep. I wanted to be clean as fuck when I expired, because that's how I wanted to go to the morgue: *so fresh and so clean*. When the coroner arrived to collect my body, I wanted to make sure they reported: *Mr. Ross must have been someone important.*

That's one reason I decided to go with the pills—also because my mother would have wanted an open casket. Another reason is I couldn't manage to pull the trigger. I touched the trigger, but I had a vision of my brains splattered all over the wall and the mess that would leave behind—it wasn't fair to the person who had to clean it up. So, I went with the Tylenol exit strategy.

I planned everything out—I even thought about who would

attend my funeral—and I still screwed it up.

You think LaDeisha would have attended my funeral with Timothy or alone? In any case, I did say goodbye to her in my letter; her section was right before my farewell to my sons. Then I was awakened by this grouchy-ass woman with the cup of tar.

I'm still alive, but I don't want to be.

I'm tired, so tired.

I'm tired of chest pains every day. Tired of trying to delete her out of my mind, tired of trying to move on but not being able to, tired of constantly checking my phone to see if she called. I'm also tired of asking myself what she saw in Timothy that she didn't see in me. Does she make the same sounds during sex with him? I'm tired of women only giving me what they want me to have, but saving the good stuff for the next guy.

Why, LaDeisha?

If only I had a little more time with you. One more dinner, one more funny meme from Facebook, one more protest rally together, one more zombie Netflix series. If only I wasn't the problem.

It wasn't LaDeisha; she's not the reason I took those pills. I needed pain relief. The only place I could think of was the grave. It wasn't LaDeisha; it was the way I fucked my life. My life has been reduced to a little booth in a flea market, and if it rains two days in a row, then I'm shit out of luck in cash. A flea market hustler, that's all I am. No one will miss a flea market hustler.

It wasn't LaDeisha; she's not the reason I'm here. I am. I'm tired of being looked down on as an illegitimate business owner, an illegitimate lover, and an illegitimate father—a field trip dad. If you really want to know why I tried to kill myself, then I'll tell you: it was because of two Happy Meals from McDonald's.

You heard me correctly.

A $4.50 Happy Meal.

I needed two of them for my younger sons. My card declined from insufficient funds after I handed my sons the meals. I had already spent the money from Uncle Glenn on a truck and trailer, and the surplus ran out last week. For two consecutive weeks, it has rained. I only sold fifty dollars' worth of merchandise in two weeks. I didn't have enough for two fucking Happy Meals; that's what did it. Losing LaDeisha to Timothy hurt like hell, but not as badly as having a woman behind me step forward to pay for my food. That act of kindness stripped away a layer of my manhood. I became a chicken nugget: *a boneless man.*

But I will never forget her face; she had a smile like my mother on Christmas morning. She protected me in the eyes of my children. An angel? I will never forget my tall, beautiful, angelic beauty, but she was also part of the reason I took the pills; a supporting actor in my tragic minstrel.

In walked another doctor.

"Hi Mr. Ross, my name is Doctor Morton. Are you feeling a little better?" I didn't, nor did he expect me to.

"You're going to spend a few days with me, so we'll talk and sort things out." For a minute, I thought he was George Lopez.

I cleared enough tar and puke from my throat to speak. "Doc, I feel better already. Discharge me, please." I sounded like a Harry Belafonte interview on Twitter.

"I'm afraid I can't do that."

"I know how this looks. Taking those pills was a mistake, but I feel better now."

"Mr. Ross, you will be with us until I feel you're no longer a threat to yourself."

"So I'm being committed?"

"You are committed—"

"Institutionalized?"

"More like, *in the care of mental health professionals for wellness supervision —*"

"The crazy house," I cut through his politically correct gibberish.

"Roderick, I signed the paperwork," my mother said. "We came this close to losing you. The one-on-one time will do you some good."

"Momma, I'm not crazy, I don't need to be in a mental institution. I had a bad day, that's all it was."

With soaked eyes, my mother cuffed my hand.

"Roderick, you are my son, and I know you better than you know yourself. When you backed into my driveway on Friday and started giving away all your clothes, that was the first sign for me. Then you gave away appliances—televisions, and your leather sofas. I watched my neighbors surround you like Santa Claus in the hood. But it was when you gave away your woodworking tools and caught a cab home that night—that's when I turned white as these sheets. I ran to the phone and called Diana. We drove to your house as fast as we could. When we finally made it over there, we had to kick in the door." She couldn't continue.

"My brother, we were five minutes away from losing you." Uncle Glenn told me. "I asked my wife and your mother to wait outside while I checked your room. I saw the note on the side of your head." Uncle Glenn wiped his eyes with the belly of his shirt. "The EMS guy was able to get you to regurgitate some of the undigested pills; that's what saved your life."

"I know how this looks, but trust me, I was having a bad day, that's all. Doc, hear me out because it's not that complicated. One of my closest friends is marrying a woman I love; I discovered it last night—"

Glenn cut me off. "Rasta, that was three nights ago; today is Sunday. You just opened your eyes for the first time."

Then Dr. Morton cut in. "Mr. Ross, there's another reason I have to place a physician's hold on you. When we finally managed to revive you this morning, the nurse recorded your first words."

Doctor Morton held a clipboard in my view. At the bottom of the page, at 7:10 a.m., the nurse had noted:

*The patient is alert. First word spoken when he regained consciousness: FUCK!*

But I don't remember waking up; I only remember the annoying sound of the voice forcing me to drink the black paint.

"How long are you keeping me?" I asked Dr. Morton.

"Mr. Ross, that's really hard to say . . ."

"Could you at least give me a range?"

"You can plan to be in our care for at least the next two weeks, but it could extend beyond two weeks. It all depends on you."

"How?"

"If you're honest with me about your feelings, then it could take fourteen days. Dishonesty will keep you here longer. I guarantee it."

"I don't have insurance; I can't afford this place."

"I have already taken care of that part," Uncle Glenn assured me.

"Will I have to drink this black paint every day?"

Dr. Morton chuckled. "No sir, we have been pumping you full of activated charcoal. It stops the effects of the pills you swallowed. Dr. Ferncrest will pass by within the hour with the results of the tests we ran—your liver is our main concern right now. Once you're discharged from intensive care, then we'll talk more."

"I can't go home to change and grab a few things?"

"I'm afraid not."

"Why not? I can agree to the treatment, but first I need to take care of a few business matters."

"The only business matter that matters is getting you healthy. If I release you today, chances are your mother will be at the funeral home tomorrow. Not on my watch, Mr. Ross."

"Rasta, we have already delivered clothes and everything you need to be comfortable," Uncle Glenn said.

"Delivered already? You mean I have no say in whether or not I want to go through with this treatment?"

"Under the circumstances, I'm afraid not. Please try to understand that we are taking your actions very seriously. Mr. Ross, you arrived in the ER unresponsive, as close to death as one can get. It is my belief that you are determined to kill yourself, and all the people in this room are committed to making sure you're unsuccessful."

I can't believe this shit—I have been committed to a mental institution. They're sending me to a mental ward full of crazy people. But I'm not crazy, I'm tired. Tired and mentally crazy are two different things.

"If that's all the questions you have for me, then I will meet with you tomorrow right after breakfast."

"I have no further questions."

I don't want to be alive. When I get out of here, I will hang myself.

# CHAPTER 21

Sunday, May 28, 2017
8:22 p.m.

Leaving Rasta in the hospital was one of the hardest things I have had to do in a long time. In fact, it broke me. I can count on one hand the number of times I have cried in front of my wife, but on this bright Sunday morning, I folded over in the passenger seat and wailed. What broke me was his brokenness. His devastation. How he had swallowed every pill in the bottle. How determined Rasta was to die.

When we arrived at his place on Friday night, his next-door neighbor helped me kick in the door. I wanted to view him first for signs of life—I thought he was dead. Diana did her best to console his mother, but the letter he placed on the side of his head was too much. The only thing missing was a casket and a few flowers.

"Glenn, this is not your fault." With one hand on the steering wheel, Diana tried to shake me away from a quicksand pond of guilt.

"I should have butted out of their lives."

"I strongly disagree; you should have done exactly what you did. You challenged them to be better men. Cheating on wives and dogging out girlfriends was no way to live, but you caused them to examine the error of their ways. Glenn, baby, I'm proud of you. That's my nephew we just left in the ER, and I have never been more proud of you than I am right now. You did the right thing."

"Then why does it feel so bad? Like I set all of these horrible even in motion?"

"These events were going to come to light with or without your involvement, but the difference is you motivated them to change. At some point, the whoremongering had to stop."

"Rasta tried to commit suicide over this challenge."

"Glenn, that's not what happened—backstabbing Timothy got in between LaDeisha and Roderick. That's how we got here—not challenge, but a friend who wasn't a friend after all."

The morning that Timothy returned from Miami with LaDeisha, Diana and I were at West Jeff Hospital praying for Rasta's life. Regretfully, I didn't get the opportunity to meet with him. I told Timothy I had an emergency and would get with him later today if possible.

"Glenn, is the meeting with Timothy still on?" I swear that woman can read my mind.

"Yes, I received a text from him saying he's just finishing dinner and will meet me in a few."

"I know you guys are close, but I don't want anyone to know what happened to Roderick. When he's out and feeling better, he'll share with those who he feels are entitled to know."

"I agree, and I didn't plan to talk his business. Rasta has enough going on. I think this break away from familiar faces will make him stronger."

"I'm confident it will," Diana said as we pulled into our parking spot.

"I still can't believe he tried to kill himself over a woman."

"Excuse me?"

"I'm just saying."

"So you can't fathom how one could have those thoughts?" She turned the ignition off and half turned to me. "You didn't think the thought entered my mind after I delivered your daughter? You didn't think for one second that I wanted to fall asleep and never wake up after watching that perfect picture of a family that involved my husband?"

"Bu-but you never said anything about having those thoughts."

"Because those were *my thoughts, and my hurt, and my sorrow* that I couldn't escape." She spoke with an edge in her throat. "Here's how close I came." Diana leaned in—I could see thin red veins around her brown pupils. "After I left the three of you in that room that day, I ran up seven flights of stairs to the roof and sat there for hours. I wanted to end it all but couldn't. Why? Because I loved to love you. I was happy for the first time in my life—then I saw you standing there, and it wrung my heart. The only difference between the woman you see now and my nephew in the ER is I didn't want you and Derinda to be the conclusion of my life."

Before I could apologize, Diana stormed out of the car in a straight line to our apartment. Normally she would come around to my side of the car and assist me, but not tonight. I reached for my custom-made crutch, and with a deep, roaring grunt, I managed to stand. Once I made it inside our apartment, I saw Diana facedown across our bed, spilling all she had into a heart-shaped pillow I once gave her for Valentine's Day. I touched her heel, which caused her body to staccato in sorrowful convolutions.

"Diana, I'm so, so sorry. I know you still struggle with that day. I struggle with it too. Knowing how deeply I hurt you is something that haunts me with regret. I've said it a million times, but I'll say it again—I didn't sleep with Derinda while we were married, it was all before I said my vows to you—"

Her head turned to the side. "Glenn, I'm aware of that, I did the math years ago, but what rips me apart is she gave you something I couldn't. I wanted your first child to be our child."

"But Diana, I never cared if we didn't have children—"

"But I cared, Glenn; as a woman and a wife, I care. That too is a part of the pain I can never escape. Derinda never allowed you to have a relationship with your daughter, and I wasn't able to give you one. That still matters to me."

Just as I was about to lie next to her, there was a knock at the door; it could only be Timothy.

"That's Timothy."

"Please shut the door behind you; I have nothing to say to him."

"I understand."

About eighteen hops later I finally reached the front door. Just as I anticipated, it was Timothy. We embraced as we've always embraced, after which he followed me to the living room. By instinct, I cued up Lil Wayne, then offered Timothy something to drink.

"I'm good, Uncle Glenn, just coming from dinner with the future Mrs. Feltus. I'm stuffed."

His face and demeanor were those of a proud father who just watched his son win the Super Bowl. At no point during the time I've known Timothy had he ever seemed so at peace, so happy, so in love. His dazed eyes were filled with so much optimism. Even as he stared at my 1998 CD player, the one he's seen many times before, he smiled as if it were a top-of-the-line system with the best sound he'd ever heard.

I twisted the cap off my Heineken and slumped across from him on the loveseat. I needed to look him in the face when he explained this mess. I wanted to see if he would try to justify his actions with a straight face, or if he would admit that he stole Rasta's woman. Most importantly, I wanted to know why he cheated to win. I needed to know all of that and then some, and since he was less than two feet away, this was the best time to redeem the truth.

"So Tootsie is LaDeisha."

"Yes, and I prepared months ago for this part of the conversation."

"Really?"

"It looks bad, I know it does, but it's all legit."

"Legit? You proposed to a woman Rasta was madly in love with. He confided in you. He trusted you."

"As I said, I know this looks bad, but I can't help who I love. From the day she walked into my studio, I knew right then and there she was going to be my wife."

"Rasta referred her to your studio, and you make a move on his girl? What kind of bullshit is that, Timothy?" My voice was deep and loaded with rebuke.

"What you need to understand is the moment she entered my life, even in a professional capacity, I was going to make her my wife."

"But she wasn't single."

"It didn't matter, Uncle Glenn." Timothy's voice climbed to the second floor as his chest inflated with contentious steam. "None of that mattered. Rasta didn't matter. Even if she were married to another man, I was going to take her."

"The fuck you mean, take her?"

"Meaning it didn't matter if she was single or married, with Rasta or not—I claimed her in here." Timothy pounded his chest like an albino gorilla. "I never wanted a woman in my life the way I wanted Tootsie."

"LaDeisha, her name is LaDeisha. Lay off the Tootsie bullshit"

"Yes, LaDeisha. I wanted her all to myself, and there wasn't anything anyone could say or do to stop me. What you also need to understand is my plan to win LaDeisha started long before you initiated this challenge—at least six months prior—so trust me when I say there wasn't a damn thing that was going to stop me."

"And how does LaDeisha feel knowing she has been passed from one friend to the other?"

Timothy's chest deflated. "She doesn't know."

"Doesn't know? She doesn't know you two were friends? Why not tell her the truth?"

"Because the truth is irrelevant. The truth as it relates to Rasta is a non-factor. It's not like they were married. Rasta is merely an associate."

"Timothy that's fucked up, and you know it."

"No, I'll tell you what's fucked up." His chest inflated with steam again. "What's fucked up is to have a woman like LaDeisha and still be fucking with a *thot* like Shameka. You can judge me all you want to, but I have never been in a dilemma with a Mrs. Huxtable on the one hand and a hoe on the other. That hoe lost every time. What's fucked up is Rasta couldn't decide which one was the better woman, so I decided—for him."

"No really, you used his circumstances to your advantage, knowing he needed Shameka's truck."

"The way I looked at it, two million dollars was on the line, so if LaDeisha came across pictures from an anonymous Facebook page, then so be it."

*"Right when she was getting ready to take Rasta back—"*

"Yes, right when it appeared she was softening up to him, I sent those pictures. How do you think Yolanda discovered Erica? If Biyell hadn't confessed to GiGi and started that whole mess himself, I would have sent Tamera some evidence, too. I knew Jarvis's situation would take care of itself, but if for some reason it didn't, I was ready to help. But my main focus was LaDeisha. I held her hand all the way through the process of ending it with Rasta."

If I had my other leg, I would kick him in his fucking head.

"LaDeisha had a copy of my divorce as proof that I was serious. There was no way I was leaving a crack for Rasta to creep back in—I was all in. But I needed her to proof up. When she ended it with Rasta the first time, she called me to confirm it was over. Once she saw the pictures and ended it for good, I got a final confirmation call, and I knew she was serious."

"An anonymous Facebook page?! You had Rasta ready to kill Shameka thinking she sent those pictures!"

"It was me; I sent those pictures from the night Shameka came here with all that drama. I also sent video. After that, there wasn't a damn thing he could tell say to LaDeisha. She was done."

My mouth plopped open like an interstate tunnel. "Tim . . . that's that hoe shit, bruh. I thought we were closer than that."

"Glenn, this doesn't involve you . . ."

"How do you figure that? I love you both like blood brothers. You broke our code, the rules that govern how we conduct ourselves—"

"Oh, the G-Code?"

"Yes, and you know you never touch a wife or the main lady. She was his main lady!"

"Uncle Glenn, there's only one rule I live by."

"Which is . . . ?"

"No matter how many times a woman whispers in your ear, *it's your pussy*, don't believe her. It's never your pussy; *it's your turn*. The good news is, it's my turn now, and I'm the only one standing." Timothy's voice lowered to right above a whisper. "Whether you like it or not, I am the only one who could win. His bitch chose me. Now we can handle it like gentlemen or get into some gangster shit."

I can't believe this little nail shop nigga is sitting in my house quoting some pimp shit. Suddenly my bedroom door flew open and slammed against the rubber door stop. It sounded like the Southern University Marching Band was entering the stadium.

"GET THE FUCK OUT OF MY HOUSE!" Diana was here for the gangster shit. "You will not get one fucking dime of my money, you lowdown piece of shit."

"Diana, honey, please. I got this."

"Got this, my ass, Glenn. You're sitting here listening to this motherfucker brag in your face about how he stole LaDeisha, and not once have you set his ass straight."

"Look, I'm sorry you feel that way, Mrs. Braxton—"

"Fuck you."

Timothy stepped fifteen feet of space away from Diana. "One more thing before I go." His eyes avoided my wife. "Unlike all the other men who sat in this house every week and bragged about all the women they're knocking down, I have never—not one time—boasted about cheating on my wife. When my heart was no longer in my marriage, long before I touched another woman, I did the right thing by setting my wife free to find the love she deserves. Ask yourself this one question: if LaDeisha was your daughter, would you rather her be with a man who doesn't cheat, or one like Jarvis, Biyell, Telly or Rasta?"

"Get the fuck out of my house, Timothy . . . I will not ask you again," my wife growled in a low, rumbling voice as she moved toward Timothy. I reached for her, but she stiff-armed out of my grip and damn near sent my one-legged ass flying across the room.

"Mrs. Braxton, I can understand you're angry, but I won, and I expect to receive my money."

"You're not getting a dime, not one dime."

"We will see about that."

"Ain't shit see!" Diana stalked him to the door. With her left hand, she pointed one of my walking canes at Timothy. "If my father were here, he would call you a *jive bitch*. I would call you a pussy, but I have one, and I'm more man than you. So, I'll call your ass out because you will not get one fucking penny!" Diana yelled as she slammed the door on his back.

"Glenn, if he ever steps foot in my house again, I promise on everything . . ."

# CHAPTER 22

Monday, May 29, 2017
8:45 a.m.

## BIYELL

I used to often lie to Tamera and GiGi about getting stuck on a job, but this time I was stuck for real. It was my first and only job of the day. I was greeted by a Mrs. Brady-type woman with big, blue eyes and cheekbones so high she smiled with her mouth closed. She was caught off guard by me the same way most women are caught off guard—no one expects a cable guy who's shredded like lettuce. And that was all it took to trigger Lil Glenn.

*Even if she offers you the pussy, don't take it.*

"Good morning, and welcome to our home. Everyone is still sound asleep, so I apologize that you have to work around them." She had that look in her eye—that *I will fuck you* look—but I ignored it.

"Oh, it's no problem. Point me in the direction where the cable boxes are going, and I'll take it from there."

"Wonderful, let's start with the ground floor, shall we?"

Though she resembled Mrs. Brady in the face, when she turned to lead me through the house, her hair damn near swept the floor as she walked. Her feet were hidden under this long, denim dress. That's when Pimp B appeared on my other shoulder.

*Don't let that long skirt fool you, it can pull up just as fast as a short skirt. Bet she has some good pussy under there.*

I ignored Pimp B.

The home was a two-story shotgun house, and the entire bottom floor had been converted into a dorm room. The install called for eight converter boxes; two upstairs and six in the dorm. The reason I refer to it as a dorm is because the room had ten twin-sized beds and two full-sized ones. Each bed was occupied with either two teenage girls or pre-teen boys. One of the full beds housed one teenage boy, and two teenage girls slept on the other. It freaked me the fuck out.

Then I was escorted upstairs, where Mrs. Brady opened one of four bedroom doors.

"One of the boxes goes there," she pointed to a flat-screen TV on the floor, but I was too distracted to notice.

*And what do we have here?* Pimp B inquired.

In the bed were two women, sound asleep on their sides, facing the opposite direction. Both appeared to be in their mid-forties, and both had golden hair.

Then she moved to the adjacent room. "This is our main bedroom. The other box is going there." She pointed to another flat-screen in the corner on the floor.

"Please excuse the mess; our things are everywhere, but it was a three-day haul down here and all of us are exhausted. If you need me to move anything I will be right here, but if not, I'm going back to bed." Mrs. Brady sat on the edge of a king-sized bed that already had a spooning couple snoring in the dead center.

*We have it a jackpot of pussy at this house.* Pimp B was

excited.

"No ma'am, I've got it from here," I said as I closed the door behind me. I trotted down a short flight of stairs, confused and flustered.

What the *crawfish fuck* is going on in this house?

*I tell you what's going on—ninety-nine ways to catch a rape charge*, Lil Glenn warned.

No sooner did I ask than the answer was revealed in full color. Hanging on the wall that lead to the dormitory was a huge photo of Mrs. Brady, the two women in the upstairs bedroom, the spooning couple in the king-sized bed, and all the kids sleeping in the dorm. This was some shit right off the TLC channel.

"Get the fuck out of here, this is all one family," I whispered. "Dude upstairs has four wives." You could have pissed on my blue suede shoes and I wouldn't have noticed. This motherfucker has four Mrs. Bradys, all under the same roof. Every day I'm out here installing I learn three new life lessons, and one of this day's lessons is: *Women may agree to it if you ask them.* Here I am getting busted in the face with bricks and this fucker has four wives? My brain was stuck on *loading* as I processed how he managed to convince four women to share him under one roof.

*Lord, I want to be white, right now. Make me white, Lord. Hell on being black, dude has four wives*, Pimp B prayed.

Once outside, I surveyed the exterior of the home for existing cable lines I could tap into and quickly became pissed. Not one piece of cable wire could be found. Then I noticed the house had been freshly painted.

*Those knucklehead-ass painters always cut the damn cable wires.* Not only was the polygamy house an eight-box install, it was also a complete re-wire.

*Fuck.*

I pouted back to my truck to gear up, threw my ladder over my shoulder, grabbed a spool of cable wire, then dove into the job. It took me two hours just to run the new lines, but afterward, everything ran smoothly. That's when I received the call.

The second lesson of the day: *It's possible to miss the main event but still arrive on time.* I'm here, and here is eighty-five miles from that polygamy house in New Orleans. I just made it to Baton Rouge General Hospital. The five-inch-thick window wasn't thick enough to stop my heart from melting. In a clear bassinet, with an identification band around his right leg and a name card taped to the front panel, was my new obsession.

*Biyell Baltimore, 10 lbs., 2 oz.*

He looked like a child on steroids compared to the other babies in the room. The average kid only weighted seven pounds, but not my son. I swore I saw pubic hair hanging out of his Pamper, he was so big.

A nurse walked over to where I fogged the window and gently lifted my son to chest level. Even with his pale, lizard skin, I could tell he was my son. He had my chin and my big hands (minus the calluses); he had my shoulders and my legs, and undeniably, he had my face. I gazed into my eyes and face, and he squinted back at me. *My little man.* The nurse snapped our trance when she returned my little man to the slumber of his bassinet, then clicked on the intercom.

"I'll just be another hour with him, then I'll roll him to Mommy for his first feeding."

"Thank you, I can't wait to hold him."

The nurse giggled at my enthusiasm.

*Oh shit, I never checked on GiGi.* I stopped at the nurse's station about thirty feet away and was given directions to her room.

"From that silly smile, I take it you've seen that grown man I delivered?" GiGi asked me as I entered the room.

"Yes, and he's beautiful."

"Whatever," GiGi winced in pain as the nurse treated her vaginal area.

"Need me to step out until you're done?"

"Why? There's isn't anything down there you haven't seen before; it's just bloody and ripped to pieces." That's GiGi—always blunt, with no filter.

Her hair was wrapped in a tie-dyed scarf, which was her only recognizable clothing.

I can't believe GiGI delivered my son the old-fashioned way and I missed it. Deep down I knew I would miss it—that's just how things have been between us lately. *Hit and miss.* The irony is, before GiGi and Tamera discovered each other, I was on-site for everything . . . but now we're offbeat like rhythmless drummers.

"No one was here with you . . . for the delivery?"

"Do you see anyone?" Her eyes roamed the room.

"I got here as fast as I could."

"I know, but there wasn't much time. One minute I was baking your daughter some hot cinnamon rolls, then I heard her say, *bad Mommy, use the potty*."

I straightened my face, but the thought of her water breaking on the kitchen floor still made me cringe. As much as I love pussy, I don't have an appreciation for everything that comes out of it—but I love my kids.

The nurse finished treating GiGi and promised to follow up right after lunch.

"I had a feeling he was coming today," I said to GiGi once the nurse left the room.

"You should have told me."

"I called you last night and this morning. Like the other ten calls, you sent me to voicemail."

"I know, I'm not feeling you right now."

"Because of the baby?"

"Because you're married."

"Only on paper."

"Bullshit."

"It's not bullshit, I haven't spoken to her since that night."

"Biyell, you're still married until you're not married."

"I feel like I'm trapped in no-man's land where I don't want to go backward and can't go forward with you. And then the other half of me questions why I would even want to. You're never going to be the woman I had—that's over—and if you do decide to take me back, it'll only be to torment the fuck out of me for lying."

"Sounds to me like you have it all figured out." With a shrug, she changed the subject. "So . . . did you see his big-ass hands?"

And that's the attitude I've dealt with since that night; she wants me around, but not really. She eventually decided to let me come over without her mother mediating, but she won't really talk to me much. She still likes to see me and my daughter wrestling in the middle of the floor, but she wants me gone when playtime is over. I started to get frustrated, then I heard Lil Glenn.

*You have to take your lick, Biyell, it's not going to be easy. This is the part where we hunker down and put in our time. You can earn her trust again, don't quit.*

How many years do I take the lick? Isn't it easier to get a fresh start with a new woman?

*Listen, Tamera has served you with divorce papers—the only shot you have of waking up every morning under the same roof with your kids is to fix this with GiGi. If you meet someone new, chances are she will have kids. Why raise another man's kids when you have two with GiGi?*

I nodded.

*When another man has to pick your son up from football practice because you're stuck on a job, you're not going to like it.*

I nodded again.

Then Pimp B offered his advice. *Fuck the dumb shit, I say we find a new woman. Remember back in school when the new teacher walked in and wrote her name on a clean chalkboard? That's what you need; a new bitch with a clean chalkboard.* Pimp B wanted out. *And did you see the size of that baby? Fucking GiGi now is going to be like trying to fuck a dishwasher; you ain't feeling shit from today going forward*, Pimp B warned again.

*Don't listen to him, GiGi will heal just fine*, Lil Glenn assured me.

*Go to the store, buy some Pringles, dump the potato chips out, then fuck the can. That is what sex with GiGi is going to feel like.* Pimp B was convinced.

I think Pimp B is exaggerating, but the thought did cross my mind. Another thought that has crossed my mind is the fact that I will turn forty next month, which means the majority of single women my age will be fresh out of marriages with kids. I don't feel like dealing with a baby daddy, nor do I want two baby mamas. Fuck it, GiGi has to take me back. I'm not ready to walk away from all the hard work I put into this relationship.

"Tyra, I was thinking we could—"

There was a soft knock at the door, and then six women entered with balloons, food, and toys.

"Lordy, Lordy, my poor daughter. A ten-pound baby?" GiGi's mother walked past me like I was a hallway closet. I greeted her first. She said hi to my boots.

"I see you finally made it," her mother said in wavy, facetious voice that sounded like Willona from *Good Times*.

"Yes ma'am, arrived about an hour ago."

"Umm." Her mother turned to kiss GiGi on the forehead.

I said hello to her other relatives. Some said hello, others smacked their teeth and neck-rolled back to GiGi. Her mom and cousins formed a wall around her bed, which pretty much confirmed the new order of things. I would be on the outside looking in at my own children. Discreetly, I slipped out of GiGi's room and returned to the glass window. By this point other families were packed in tight around the window, all jousting for a closer view, and all enamored by the size of my son.

"Congratulations, Mr. Baltimore, on that huge baby boy," a silver-haired lady said.

I wondered how she knew which baby was my son. Then it dawned on me that he was the only African American baby in the nursery, and I was still wearing my work ID.

"Thank you, I can't wait to hold him."

"Well, it's a good thing you have those strong arms, he's a fat tater tot."

It was about thirty minutes before the crowd dwindled to just me, and not a minute too soon, because I couldn't hold the tears another second. She named him after me, but I didn't want him to be me. Anything but me. Do you hear me, little man? Don't ever grow up to be me; be better than me. Only have eyes for one woman. Don't ever do the things I've done; don't be like your father. I typed a text to GiGi:

*Don't name him Biyell. Please find another first name.*

"All right, Daddy, your big bundle of joy is all ready for you. I'll meet you bedside with Mommy."

I thanked the nurse and made my way back to GiGi, but when I entered the room, even more of her aunts and cousins, along with her great-grandmother, had arrived. I stepped back into the hall. To my right I heard the squeaky wheels of a rolling cart. It was my little man.

"Sir, if you would like to hold your big bundle, all I need is for you to stand bedside with Mommy, and after I scan his band, he's all yours."

I looked down. My son was wrapped tightly in a blanket.

"Ma'am, I appreciate that, but all I need to do is one thing and I'll be out of your way." I leaned into his bassinet and kissed his belly goodbye. Then I left the hospital.

# CHAPTER 23

Tuesday, May 30, 2017
11:15 a.m.

## RASTA

I'm still shitting out charcoal four days later; four *moth-erfuckin'* days later. Literally, it's the worst shit ever. I'm not talking dark brown stool or bad constipation stool— naw, not at all— this is crayon-black shit coming out of my ass. It's as if I ran into a burnt house carrying a cereal bowl and ate the wood. I have to get out of here. Fuck this place. I'm being held in here against my will. I need to get back to some form of a normal life, where I shit like normal people, but this is where they warehouse folk who commit abnormal acts—like get fully dressed in a three-piece, pinstripe suit just to commit suicide.

They rolled me in here a couple of days ago in a medical bed. I spent the end of the weekend and entire week so far in this room—and since yesterday, I've spent it with *him*. Now I know why they call it the *crazy house*, because there are three groups of people in here: a group that doesn't know they're in here, a second group that comes in and out like a revolving door, and a third group comprised of patients like me who want to kick out one of the windows and jump out this bitch. I'm not like them. I'm not crazy.

At first, I had this room to myself.

I placed my hygiene bag on the empty bed across from me when I arrived, but when I woke yesterday morning, there he was: on the edge of the bed, rocking on his ass cheeks, in a big-ass Pamper. I rolled over onto my back to find my door open. Having that door open was freaking me out, but I soon found a sticky note from the nurse stuck to my pillow:

*Hope you don't mind leaving the door open. Your new room-mate is a regular, and he's fearful of closed doors.*

That's just fucking great; now I have to sleep in a crazy house with my door open all day with a grown man who is very much a child. At first I thought he was Jonah Hill from that movie *Su-perbad*, only thinner and much shorter. On his head he wore a black Saints hat, his shirt was a white tank top, and if it weren't for the adult diaper, he would be butt-ass naked over there. In his right hand, he held a little wooden hammer delicately between his thumb and index finger. He likes to shake his hammer left to right inches from his nose. When I opened my eyes yester-day, that's what I saw—that's my roommate, and there's no way to escape this place.

Yesterday when I gazed out the narrow, prison-glass window for the first time, I figured out my location—I'm in that brown building at the edge of the West Jefferson Medical Complex. I'm from Marrero—my mother lives on Admiral Drive in the Haydel subdivision—so I've passed this three-story building with the dark, tinted windows a thousand times. I never knew what was inside—now I know. From my window, I can read the incognito sign out front.

*West Jefferson Behavioral Medicine Center*

The exterior view of this the Behavioral Medicine Center is quite deceptive, in that it gives the appearance of a typical office complex you would find within walking distance from the main hospital, but inside, this bitch is crazy. Fucking nuts, *you heard me?* And if that's not hellish enough, my roommate, Pamper Man, stared at me for eight hours yesterday as I tried to read some magazines. Little dude never said a word all day; he just sat there on the edge of the bed with that wooden hammer, a smooth-shaven face, and a moist smile. This morning he spoke for the first time.

"Hi, what's your name?"

"My name is Roderick, and your name is?" I spoke to him in the soft voice of a kindergarten teacher, because he's wearing a diaper and has a toy hammer.

"My name is Levi," he replied with a full smile. "I like your name."

I was caught off guard at the clarify of his speech. At first I thought he was mute, but I was about to learn the ultimate lesson in pre-judging.

"Thanks Levi, I like your name too," I replied.

"But your name is awesome."

"Thank you, Levi; your name is pretty cool too."

"Rod. Rod-rick. Rod-er-rick."

I tried to bury my face deeper in my magazine, hoping he would drift off again into his magical world of wooden hammers, but not today.

"Rod-er-ick, that's Scottish. King Rodrigo was a warrior king. The Germanic root is *hrod,* which means fame and power. Your name means famous and powerful king."

I peeked around the side of my magazine with one eye. *Did he just break down the meaning of my name?*

"Roderick, you are a king; a rich and famous warrior."

"Nice to know that, thanks." I tried to blow him off, but compassionately.

"You are a famous king. What are you doing in here? Have you been deposed?" A bewildered expression replaced his childish smile.

At this point, I'm thinking it would make no sense to lie to him. And what better time to start an honest life?

"I'm in here because I tried to kill myself."

"Why would you ever want to do that?"

"Levi," I let out a sigh the length of Route 66, "I don't know; I guess I was feeling down and out."

"You shouldn't feel down and out; you are a king. Your name means rich and powerful king."

I'm thinking, *First of all, I never investigated the root meaning of my name to know if he just accurately gave me the Germanic meaning of Roderick. I never even thought to look the shit up, but this lil' fucker sounded like he knew what he was talking about. Second of all, how in the fuck did he know that? One minute he's rocking back in fourth in a diaper and the next minute dude is breaking down my name based on the root word. I have to get out of here today.*

"You should never feel down, King Roderick, because you're rich and famous. You rule over a kingdom; your people love you."

"Easier said than done, Levi, but thanks for the info."

With that, Levi slipped back into deep thought resumed rocking back and forth with his little hammer. I had no way of confirming if what he said was accurate or not, and to be honest, I gave less than fuck, but at least I knew he could talk. It's bad enough that I am locked in an office building that's actually a mental hospital, with around-the-clock staff and no exits, but to have a roommate who stares at me for eight hours without saying a word is cruel and excessive punishment.

My room is the last in the corridor before you reach the main dining hall—the one with the blaring television that remains on PBS all day. No one cares enough to find the remote.

By the way, *Petticoat Junction* still airs twice a day on PBS.

The staff herds us all into the dining hall three times a day for meds and meals, and three times a day, I refuse all meds. I know what I did was extreme, but I refuse to take whatever that is in those little pill cups—not happening. Each time I refuse, the nurse who administers the meds shoots a look at me that says, *your ass will never get out of here unless you take these pills.*

"Hi, what's your name?" Levi asked again.

My eye looked around the magazine again. "Roderick; my name is Roderick . . . remember?"

"Rod. Rod-rick. Rod-er-ick. That's Scottish."

"Yes, you just told me that a minute ago."

"King Rodrigo was a warrior king who lived in the eighth century. In German, your name means famous and powerful king. Did you know you were a king?"

"No, I didn't. But thanks for letting me know. Again." My lips fluttered.

"King Roderick, what are you doing in here?" he asked again as if I didn't answer him ten minutes ago.

"Levi, I tried to kill myself by swallowing a lot of pills. It was a dumb thing to do, and now I'm stuck in here—in here with you—and there's no way out. If I thought I was miserable before, I am really in the sad place this morning."

"But you are a rich and famous king. You are a ruler; you should be happy."

This continued every fifteen minutes. Levi would introduce himself to me as if we'd never met, then it was wooden hammer time, and then we would start all over from the top. By the sixth time, I covered my face with a pillow, but it didn't stop him from asking.

"Hi, what's your name?"

"I see you have met Levi, one of our regular members at West Jeff Country Club for the Exotic."

I sat up just as this beautiful nurse entered the room. Immediately, I noticed her thick, pink lips and her name badge:

*DESHONTA*

Her pretty, green eyes were deserving of a song.

Her naturally red dreadlocks were a natural aphrodisiac.

Her dreadlocks were twisted up in a bun. In the center of that bun was a red bow attached to a ribbon that held her dreads up high. Her skin complimented her hair, which blended perfectly with those lips. I have always been a sucker for lips that don't need lipstick. Everything DeShonta had on she was born with, except her work uniform and that innocent red ribbon. My heart skipped. Then I reminded myself of where I was and why she was in my room.

I am not on her level.

I am a mental patient.

A nigga nugget.

I am boneless.

I cleared my throat. "Yes we've met, about twenty times."

She chuckled. "He has a habit of doing that, but we're all used to little Levi." She placed Levi's suitcase on the bed and removed a pair of sweat pants. "So, what does Roderick mean?"

"According to Levi, my name means 'king' and I was once rich and famous in the eighth century."

She chuckled again from the inside joke. "Rich and powerful king? Now that's the type of husband I need." DeShonta assisted Levi into the sweat pants one careful leg at time. "If Levi says you name means rich and powerful king, then you can take that to the bank. Both of his parents are professors; his father teaches German and his mother is a linguistics professor at Loyola. My little Levi is the smartest person I have ever met in my life."

"Wait, Levi is like one of those . . . those . . ." I snapped my fingers to recall. "One of those . . ." I didn't know the exact medical term for his condition.

"It's called Savant Syndrome, like the Dennis Hoffman character in *Rain Man*."

"Yes, that's it. I loved that movie."

"Well, little Levi has the same remarkable gift, except his

focus is on the historical origin of names. That is, unless your mother named you a Lower Ninth Ward name like De-Shon-ta." She did a little cha-cha dance on each syllable. "Watch this— Levi, what does *DeShonta* mean?"

Levi closed his eyes and swayed his head like Stevie Wonder for a full sixty seconds. He had nothing.

"No answer means your mother named you something ghetto. Without Levi having to say it's ghetto, I know it is—all of my sisters have neighborhood names: Jaracie, Davinna, Kerrionah, and of course yours truly . . . DeShonta. The type of names you don't realize are hood until you leave the hood. The type of names where people know you're black on the job application, but your BFF referred you. You follow?" Levi held both arms in the air as DeShonta applied deodorant.

"That's how I got this job, because they would have never hired me with a name like DeShonta. Isn't that right, Levi?" There was that Stevie Wonder smile again.

Once Levi was dressed, DeShonta reached for his hand, and the two of them moved toward the door. Levi's steps were light and soft. He gently placed each foot as if blisters lined the soles of his feet. His timid steps delayed their exit long enough for me to get a status on my release.

"So . . . DeShonta, have you heard any word on my discharge?"

"Yes, I have."

"So, when?"

"Never."

"Huh?"

DeShonta giggled. "Mr. Ross, if I were you, I would make myself comfortable. You haven't even had your first session with Dr. Morton yet, and he never releases a patient like you until he's one hundred percent sure."

"And how long is that?" A tsunami of discouragement waved through my body.

"I've seen anywhere from seven days to three weeks, that

is, if the patient doesn't have anything unusual written in the notes—anything the staff observed that raised a flag. If that's not the case, then there's a chance you could leave in a week. The good news is, your session is next, as soon as I discharge little Levi. He'll back same day next week. Say bye-bye to Mr. King Roderick."

"Bye-bye, King Roderick," Levi said.

"See you later Levi, but I hope I'm gone next week when you check in."

It was then that I remembered what the nurse wrote in my file: *First word spoken when he regained consciousness: FUCK!*

And I probably did say fuck, because I didn't want to be here or anywhere; I wanted to be far away. I just watched Pamper Man get discharged before me; could I be worse off than Levi? Before I could answer that question in my own consciousness, a deep baritone rattled the walls in my room.

"Mr. Ross, it's time for your first session. Follow me, right this way."

It was obvious that I didn't have a choice. The bold letters on his name badge read *PHILLIP*, and his voice was bigger than his stature. He couldn't have been any more than five feet, seven inches tall, with a caramel bald head and a Just for Men black beard. He trailed behind me like a prison guard and guided me through a hallway maze lined with stained oak doors on both sides. I figured that he'd walked this route to Dr. Morton's office so many times he could walk it with his eyes closed.

"Dr. Morton's office is the door on the left," Don Cornelius said.

There was no name plate above the room number, or any indication that the person on the other side of this door was my key to freedom. Maybe that was by design—keep us drugged and uninformed until we wander the halls like zombies. In any case, I mentally recorded the route to this door, because at some point I'm going to bust the fuck out of here.

*Dr. Morton's office is the one next to the red door below the exit sign.*

Phillip tapped the door five times with his knuckle, and a voice invited us in. From behind his cluttered desk, Dr. Morton stood and extended his hand as he thanked Phillip for delivering me. The wall behind his desk was the same as you'd find in any doctor's office—pretentious in that it left no doubt as to his level of expertise. What I found strange was the absence of family photos or anything sentimental. It didn't take me long to figure out why. Gone was his pleasant bedside manners from the ER, and the warm smile he'd shared at breakfast on Saturday morning. This was a different Dr. Morton—a stiff Dr. Morton, a not-in-the-mood-for-bullshit Dr. Morton. It was time to get down to business. After some small talk about my accommodations, he hit the ground running.

"Mr. Ross, welcome to your first session. Let's have a little chat about the thoughts running through your head."

"Thanks, Dr. Morton. As I said before, I was having a bad day, but I feel better now."

"I see."

His face was empty, his back perfectly vertical; his body fused into his desk as if they were cut from a single piece of wood. In front of him was a file with my name written in the tab, along with patient number 432-B39. My heart sank at the thought that I was assigned a patient number in a mental institution.

"Mr. Ross, I see we're getting off on the wrong foot. The conversations we're going to have this morning and over the next three weeks will be related to your thoughts when you wrote this letter."

*Dammit, he has the letter. Why would they give him that letter?*

"Three weeks? Dr. Morton, with all due respect, I can't stay here for three weeks. I have things to do, a business to run, and I have never been away from my kids for three weeks. There has to be a way I can get discharged sooner."

"I see. You would like me to fast track you out of here because you have a life and a business waiting for you. Did I hear you correctly?"

"Yes, the longer I'm in this building, the harder it will be for me to rebuild my life when I get out. Things were already falling apart."

"I see, but with all due respect, Mr. Ross, I strongly disagree. Being in here will not hinder your life . . . because you don't have a life."

"Doc, that's where you're wrong. You don't know me; I'm not like these people in here."

"Is that so? And how are you any different?"

"For one, I'm not crazy. I have a business, and things to do—"

"No, you don't. You don't have anything to do. There was a life, and a business to run, and kids to take to the park, but not anymore—because you are dead. You ended your life. You committed suicide."

Dr. Morton stood and leaned across the table, forcing me further back in my chair. "You put the pills in your mouth two at a time, and you washed them down with a bottle of water."

At this point, I'm wondering how he knows I swallowed two pills at a time.

"Mr. Ross, everything you set out to do was accomplished with swift efficiency. You wanted to kill yourself, so you killed yourself. The glitch in your plan was we refused to let you die."

Dr. Morton was right. I had a life, and a business, and a relationship with my kids, and I still swallowed those pills two at a time until the bottle was empty. Then I dressed in my navy blue pinstripe suit; then I relaxed in my bed.

I remember it all so clearly now. I stretched across the bed into the position I wanted the coroner to find me in, with my fingers woven together across my waist and my head on a pillow. For the first ten minutes, I didn't feel any changes in my body— it was like I took a few Tylenol to chill a headache. Then I started to feel it. My heart started beating in the tips of my fingers, then a cooling feeling crept down my spine, then a thumping appeared under my neck. And that's all I remember.

"Mr. Ross, the bad news for you is the people who love you interrupted your funeral plans. The good news is that you are, in fact, dead—but here's how were going to bring you back to life."

Doctor Morton held my suicide note inches from my nose. "This episode started for you with her, and it ended with her. So, I ask you again, what are the thoughts in your head right now, at this very second, about LaDeisha?"

*I'm never getting out of here.*

# CHAPTER 24

Wednesday, May 31, 2017
11:36 p.m.

## TELLY

Her bra was black, her hair was black, she wore black panties, and that ass was definitely molded in Ghana. When I was a teen, I don't remember white girls having juicy asses, but somewhere around 1998, God must have made an adjustment. White girls started to get thicker in places that African American women had previously owned exclusively: *hips and ass*. I know I'm late to the white girl booty revolution, but I'm here for this—let's get it on and popping.

Some men are breast men, some love a pretty face, some men are like Biyell (it doesn't matter as long as there's a working vagina) but I am a Man of Ass. There's nothing better than a nice ass in a sexy pair of panties. Not that thong bullshit, but an honest pair of panties with the panty lines.

Fuck thongs.

And fuck that overly religious asshole Mayor of New York,

Fiorello LaGuardia, who in 1974 couldn't mind his fucking business. Instead, he harassed strippers with dumbass decency laws, which resulted in some dude named Rudi Gernreich creating the thong. Then came that annoying "Thong Song" by Sisqo in 2000, and overnight, just like that—without a memo, fax or letter of permission—the reason for my existence, the thing I'd watched consistently since I was eleven years old, vanished from asses for over twenty years.

The panty line has only recently made a comeback, but I'm still pissed about that two-decade moratorium on booty lines. All three of them—LaGuardia, Gernreich, and Sisqo—should be handed over to the Delegation of Ass Men so we can soak them in a tub of honey and douse those bastards with fire ants. Watching a woman's ass walk by is our indelible right as men; it is part of our dominion to behold the perfect ass and trace those two curved lines all the way to her HEC: her Home Entertainment Center.

But I digress.

I used to think Yolanda was the sexiest bitch I'd ever entered—until Megyn, whose real name is Ciara. She's a different type of awesomeness. She does that CrossFit workout. I tried to do it with her but I damn near caught an asthma attack. I don't even have asthma, but that shit nearly killed me. But she loves it, and I love the rewards of her CrossFit lifestyle—the way they look for shit to pick up or flip over. As for me, I'm into the law, and gravity is a law—I like to sit down.

I also like to watch her walk around my apartment in her panties. Megyn is so fucking sexy that I could charge men just to watch her walk in a pair drawls—if that weren't considered pimping. There have been times, right after the foreplay, that all I wanted to do was look at her naked.

*When you are blessed with a woman like Megyn: simply humping on her is overrated.*

Where was this woman when I was just starting out on the road to happiness? That's right, she was with him: a former NFL player who blew through his career and his money faster than she could preserve either one. They started dating at LSU and married after the NFL Draft. Within three years she had three kids. He was a typical black dude from the inner city: he was recruited to a white campus, became the star of the football team, discovered white pussy, then married white pussy. She was the typical white girl who liked black football players. Jacoby Sincere married Ciara Boudreaux during a picturesque ceremony on the campus of LSU. Their marriage had the look of forever.

The thing about NFL linebackers is they're constantly ramming into grown men with their heads. Over time, this inflicted a cognitive toll on Jacoby, one with no known cure. Megyn told me he started punching the walls first, then he started punching her—but she wanted her family. Then came the heavy drug use and the back-to-back DUIs, but she still wanted her family.

Apparently, the final straw didn't come until he slapped one of the kids. Her daughter's face swelled. She was left with no other option but to call the police. Regarding that decision, she once told me:

*Even though he was abusive, I was still terrified to dial 911—not out of fear that Jacoby would retaliate with more violence, but out of fear that the police would kill my husband on sight. It's the ABCs of Domestic Violence: A Bruised Caucasian woman has the ability to instantly invoke rage in white cops. After he slapped my child, I shelved my concerns for his safety and made the call. To be battered doesn't end with just physical scars; the mental lacerations are far more severe. Battered is boundless.*

She made that call a year ago; her divorce was finalized three months ago.

Her husband was my client. Keep that on the low. I was the mediator who arranged the supervised visits. I should have never stepped to Megyn in a romantic way, but I did. She should have never invited my dick into her mouth, but she did. She should have never opened nearly every door in her body, her soul, and her life, but she did. But the door that leads to her kids is off limits and locked.

Megyn isn't ready for me to meet them, because there's still a ton of bad blood between her and the ex-husband over child support, custody, and his NFL pension, which she is now entitled to receive starting next month. At the same time, I'm overbooked with Erica's kids, so it's worked out in my favor.

And I don't know if it's the CTE or what, but her ex is becoming increasingly more threatening. Jacoby Sincere is mad as hell; Megyn's shown me several of his text messages calling her every white bitch under the sun. Little does he know it, but she's my white bitch now—I'm diving into Megyn every other day. I'm providing her with all her intimate needs.

She's in good hands.

Three nights a week, we meet at my apartment. Erica doesn't know I still have my apartment. I was about to let the apartment go, but that was before Megyn sucked me off in that parking garage after court. After that, the lease was renewed!

Since then, my old bachelor pad has become our secret place.

My lie to Erica is that I need to fly to New York to see a big client.

My lie to Megyn is that I have to keep things on the low because of the ethics rules.

The truth is, I was planning to ask Erica to marry me the week Megyn fucked me in that garage—then something snapped in my brain. I decided right then to put the marriage thing off for a little while longer to explore Megyn, and I'm so happy I did. Don't get me wrong; I still plan to marry Erica, just not right now. Can't do it. I plan to enjoy this trick Megyn does with her tongue a little while longer. She just did it again. *Oh-weeeeee.*

"Do you like that?" she whispered on my nuts.

My nuts replied, "Fuck yeah."

She has my balls cuffed in one hand, while the other hand is stroking my dick in her mouth. "Don't cum, not yet. Okay?"

"I can't ma-make any promises," my voice staggered.

"Baby, you have to try. I want you for a long time tonight, and you said we have all night. You promised."

"I will try, but you have to stop that tongue. That's sending me over the top."

"You're a big boy, and it's just a little tongue," she said with an evil grin. "I think you need a little bit more."

Before she could do the tongue thing again, I grabbed her by the arms. She tried to resist. My strength turns her on; she likes when I handle her rough. Megyn is aggressive, and I'm learning to be. Against her struggling, I rolled her onto her back, slid those black lace panties to the left, and put some old-fashioned missionary dick on her hard and deep. I saw the fear in the whites of her eyes. I had her pinned down and was pillaging her vagina of all valuables. It's in this same position that I first discovered her sexual weakness.

Hard and deep she can handle, but hard, deep, and fast pushes her to the max.

The first time I noticed it, she caught me off guard. Once she started to orgasm, Megyn got violent—slapped me in the face. Then thirty seconds later, her eyes rolled into their lids and she started to bang her head like a Nirvana concert back in the day. Then came the snoring. Knocked the fuck out snoring. Been working on the railroad all night snoring. Ambien-ed the fuck out. I stopped in mid-hump and went straight into slave mode.

*Oh Lordy, I done killed her.*

It just happened again. She's out. My dick looked at me, I looked at my dick, and we both shrugged. It takes her about twenty minutes to fully recover. The last time it happened, she was so embarrassed that she gathered her clothes off the floor, got dressed, and darted to the car, but that's not happening this time. When she recovers, we need to talk.

Megyn was out for forty-five minutes. Then, she rose from the dead and regained consciousness. Once again, her first reaction was to haul ass out the door.

"No, no, no, put the clothes down."

"I'm sorry, but I have to go." She continued to gather her

belongings.

"Ciara, put the clothes down now. We need to talk about what just happened."

"Maybe another time. I have to get home. It's late."

"Ciara, you're not leaving until we talk."

"That's kidnapping."

"Yes it is, but you will not leave me hanging again. What just happened? We're having a good time then all of—"

She clipped my sentence. "It's my unique, extended version of a cataplexy attack."

"I've never heard of it."

"That's because it's rare."

"But why does it happen when you cum? I don't get it."

"It's not just during sex, but any intense emotion. Even if I laugh too hard, it sends me into a narcoleptic state that takes about—"

"Thirty minutes to recover."

She turned her back in shame.

"Sweetheart, you don't have to be embarrassed to share things like this with me. I'm more than just dick, you know." That got her to smile a little.

"I guess that's the reason I stayed with him so long, it's the explaining part that's the most depressing."

"How long have you had this condition?"

"Since I was fifteen."

"You naughty girl. *Getting booty* at fifteen. That's how you learned those tongue tricks."

Megyn jumped in the bed and whopped me with a pillow. "I wasn't having sex. Well, not with a partner."

"Masturbating?"

"At a pool party, while everyone was dancing all around me, I found this cozy little area in the pool that had water jets. Right in that little current, I felt it for the first time. It was amazing."

"Your first orgasm?"

"Eureka. Then I passed out and nearly fucking drowned."

"Floating with a smile on your face."

"Pretty much, at least that's what my best friend told me when she came to visit me in the hospital. They pulled me out of the water with my hand deep inside my bikini. In front of the entire world."

I tried not to laugh, but that was funny as fuck. She turtled back under the sheets.

*It makes sense now.*

I had always found it strange how she avoided sexual positions which made her surrender control. Sex with Megyn was more or less her pleasing me. The first time in the parking garage, she was on top. Now that I think about it, she was always on top. Periodically, she would jump off like my dick had heated to four-hundred degrees. If she wasn't on top, then it was oral and that thing with her tongue, which I didn't mind because it was all new to me.

I'm not a guy who's into a lot of positions. I consider myself the Director of the Fucking, which basically means missionary and from the back. Then came Megyn with a repertoire of kinky shit I'd never experienced.

"Ciara, thanks for sharing that story. The more I discover about you, the more irresistible you become."

Blushing, she said, "Would you look at the time?" Megyn rolled out of bed again and started to collect her clothes.

"Hello, aren't you forgetting something?"

She looked at me chicken-eyed. "Umm, no?"

My dick was standing straight up with his arms folded. "You passed out before I . . ."

"Oh my God, I'm so sorry!" Megyn giggled as she walked around the bed, then crawled back to my dick under the covers. From between my legs, she shot me a serious look.

"Promise you will relax and let me please you."

"I promise."

"And you won't roll me over?"

"Not tonight at least, but I see a lot of rolling over in your future." I smiled down at her; she blew a kiss up to my lips.

Then Megyn slurped me into her mouth as deep as she could without gagging, and my eyes slowly closed. She's really good at oral—so is Erica, but the difference is that Erica sucks my dick to get me in the mood, to get what she needs. Megyn, on the other hand, sucks my dick like it's a narcotic and she needs a three-day fix.

Putting sex aside, I feel like tonight we've graduated from just fucking to a more intimate level. Tonight, we became a couple.

Suddenly, I heard a loud popping sound as she released the head of my dick from her thick lips. Then she mounted me, but in reverse.

"Just relax and enjoy this, okay?"

"Okay."

"Don't stop me no matter what you feel, okay?"

"Handle your business on that dick, baby." Her body began to stroke me long and smooth.

After about ten minutes, she paused and allowed me to pulsate inside her before she started up again. I wasn't sure if she was trying to control my orgasm or her cataplexy attack, but I was ready to blow and could hold it.

"Just go with it, okay?"

"O-O-Okay." I was about to explode.

My last image was of Megyn leaning forward as I drifted away in a pleasure wonderland . . . and that's when I felt it.

Her finger in my ass.

Yes, my ass.

Horror.

My entire body tensed up. Just as I was about to throw her on the floor, she pressed down on it—and fucked over my life. I can say that with all certainty because over the years I've had at least 3,600 orgasms, including all of that dick-beating I did at thirteen, but I have never felt one like this.

"Awwwwwwwww, oooh-ooooh, C-Ciara, stop . . . awwwwwwww."

"Relax and go with it—give it all to me, shoot it in me Telly.

I want every last drop."

And I did, for what felt like five minutes. And then it was over. And then I was the one suffering from a cataplexy attack.

Sounding like a Harley motorcycle was parked alongside the bed.

Ambien-ed the fuck out.

Knocked the fuck out.

# CHAPTER 25

Madden Thursday
June 1, 2017
7:30 a.m.

It's Madden Thursday, and even though I'm not expecting anyone, I still prepared an ingredient list and handed it off to Diana. Today I plan to fry up a batch of chicken wings with some fried okra and rice. In the worst-case scenario that no one shows, at least we won't have to cook until Sunday.

From my favorite stool at the end of the counter, I watched my wife tie her shoes, then sofa dive between the cushions in search of her keys. Her keys are right next to me on the counter, but I'm enjoying her bent-over view, so the search continues.

She's slim fine; the way girls were shaped back in the eighties before the toxic birth control shots and chemical-laced food from Walmart. Now that I think about it, we never used any form of birth control over our entire marriage, but she never got pregnant. In a family where the average woman had at least three kids, my wife proved to be the only one who couldn't conceive. Her mother once shared a story of an aunt who suffered from the same issue; it had cost her a husband.

As for me, the thought of leaving my wife never entered my mind. At one time we discussed adopting, but the state wanted us to jump through too many hoops—they wore me out. Diana even raised the idea of adopting three kids from Africa who were siblings, but the cost through an adoption agency was sixteen-thousand dollars plus travel for the agency to facilitate the adoption. At that time, we didn't have an extra twenty grand sitting around.

As the days went on, we had fewer conversations about adopting, but I always wondered how much Diana thought about it—until last week, when she exploded on me, then threatened to kick Timothy's ass. I shouldn't have held her back. She would have slapped the scented lotion off his face.

Nevertheless.

My lawyer, Larry Aisola, sent another packet over yesterday. We opened it and found out he reached a second settlement with an additional insurer for the shipping yard for $9.5 million, which brings the total settlement to $18.7 million. It wasn't until Larry scheduled our estate planning meeting that it dawned on us that we have no biological heir. As far as my daughter? I don't even know her name; I was kicked out of the hospital before I could even sign a birth certificate.

"I swear to God there's a ghost in here who hides my keys." Diana's frustration started to boil.

By the loveseat, Diana was down on all fours again as her search intensified. My eyes had enjoyed their fill of her booty in those cotton sweat pants; it was time to end her anguish. I wrapped the keys in two twenty-dollar bills and tossed them where she kneeled. She raised from the floor with that *I'm gonna get you, sucka* look, but I didn't try to run—as if I could actually get away.

"What the forty dollars for?"

"That show you just gave me."

"You had my keys the entire time?" A straight jab to the chest.

"No, the kitchen counter had your keys the entire time, but why would I interrupt the only sex I've had this month?" Another straight right to my shoulder.

"Ouch!" I yelled as she kissed me. "Do you have everything?"

"Yes," she answered.

"Your cell phone?"

"It's right here." It was in her left hand.

"The list?"

"It's right here." In her right hand.

"Looks like you're all set."

"Do you think any of the guys will show tonight?" she asked as she lassoed her purse strap.

"It's hard to say, but I have been craving some fried okra, so that's more for us if no one shows."

"I know who better not show."

"I doubt very seriously that Timothy shows his face."

"Back-stabbing pretty boy, I hate him," Diana growled.

I laughed. "Call me when you get in the car."

I haven't seen her that pissed off in a while, but if Timothy had continued to run off at the mouth that day, it was about to go down in here. I'm still in a state of shock. The audacity of that dude. Now Rasta is in the hospital, and I don't see how things could get any worse for my band of brothers.

Suddenly, I heard Diana re-enter the house.

"Don't tell me you forgot something?"

"No, but are you expecting Telly this early?" Her eyes narrowed.

"No, I wasn't even sure if the tournament was on for tonight."

"Well, parked next to our car is Telly's. He said he was waiting for a more appropriate time to knock on the door. I think he's been out there all night."

"Huh? What? Telly?"

"It looks like something is bothering him."

I hopped over to the window and peeked out. It was Telly for sure; he leaned against his car with his head slumped, holding a cigarette that smoked itself.

"I got it, let him know I'll be right out."

I was still in my morning robe, so I hopped to the bedroom and threw on something right quick, then hopped out the front door.

"Yo, yo, yo! Where are those Packers?!" He yelled, but I know he didn't come here to play *Madden* this early. Something was bothering him.

The cool of the morning had given way to the sun, and the heat had just reported for duty. All around us, neighbors were leaving for work, staring with nosey eyes, but running too late to inquire any further. On the third-floor balcony, I noticed Felicia, aka Spider-Bitch, watering her plants before she headed off to work. I waved *good morning* as I always do when our paths cross, and she flicked me her middle acrylic nail—same as last week.

For what it's worth, I'm still friendly to Felicia, but deep down I feel she blames me for her introduction to a fuck boy name Biyell. I'm taking the charge for crimes I didn't commit, for women I've never touched, all because I refused to snitch—but they would do the same for me if I had a mistress. Such a foul box in which to find admiration. But enough about me, back to Telly 'Crowd Noise' Ned.

"Let's head inside before I catch a stroke in this heat," I motioned him toward the door.

"Heat? What heat? You have become one of those house dogs since your injury! Inside all day like house arrest."

"Call it what you want, but I'm getting the fuck inside."

And so he followed.

Surprisingly, he didn't turn on the music, and I didn't hear the PlayStation load up. *Madden* was just his excuse to get over here, which is also puzzling because today is a work day. In my

Green Bay Packers shirt and a pair of denim shorts, I hopped back into the living room and embraced him.

"Brother, I know you didn't come here this morning for *Madden*, so lay it on me."

Telly had a nauseated look on his face like he'd just stepped off a cup and saucer carnival ride and needed to puke. There he sat with his elbows on his kneecaps and his head hung low. I can count on one hand how many times I've seen Telly struggle to find words, but today the cat has his tongue and his throat. I can tell his clothes are from yesterday, and his mind is somewhere even further. I have to get to the bottom of this, whatever it is.

"Telly, my brother. You know you can talk to me. Whatever it is that's bothering you, isn't anything new to me or something we can't work out."

"*Man, man, man . . .*"

"Come on, Telly; this is not like you. Talk to me." As I spoke, his head shook.

"Uncle Glenn, Uncle Glenn, Uncle Glenn . . ." His words were followed by deep breaths, then his lips flapped in the wind like those little fan flags people sport out of their car windows. "Uncle Glenn, these fucking women, where do they get that shit from?"

"Get what from?" I asked.

Crowd Noise nodded as he came to a profound conclusion. "Bitch violated me, Unc."

"Come again?"

"Bitch violated me bad."

"Oh no—you went home, and a big, black nigga named Tyronne was pulling twelve inches of dick out of Erica?"

"No, not at all. She would never."

"Then I don't see how else a woman could violate you."

"Oh, there's another way. I learned that the hard way just a few hours ago," Telly countered. Then he fell silent again.

"Telly, I can't help unless you break it down for me. What happened? Who violated you?"

After several deep breaths, he was ready to talk.

"Everything was chill with Megyn; I'm doing what I do, kicking and punching the pussy like Teebo. Then she asked to suck me off a little while, and I was cool with that, then she wanted to fuck me a little, and I was cool with that, but then she . . . then she . . . she . . . she . . . she put . . ."

Dude's face was dried and wrinkled like a raisin; he didn't even blink. It was so bad I had the thought of slapping him behind the head, thinking that could free his thought.

"Telly, what did she do?" I asked in the brash voice of a prosecutor. *The woman who violated you, is she in this courtroom? Point to her,* is what I wanted to say. "Telly, you have to trust me with this—what happened?"

"She was in a reverse cowgirl position, and I thought I heard her say, *just hold still, regardless of what you feel.* I'm thinking she is probably going to jump off the dick and suck it out of me."

He fell silent again. I waited for two minutes for him to resume.

"Well, did she?"

"Huh?"

"You were saying . . . she was riding you reverse cowgirl and said hold still . . ."

"Yeah, yeah . . . I remember now. Uncle Glenn, what do you have to drink?"

"Like, beer?"

"Beer. Wine. Whiskey. Moonshine. Fingernail polish, any fucking thing. I need a drink."

"It's not even eight o'clock in the morning."

"Morris Day, I know what time it is. What do you have to drink in here?"

"In the fridge I have some Heinekens in the door—help yourself."

On weak legs, I watched him wobble into the kitchen and grab a beer. He didn't return to his seat, but instead came to a rest near my favorite stool. So I turned to face him, being that the seating arrangement for the conversation had shifted.

"Uncle Glenn, she stuck her finger in my ass. Dawg, my ass."

*So that was it.*

"Without permission?" I had to ask.

"Fuck you asking? I'm not a man who gives anyone permission to play with my asshole."

"Then why did she feel safe sticking her finger in your asshole?"

"Glenn, what are you asking me? This Telly, nigga! This Telly! You know I didn't give her freaky ass permission to do that shit. She started riding my dick, then before I knew it, her finger was up my ass."

"I hear you, Telly, but most women don't go there unless that finger has been approved prior to insertion. All I'm saying is there had to be some kind of mixed signal she detected from you that convinced her you were that type."

He fell silent for a second. Then I saw the exact moment he figured it out.

"It was the little trick with her tongue."

*Now we're getting somewhere.*

"Which trick?" I'm being deliberately naive, but I already know where this is going.

"Big Dawg, she has this really long tongue, right? And when she was down there licking my balls, a few times I felt her tongue poking me."

"Poking you where?"

"Nigga, you know . . . down there."

"I don't know because my nuts mark the U-turn."

"Well the bitch drove through my U-turn, and at first I didn't think much of it. I thought it was a cool little trick how she could have a mouth full of my balls and tickle my asshole at the same time. It was cute."

"*So that's the tongue trick?*"

"The tongue trick was a nice little change-up, but I never gave her permission to stick . . . to stick . . . her finger in my ass, bruh. I don't rock like that."

"Then why didn't you stop her?"

His voice became weak and airy. His words came out in a hesitant whisper, like we were in church.

*"Nigga, I tried, but once she pressed down on my . . . on my . . ."*

"Your prostate."

"Yes, I couldn't move. I was paralyzed, nigga."

It was then that Telly started to cry. I couldn't fuckin' believe it. Dude is really in my kitchen crying.

"Unc, I tried to toss her off me, but cum started gushing out my dick like Jergens lotion. I felt it, like *blump, blump, blump.*" His thumb flicked like he was trying to shoot a marble. "I never came like that in my life."

*Heavenly Father, this is Glenn, and I come to you as your humble servant, oh Lord. I plead the blood over Telly's asshole that was molested by the white girl. Keep his mind, Lord. Amen.*

"Straight up, tell me the truth Unc—that bitch made me gay, huh? I'm turnt out, huh? I'm going to be a punk, huh?"

How do you listen to something like that and keep a straight face? I managed it somehow. This is Telly—the one we call Crowd Noise because he is the most heckling fucka I've ever met, but right now he is on the verge of a nervous breakdown and I have a narrow window to bring him back to the light.

"Remember a while back when we were having the conversation about prostate exams?"

"Yeah, about the doctor feeling around in my ass."

"Brother, that's the same gland. Telly, you were in a heightened state of arousal and your partner took the experience somewhere that made you uncomfortable, but you're not gay."

*"But, but I nutttted,"* he whined.

"But that doesn't make you gay."

"I only nut when I like something."

"Telly, the urologist pressed down on my prostate during a

recent exam—that's why they give you a tissue for the front and the back. In my case it was an involuntary ejaculation, but if pressure is applied to the prostate, then cum shoots out. If your scary ass had made an appointment with my urologist, then you would now have a better understanding of what happens. Megyn pressed on a very sensitive gland, and the normal reaction is for semen to ejaculate, but you're not gay."

"Even though she stuck her finger in my ass?"

"You're not gay."

"*But it felt good,*" he whined again.

"Telly, you're not gay unless you want to be." I hopped over to him in the kitchen and with a tight fist, I began to jab him in the chest the way Diana sometimes jabs me. "You're not gay; you're healthy, all your parts are working as they should. Having said that, you did some borderline shit with a woman, but you're not gay."

He wiped his face on the sleeve of his shirt. "That's all I needed to know."

"Now do me a favor."

"Just name it and consider it done."

"The next time you plan to fuck with . . ." I plucked my finger.

"*Megyn . . .*"

"Yes, Megyn. The next time you plan to fuck Megyn, wear a chastity belt."

"Fuck you, Uncle Glenn." His laughter was back. The eardrum-shattering volume of his voice blared with a vengeance. "I will keep Megyn's fingers and her long-ass tongue in full view at all times. Rape me once, shame on you, bitch, but rape me twice—"

"You turnt out." We shared a laugh.

Suddenly there was another knock on the door, and Telly sidestepped me to go answer it. Once he opened the door, I heard what sounded like a confrontation.

"You heard me, fuck you."

*Oh no, don't tell me the finger chick* is looking for her bitch,

I chuckled to myself.

"Motherfucker, I told you, I'm not Glenn. Don't you remember me? Then ride out!" Telly demanded of someone before slamming the door. He returned to the living room perturbed.

"Who was that at the door?" I asked.

"This annoying little fucker I recognized from court."

"Someone from court looking for me?"

"Uncle Glenn, I'm sorry to break this news to you. I just rejected legal forms in order to buy us some time, but Timothy is trying to sue you in civil court."

# CHAPTER 26

One hour later

**M**y wife wanted to kill him—not with a gun or a knife, but with her bare hands, over a period of three days, in a rotten woodshed down in Violet, Louisiana, where he could scream all night and no one would hear. She hasn't sat down since she got home and we broke the news that Timothy tried to serve me with a civil suit. From the kitchen to the living room window and back again she stomped, only pausing to peek out the blinds on each pass, hoping to see Timothy's car.

"I will show you better than I can tell you," Diana's argument with Timothy continued posthumously, as she referred to him in the past tense. "They will find your ass stinking before you get a dime from me, mutha-fucka."

Telly and I made quick eye contact. Laughter was trapped in our cheeks. Even though the court papers Telly rejected have my name on the upper left, Timothy will soon discover that he served the wrong person because this battle is not mine—it's Diana's.

"He fucked with the wrong one this time," Diana pumped her fist in the air. "The problem is, y'all let Timothy smile in your face, but I'm with Biyell—we should have kicked his ass."

Telly and I sat on the sofa and followed her from left to right as if we were sitting center court at Wimbledon. Diana and I offered Telly the role of representing us, but in his professional opinion, he decided it was best to go with our current attorney, who was handling my amputee lawsuits.

"It's only because I'm closely involved, and I wouldn't want his lawyer to use my friendship against you. But I plan to work behind the scenes with Attorney Larry Aisola to help prepare the overall strategy."

"Telly, you think Timothy has a case?" I asked. Only then did my wife stop pacing.

"He's going to use that video with the rules of the challenge to make the argument that if you refuse to pay him, then you're voiding the agreement."

"So he has a case," my wife huffed.

"Yes, because according to the terms of the challenge you set out in the video, the challenge was officially on once each man texted you a name and then handed you his old phone. He replied with Tootsie." Telly turned to Diana. "She turned out to be LaDeisha, as you know, but we referred to each mistress by nickname."

"And what was my nickname?" Diana turned to me with fire in her eyes.

"My wife."

"It better have been."

Whenever Diana got pissed liked this, she looked for a fight. I wasn't giving it to her, because the person she was pissed with was Timothy.

"Diana, please, have a seat and calm down. We're not fighting because you're angry with Timothy."

Begrudgingly, she sat down on the loveseat. "I'm sorry."

"All is forgiven. Please continue, Telly."

"In this day and age of electronic signatures and fickle judges, there's a strong possibility Timothy's lawyer is prepared to go the distance. He has that video, in your voice, stating the rules."

"Sounds like I need to schedule a meeting with my attorney."

"I strongly recommend you do." Telly stood and walked over to Diana. "I'm sorry this fool is coming for your coins, but I will never leave your side. We will deal with him." They hugged.

"Thank you, Telly, but that fucka will not make it to a court date."

Telly laughed. "And I heard no evil, will speak no evil, and when the police ask me about it . . . I ain't seen the nigga since court."

"Telly who?" My wife burst into laughter.

That's Telly—he has a natural gift for making you forget about your troubles.

"Have you heard from Rasta? I've been calling his phone." Telly looked at me curiously.

Diana and I locked eyes for a second.

"He's catching up with his sons," I improvised. "That oldest boy has a big-time recruiting visit coming up."

"That's right, Alabama is interested in him. Rasta better not send him to Tuscaloosa, we will fall out," Telly chuckled as he made his way toward the door.

"Telly, I'll walk you out." I grabbed my crutch and hopped down the hall, then out to the parking lot.

\*\*\*

"So, where you off to now?" I asked Telly on the side of his car.

"To the airport, where Erica is going to pick me up in an hour."

"Why is she picking you up from the airport?"

"Because I'm on a plane as we speak, headed back from New York."

"So you're driving to the airport to park and wait for Erica?"

"Grasshopper, pay attention." Telly donned his Mr. Miyagi voice. "First I'm headed to my office to park my car, then I will catch a cab to the airport. She will wait by the Shell gas station across from the airport. Then I will call her to meet me on the second floor by American Airlines, and—"

"Then she'll bring you back to your office to get your car."

"You got it, Grasshopper. Erica will never suspect a thing. That's the key to winning this game—always be where you're supposed to be and stay in constant contact."

"Telly, please stop fucking over that girl and settle down. That's why your asshole got violated, it's time to settle down."

*"Leave my asshole out of this."*

"Erica is a good woman—settle down."

"Uncle Glenn, I plan to. It'll be easy to break things off with Megyn because she can't have a full-time man right now anyway. Her ex-husband played for ten years in the NFL, and his pension is part of her alimony, but the property division isn't. If she remarries, then she's assed out."

"In other words, all you would have to do to break things off is act like you're ready to get married."

"Grasshopper, you're not as slow as I thought you were," Telly smirked.

"The way I see it, Telly, is if Erica were the one, then you would feel about her the way I feel about Diana, or the way Timothy feels about LaDeisha."

"Don't use your wife in the same sentence with LaDeisha; I think she's burying nigga's drawls in the backyard."

"What?"

"You know, how women back in the day used to trap a man."

"Telly, that voodoo crap is not real."

"Hell if it ain't—that bitch burying drawls. For Rasta and Timothy to act like that over her when either one of them could have any woman around . . . that ain't good pussy, that's voodoo."

"No, that's bullshit." In New Orleans, whenever a man is head over heels for a woman, someone always says it has to be voodoo—it can never just be the fact that he found the one his soul loves. "But answer me straight up . . . is Erica the one for you?"

There was a delayed reaction in his response as his eyes focused in on a garbage truck backing down a nearby driveway. When it came to relationships, Telly loved the game more than the women he played. All the other guys had tried to change, but Telly never lifted a finger. When Yolanda dumped him, he quickly found a replacement—he never pumped the brakes.

"No, she's not the one, but she's the best available one."

"The best you have, but not the one?"

"Something like that."

"So you're still searching for the one?"

"Not really, but remember, a huge portion of my clientele are divorces cases, and on my desk is a stack of failed marriages. These marriages always start out wonderful, but five years after the Electric Slide, either the husband or the wife will call me. There are not many women out here like Diana; she's a dying breed."

"No, she isn't; the problem is you don't know what you want. Once you determine what you want, then you can stop robbing these ladies of the opportunity to find real love. All around you are good women—in search of a good man. Hell, every time I turn on the television, there's a commercial for a new dating website. With the exception of a broken few, many of those women would thank God every day for a man like you."

"But you didn't meet Diana on a dating site. That's what I mean by Lady Diana is a dying breed—"

"Where I met her is irrelevant; I knew what I wanted when I married Diana. Answer this for me—what if you try to back Megyn into a corner with the marriage question and she decides to forgo the pension? Would you marry Megyn?"

"Would you look at the time . . . Uncle Glenn, I have to get to the airport."

"Telly, would you marry Megyn?"

"I don't know."

"If she decided to keep the pension, would you marry Erica?"

"Fuck, I don't know. What's up with you asking all these questions?"

"Well?"

"I probably would marry Erica; she's the only one I would consider jumping the broom with. But I'm not the marrying kind . . . I don't believe in it."

"Telly, your issue is fear—you're afraid to make a decision. That's why they call it *a deer in headlights,* and that's why the deer gets knocked on his ass. If the deer decided to run left or right, he would live, but it's the inability to decide that causes the collision. Take, for instance, Yolanda."

"Unc, I really have to get going . . ." Telly tried to blow me off.

"You tried to walk off that pain, but I know how much you loved her. She gave you every opportunity to have forever, but you assholed around until another joker lured her away. Telly, you're about to lose out again."

Every other minute, Telly gawked at his watch, but in his world, he ruled like Kim Jong-un: everything happened on his time schedule and by his command. That's the false sense of security cheaters enjoy—they control everything and avoid situations out of their control. They're terrified of the unexpected and petrified of the unknown. Men like Telly only get caught when the aforementioned situations occur—something off the wall or unforeseen, like the mailman turning out to be a deacon working with the father of his girlfriend. When Erica finally catches his ass, I promise you it'll happen just like that.

"I guess you're right, Uncle Glenn. I don't know if I would be happy long term with Erica or any other woman, so I just date long term. When it comes to marriage, I don't think I would be any good at it. This litter of single women is a different breed. You got lucky with Lady Diana, so the decision was easy for you. She's down for you one hundred percent, rain, sleet, or snow."

"You feel my wife is the last of a dying breed, but here is how my daddy helped me to ultimately decide between Derinda and

Diana."

"I got to hear this."

"*The cake test.*"

"What?" Telly's face frowned. "The cake test, what is that?"

"Like you, I couldn't make up my mind. I loved them both, but my dad wasn't having that bullshit. He told me to call Derinda and ask her to bake me a chocolate cake that was yellow on the inside. So I did as he asked and called Derinda."

"Hold up; you picked a wife based on a cook-off like *Hell's Kitchen?*"

"Shhhhh, listen, Grasshopper. The next day around the same time, he asked me if Derinda had baked the cake. I replied *not yet*. The day after that, he asked the same question at the same time. *She had choir rehearsal*, I replied. The fourth day he asked the same question: *Derinda baked the cake?* I replied, *no sir, because this is exams week*. The fifth day he asked, *son, did she bake the cake?* I replied, *no, because it was her pastor's anniversary week* and she *was on the committee.*"

"I don't get where you're going."

"Pay attention. Then he asked me to call Diana and ask her to bake me a chocolate cake that was yellow on the inside. And so I called her. Right after I called Diana, there was a knock on the door. It was Derinda. In her hands was a cake pan. I thanked her for the cake and ran to the kitchen to show my dad. I was smiling so hard slobber ran down the side of my mouth."

"How did it taste?"

"I don't know, because he told me not to cut it. *Sit it over on the counter*, he told me. The next day around the same time, he asked me if Diana had baked the cake. I said *not yet*, but shortly after he asked me, there was a knock on the front door . . ."

"Let me guess; it was Diana with a cake."

"Yes."

"So you had two chocolate cakes side by side—which one tasted the best?"

"I don't know, because my father told me to toss the first cake in the trash."

"Wait, you threw Derinda's cake away? Without tasting it? I don't get it."

"I didn't get it either until he explained the cake test to me. He told me: *Son, it's not about how well she decorated the icing or how it tastes inside. The only thing that matters is if you matter. If she cares about you, then you are a priority, and you will never have to remind her of something as simple as a cake.*"

From the expression slowly spreading over Telly's face, I could tell he was starting to understand.

"Grasshopper, when you get in the car, call Megyn and ask her to bake you a cake. I'll call you tomorrow, and hopefully it'll be on the counter waiting for you."

# CHAPTER 27

Monday, June 5, 2017
5:45 p.m.

## JARVIS

Briana wasn't too good to be true - I was too false to be good. Whereas she was a matter of fact, I was, regretfully, in her life under a false pretense. From day one she was honest—I knew what she wanted and when. Briana was as transparent as bottled water: *Jarvis, I want a life with you.* It was a great idea—it read very well on paper. I even started to dream her dream, but from day uno, I led her on—I made her believe we were five steps from home plate knowing I never envisioned life without Monica.

I was the one who committed adultery with the facts and ignored the truth, because the truth was too depressing, too mundane, too tedious, too systematic . . . too hurtful. The fact is I enjoyed Briana more than my wife. I was twenty-eight again; each hour I spent with her I siphoned her spirit down to the last quart, then ran off the fumes until she refilled me. But I was married, and the ugly truth is that Briana is my niece by marriage. If a lie is the epidermis of who you are, then veracity will leave you bruised and battered. I'm not a right-thinking individual. Briana was my drug. I have thin skin.

I'm still addicted.

I'm a liar.

I'm hurt.

Truth.

Now, nearly thirty days after everything was exposed at that wedding in Dallas, I'm living alone in a one-bedroom apartment, still grimacing from *after-the-fact* epiphanies that arrived too late to make a difference.

Briana was a drug I injected to feel better. I ignored all the side effects listed at the end of the commercial. I just wanted to feel better. I'm closer to fifty-one than twenty-one. That's one reason I fucked with her, because she had the ability to rewind me—she was my do-over before it was over.

Every day starts the same. I call Monica and leave another voicemail apology that evaporates in her inbox, then I stare at the phone in my hand contemplating whether I should call Briana. Every day since Dallas, I've made the first call but never the second. I miss them both. I still crave them both equally but differently, and every day I don't see my daughters feels like one of my internal organs has slipped into acute failure.

*My pain relief should arrive any minute now.*

The appointed time was set a week ago and confirmed twice over the weekend during a few short, clipped conversations where I could barely get a word in. Yet still, Monica is late for our first official handoff of Lyric and Symphony. The agreed time was five o'clock. She's forty-five minutes late after sending a text thirty minutes ago saying, *we'll be there shortly.*

*Shortly, my ass.*

If she's not here in the next five minutes, I'm leaving—but that would play right into Monica's hands and give her a fresh reason to tear me down in front of my daughters. My name is already garbage—at least I'm still Daddy in the eyes of my girls. I'm chilling right here, but damn, she knows how to piss me off. And don't get me wrong, it's not just that she's late—the bigger issue here is respect. She doesn't respect me . . . but when has she? She never liked my job, she never read one sentence of my manuscript, and if I dare to be honest, she never really liked me.

Do I believed she loved me—who knows?

What's love without like?

Jarvis and Monica.

There were so many times I wanted to haul off and smack the piss out of Monica. I would have if I were the smacking kind. I always held my hand—but oh, how I wanted to. Like that time when Briana was waiting to take her to the airport for another quote-unquote *regional meeting* in Atlanta—that morning, Monica handled me rough in the company of Briana and my daughters. I should have smacked her then—if I were a slapper, but I'm not. I am a talker and a walker. I walked into the waiting arms of Briana and it felt good, because I was loved and liked, adored and appreciated, fed and fucked—treated like a king. Then I lost that, too.

But it's all my fault. Not just Briana—my entire marriage.

I watched Monica graduate to new levels and never said a word. When I say *graduated*, I'm not referring to her Master in Finance, but her Master's-level degree in disrespect. I recall a conversation with Uncle Glenn and the guys a few years ago, when the topic was raised about how to know when a woman has lost respect for her man.

This conversation came during the period leading up to Rasta's divorce, when his wife was in rare form—she even set his things outside under the carport. I remember Uncle Glenn saying that when a woman has lost respect for you, that marriage is over. If you decide to remain with her beyond that point, then you graduate her to the next level of disrespect. Those words became flesh and dwelt in my house.

Each time Monica said something fucked up and I felt like

smacking the piss out of her, I didn't. Instead, I drew a line in the sand. I told myself, *if she ever disrespects me like that again, she is going to meet a Jarvis she's never met before.* Two weeks later, she would cross that line again, and I would make the same internal threats, and draw a new line, only to have her cross the new line a week later. In one year, I drew an entire football field of lines, and Monica crossed every last one like Emmitt Smith. She proved Uncle Glenn's words to be scripture, even though I was a non-believer at the time.

*Monica just arrived.*

Our meeting place is the Shell gas station at the entrance of the Oakwood Mall, just on the other side of the Mississippi River Bride. Her white Mercedes CLS500 came to a smooth park alongside my truck—the one she kicked my ass in a month ago. Feels like it was just yesterday.

I exited my car expecting my daughters, who I haven't seen in a month, to come running to me. I pictured them hugging me as Monica drove away without a finger wave . . . but they didn't exit the vehicle.

Symphony sat in the front passenger seat, while Lyric sat in the rear. The three of them appeared locked in a heated discussion. I know my daughters. They're not ready to see me . . . but I'm their father. I need to see them.

The gas station was busy as a beehive. In my peripheral, customers pumped gas, then abandon their cars outside while they headed into the convenient store for everything from cell phone chargers to synthetic Viagra. *Don't ask me how I know.* I can smell the hair grease I applied to my scalp. A thought just entered my mind to slide fifty cents into this air compressor machine and pressure-wipe my face. I'm melting.

The deliberations inside Monica's car continued as I stood there like a fake homeless dude holding a cardboard sign scribbled with lies. I stood there like a demoralized fool while Monica crossed another line. Touchdown.

The first to exit the car was Symphony. She huffed and

puffed and threw her bag across her shoulder so hard she nearly whipped around in a full circle like Michael Jackson. Her hair was in two rope-like braids, which is my daughters' normal summertime style for amusement parks and swimming. *Are they retuning from vacation? Could they have gone to Disney World without me?* Neither of the two girls have taken any of my calls since Dallas. Monica could have updated me on their whereabouts, especially if she was planning to take my daughters out of the state.

"Well hello, Destiny's Child . . . can Daddy get a hug?"

No hug. Symphony continued past me to the rear passenger door and slammed it shut behind her.

Monica body was at a full twist as she conversed with Lyric in the back seat. Perfidiously, my daughter protested as if Monica had just taken her tablet and cell phone. Suddenly, Lyric flung back in her seat with her arms tightly folded. Monica reached for my daughter's knee and gave it a gentle squeeze, a *do it for me* nudge, then a series of persuading taps. Finally, Lyric opened her door and stepped outside, pulling an overnight bag that plumped to the ground once it cleared the back seat.

"Hello, my little India Arie!" I extended my arms. Lyric granted me a one-arm hug around my waist, then quickly bolted for the rear passenger seat.

There I stood on a stripe of yellow with my kids in one car and my wife in the other, and I wasn't welcome in either. Then Monica's door opened like it weighed five-thousand pounds. Only once her shades were perfectly positioned on her face did she exit her vehicle. Her face crinkled in dread. My face fell in despair. I expected to our little reconnect to come with a few ripples, but I never expected a rip tide that would drag me out to sea.

"As you can imagine, you're not their favorite person. You may want to give them a little time to warm up," Monica instructed as if were a new babysitter.

"Well, that's pretty obvious." Her back leaned against her car to hide from the evening rays. "What happened to our agreed time? It was confirmed twice."

"Jarvis, they don't want to see you any more than I want to see—"

"That's beside the point, we agreed on a time."

"Jarvis, does it look like I give a fuck?" Her arm tucked across her chest.

Lyric's door opened. "Mommy, can go back with you, please?"

"Tulip, we've had this discussion. I need you to be a big girl, it's only for two days."

Lyric's door replied with a loud thump.

"Look Monica, I don't want to argue, but next time don't give me a timeframe you can't keep. Be more respectful of my time. That's all I'm saying."

"Be more respectful?" She swiped the shades off her face. "You humiliated me in front of my entire family and I'm the one who should be more respectful? Have you lost your fucking mind? What is she now, four or five months pregnant? You're lucky I don't—"

Symphony exited the car. "How could you get Briana pregnant? How could you?" Symphony berated just over my shoulder. "All of my friends know—it was all over Facebook how my daddy and aunt were sneaking around while my mother was fighting for her life." Her foot stomped that hot pavement between each sentence. "Momma, I'm not spending two days with him. I'm too old to play make-believe. Lyric can go, but my daddy died in Dallas." She turned toward Monica's car.

"Symphony, you have every right to be angry with me. I'm angry with myself for causing this, but it doesn't negate the fact that I love you and I never meant for any of this to happen. Please, just give me today. All I want to do is listen to you and your sister. I want to apologize face to face so—"

"We don't have anything to talk about. You picked Briana over us. Anything you have to say to me, say it to your baby momma instead." Symphony returned to her seat in Monica's car and pressed in her earbuds. Seconds later, Lyric wobbled back to her mother's car without saying a word, tossed in her overnight bag, and yanked open her door handle.

What do you do when your children refuse to talk to you, but have every right not to? I can order them back into my truck, but I can't make either one of them like me. What started out as only one person in my household disrespecting me has escalated to three. I deserve it, but I'm still her husband until the papers are finalized, and their father forever. What do you do when those who make up your entire household can't stand to look at you?

Above Symphony's head hovers a mushroom cloud of anger. Moving across Lyric's face is a hurricane of grief over her broken family. In Monica's body is a slow-moving nor'easter front cold enough to freeze lava. Inside of me is a San Andreas Fault that has broken our foundation—everything I worked so hard to build is crumbling down.

I wanted run around to Symphony's side of the car and scream *I did not pick Briana over you and your sister!* but there was no way to convince them otherwise. Even if I manage to get things calm between us, pretty soon Briana will have her baby and the scandal will flare up again. But I'm not ready to give up, and I'm not ready to live without my family.

All is lost.

I've fucked up beyond repair.

My children will never recover from this. Maybe I should open my glove compartment and end this for all of us, starting with Lyric, then Symphony, then Monica, and then finally . . .

I reached for the passenger door handle to open the glove compartment where I housed my Glock. Just then, another car came to a rolling stop near the air compressor on the other side of Monica's car. Out of the car stepped a clean-cut guy in slacks, a polo, and a nice pair of black shoes. He left his door open as he filled his two front tires to the proper pressure per pound. I recognize him, but he hasn't noticed me or my wife. His name Therrow, and we use to sing in his gospel group. Then I heard the song that blared out of his speakers.

*You can win as long as you keep your head to the sky*
*Be optimistic*

The song hit Monica's ears at the same time, and I knew that since it instantly teleported me back to our gospel choir days in the early nineties, it definitely transported her—Monica had sung the lead. Back in the nineties, we were so in love and filled with dreams of all we would accomplish together. Our weeks consisted of school, minimum wage jobs, and our choir group: Therrow & Tehillah. That song—"Be Optimistic" by Sounds of Blackness—was Monica's song, and we performed it from church to church as if we had written it. My Lord, she nailed it every time.

*Don't give up and don't give in*
*Although it seems you never win*
*You will always pass the test*
*As long as you keep your head to the sky*

Monica left the group first because of her studies and her first teller gig, then I quit the group. Then we stop attending church together. Then life happened, now here we are. Here I am, having murder-suicide thoughts. If not for a song, Monica's song . . .

Monica also noticed Therrow, but tilted her head in disguise. Today wasn't the day for reunions, not even gospel reunions. After our old choir director merged into the Westbank Expressway commuters, Monica turned square to face me.

"Jarvis, it's too soon. I thought they were ready to see you . . . I was wrong. Maybe another time, but it's too soon."

"You guys have every right to be angry with me, but how can we get past this if we don't try?"

"Maybe there's no getting past this. Maybe this is the way it's going to be. I really don't know and don't care. My daughters are hurting and if seeing you drags them all the way back to Dallas, I rather they stay far away from you."

"Monica, I am their father. You can't keep my kids from me."

"Asshole, I am not keeping them from you." Right there, I almost smacked the piss out of her, right there.

"Jarvis, I brought them to you. If I wanted to keep them from you then we would still be in Atlanta."

"You took my kids to Atlanta and didn't tell me?"

"We needed to get as far away as we could. Yes, we've been in Atlanta, and we'll be there for as long as we need."

"Monica, I know I fucked up. I have apologized a million times, I've called every day. I don't know how to fix this and I agree with you that I should expect things to be this way, but I need to see my kids—" Suddenly I was talking to the hand.

"*I. Will. Not. Force. Them. To. See. You.* When my children are ready to see you, then I will make those arrangements at court during our divorce proceedings, but I'm not doing this." With her finger pointed between us, she leaned in and spoke in a low, growling voice. "You crushed me in a very public and painful way—there isn't a Band-Aid large enough to stop this bleeding—but see those two girls in that car? I will do everything within my power to protect my daughters from this never-ending scandal. I've transferred my treatment, so don't look for us. We'll be in Atlanta."

"Atlanta."

"Yes, Atlanta, it's where I've always gone when I needed to get away from you. It's where we will be."

"I have some say in where you take my kids—you have no right to do this."

"And you had no right to fuck my niece but you fucked her, didn't you? Didn't you?"

Yeah, I did, but I left that question hanging out there.

"Wave bye to Symphony and Lyric, because the next time you will see me will be in court. Until then, I'll keep your life insurance paid up in case your sorry ass should die."

With that, the third and final door slammed shut on any idea I had of reconciling with my daughters. They'd relocated to Atlanta. They didn't want to see me. *They're out of my life, and I don't know whether to live or die, but it cuts like a knife.* I looked into Symphony's eyes for the first time in almost a month and I saw it all: every sheepish tear, every cyberbully tweet she read about her family, every insensitive post on Facebook about The Affair involving her father and her aunt. I felt it all.

My fling with Briana hurt my daughters.

When they hurt, I hurt.

I've always outsourced the disciplinary duties to Monica because I couldn't bear to hear them cry. When they cried, I cried. For the first time, I've made them cry, and now I'm crying because the safest place for my daughters to be is far away from me. I've fucked my marriage, my family, and my home because of this fling with Briana. I have nothing, but in the back corner of my fucked-up brain I can hear Uncle Glenn say: *When a man is wrong, he stands up and takes his lick.*

With a yellow ray beaming down on me and a sweltering yellow strip beneath me, I just stood trial, and I accepted my lick for an hour in the sun after Monica sped away.

I'm guilty as charged.

# CHAPTER 28

Madden Night
Thursday, June 8, 2017
6:20 p.m.

## TELLY

U ncle Glenn and that got-damn cake test—for six consecutive days he sent me the same text, but deep down he knew the answer.

*Did you get the cake yet?*

No!

There is no cake; not even a good excuse for why she hasn't baked it. She simply forgot. Every time I ask for the cake, she says it's on her list, but somehow it's never in the oven. Good thing I didn't need that cake to survive—I would have starved to death. Even though she hasn't baked the cake yet, I disagree with Uncle Glenn that I am not her priority. Megyn has a ton of stuff to do during the course of a day, and I don't think it's fair to throw the whole woman away based on some stupid-ass cake test.

Megyn runs a PR firm from home; she handles press content for several corporations. I've been to her house, and I've seen her desk.

I like Megyn. Uncle Glenn seems to think it's because she's white, but that has zero to do with it. She's super fucking intelligent, and she's been to the land of the rich, which is the place I ought to be. She knows everybody, and everybody knows her, and for where I'm trying to go with my law practice, she is the perfect woman.

Take, for instance, last night. Last night Megyn introduced an idea I had never considered; the thought had never entered my mind. The entire concept was her brain child, and she introduced it right after we finished fucking.

"Telly, that was amazing. Thanks for not pinning me down."

"You're welcome, and thanks for not sticking your finger in *my ass*."

"Aww, Telly-Bear, you know you liked it . . ."

"*Ciarrrraaaa . . .*"

"All right, I'll drop it, but if you just relax and not tense up . . ."

"CIARA."

"Hehe, okay, okay. But aside from your ass, I had a great idea that hit me."

"And that is?"

"Have you ever considered becoming a sports agent? The reason why I ask is I remembered you shared a story of how you and your friend Rastaman—"

"It's Rasta, just Rasta."

"That's the one! You guys once coached little league football?"

"That's correct."

"Well I did the math on that timeframe, and the kids that you guys coached are now entering college."

Just like that, the greatest idea I never thought of serenaded through her beautiful lips. Several of the kids Rasta and I coached have already landed in major universities, and a boat-load are in high school. Not to mention, Rasta's son is heavily recruited; he would be our first star athlete for sure when he declares for the draft. Rasta and I have stayed in contact with all the kids we coach via Facebook, but the idea of managing their athletic careers never entered my mind until Megyn brought it up.

"I hate to bring him up, but for the sake of this conversation, I would like to . . . that is, if you approve?"

"Yes, please continue." Megyn is so submissive and respect-ful. I love that about her.

"Jacoby had an agent for six of his ten years who I didn't trust, therefore I read every contract ten times before he signed it. I became so good at identifying contract traps that other families on the team would send their paperwork to me for verification. I became an expert of sorts on NFL, NBA, and MLB contracts and free agency deals. With the relationships you have with the kids' families and my expertise in negotiating rookie salaries and counter-offers, I think we have the makings of a successful sports management and athletic marketing firm.

If you want to know the minute, hour, and day I fell in love with Megyn, it was when she said *I read every contract ten times*. It felt like I'd jumped out of an airplane and parachuted to the ground. I was in love with Megyn. She was the missing piece I needed to get to the next level, and she just gave me that one thing Yolanda said I didn't have.

"*What's your plan, Telly? Do you have one? Broke-ass nig-ga!*" Yolanda had called to me in the restaurant that morning before she ran off with that guy in the GL550. At least that's how I remember it going.

*Bitch. Bitch, I do have a plan, and fuck you.* That's what I wish I'd said, if I hadn't been comatose from heartache. I sat there and took it all. Like I was living the effects of a date rape drug, I couldn't stop her from fucking me over, but Yolanda was right—I didn't have a plan until Megyn gave me one last night.

And yes, I gave her the green light to start developing the sports management firm. After all, she knows the first thing to do and I don't, but I know everything there is to know about football players and building relationships, and that's where I see the earning potential of Megyn's idea. This could be the beginning of a long and prosperous partnership.

Megyn's idea last night also closed the gap that existed between her and Erica. Don't get me wrong, Erica has made me very happy over the past seven months, but we've never had a conversation like the one I had with Megyn last night. One problem I have with Erica is that she has struggled financially for so long—even in her dreams, she's broke. Her only goals are paying the light bill on time and taking weekly trips to Walmart. Also, she is a mother and nothing more; it's all about her kids at this point. And I'm not saying there's anything wrong with that, but a few days ago I saw Erica in her first pair of mom jeans, and I didn't like it. Those jeans said *Fuck it; I have a man, and a family, so fuck it.*

Megyn is also a mom, but she still has personal goals for her life. She still has that fire. There are still levels she's trying to reach professionally, and she needs me to get there.

I just pulled into my drive way in time for dinner, and through the kitchen window, I can see Erica moving about with an afro-puff ponytail. I gave her money for clothes and the hair salon, but she refuses to treat herself. She's too guilt conscious for the nail salon, which is a first for me. She lives in constant fear of falling back into the impoverished place where I found her, even though I've deposited ten percent of my earnings into her personal account.

But back to the mom jeans; those fuckin' pants are baggy in the worst way, even though Erica has put on some much-needed pounds. I think it's a woman's duty to stay sexy as fuck for her man, but it's hard to convince her to step it up. Nevertheless, I love her.

Erica better not have on those jeans.

I swear to Jesus, the Lord, and God.

If she has on those jeans . . .

Little does Erica know, but she got me over the heartbreak from Yolanda. It was Erica and her clinginess that made me feel needed and wanted after getting demolished in that restaurant. It was Erica who picked me up from the gutter when my heart was shattered; it was Erica who loved me back to wholeness.

Here I am again.

That *deer in the headlights* that Uncle Glenn spoke about last week—if I would only decide right or left. Is that a truck up ahead? Wham! Deer guts and blood everywhere. Yolanda, that bitch, she was the truck driver who hit my stupid ass. But enough about Yolanda and the ugly mom jeans, it's time to go inside.

I entered the kitchen to find Erica hand-washing dishes. On the side of her is brand new dishwasher. She uses the dishwasher as a dish rack, but not to wash the dishes, because in her mind it makes the light bill go up by ten dollars. Yes, you heard me: ten dollars.

I sat my bag on a chair and hurried over to her from behind, but she turned just in time. Her lips long for my lips. It's like she holds her breath from the time I leave in the morning until the time I walk through that kitchen door. Every muscle in her face readjusts as soon as she kisses me. Even her eyes smile.

"There's my Superman, how was work?"

"It's over."

"One of those days, huh?"

"Oh, yes. Where are my little princesses?"

"Their father called and said he's running late, but he's on his way."

"Dude still doesn't want to meet me, huh?"

"You're starting to understand why I can't stand him. Thank

God I have a man who seeks a pleasant parenting partnership, even though he refuses to speak to you. He's such an asshole."

*An image of Megyn with a fat Crisco finger just popped into my mind.*

"As Uncle Glenn says, I'll treat him like a gentleman not because he's one, but because I am."

"Darren is no gentleman; he is a moist asshole."

*Every time she says that word, my ass cheeks clamp tight.*

A beam of headlights lit up the driveway; the girls were home. Erica kissed me one more time before she headed out the side door, and that's when I noticed them—those fuckin' jeans. Street Trendy Vintage High Rise Denims that roll up at the bottoms. It seems like the jeans come up to her bra. But after tonight, she will have to look for those motherfuckers, because I'm burning them in the backyard.

On the table, set at my place, was a glass of wine. My plate is in the microwave. And that's the golden part of Erica that Megyn can never rival. Erica can make a tent under a bridge feel like home with just two cans of pork and beans. I made my way around the table to the microwave, and there it was, under a clear, plastic cover.

A fucking chocolate cake.

I asked for it yesterday

It's in the pan today.

On cue, I received a text from Uncle Glenn. How is that even possible? I spot the cake, then he sends me that annoying-ass text.

*Did you get the cake yet?*

*Yes, I have the cake.*

*Erica is your wife.*

*I know.*

Fuck.

# TO BE CONTINUED IN VOL 3 . . .

**www.tjnovels.com**

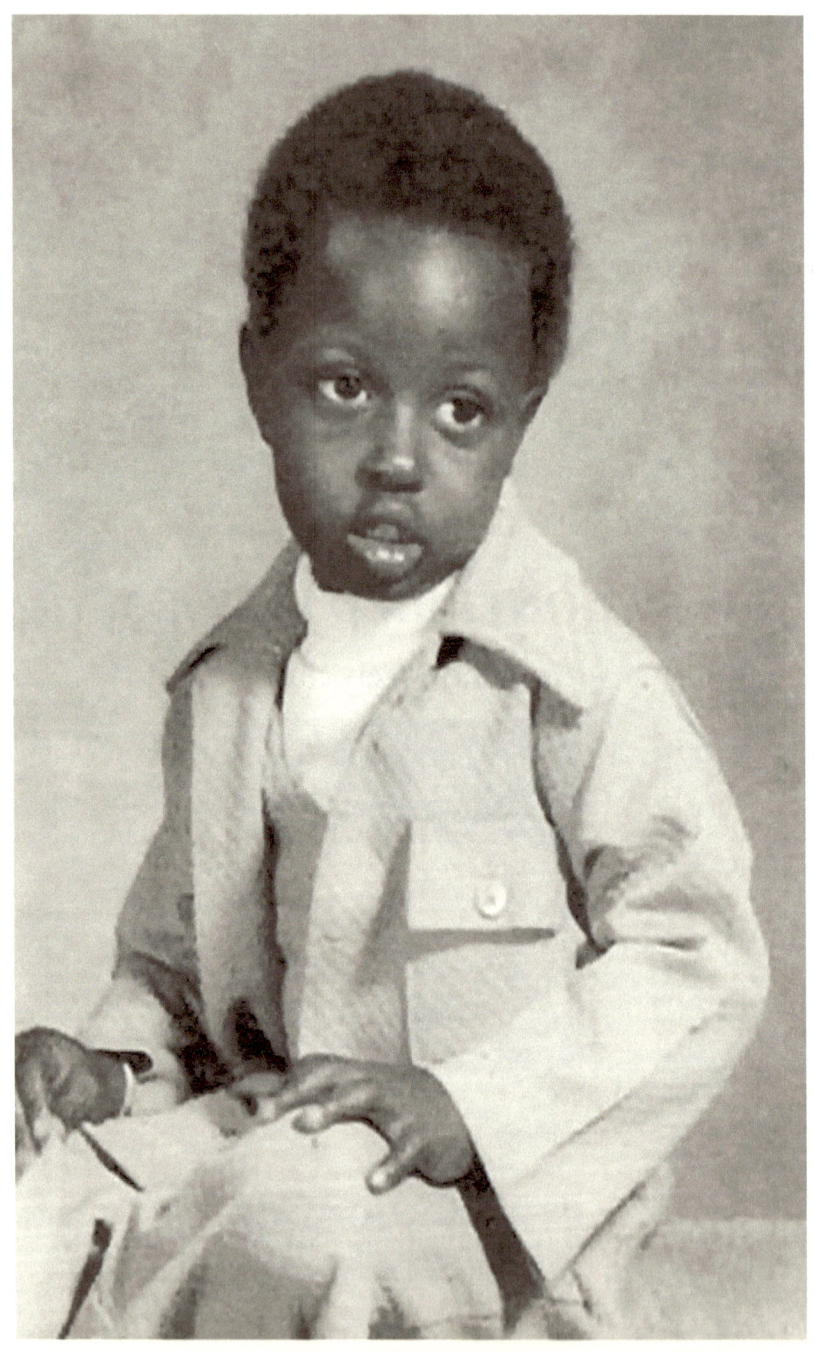

*TJ Spencer Jacques - Age 3 (1974)*

I'm author TJ Spencer Jacques and I have a Doctorate Degree in how to fuck up a good relationship.

Nice to meet you.

Thank you for reading the Infallible Series, your continued support of my novels motivates me every day. This project is a collection of my mistakes as well as the errors of my Madden Brothers: packaged in fiction – but tangible. I make no apologies for the rawness of this content. There are numerous books on the market about men who cheat, but I wanted to explain why we cheat from our point of view, and all the many ways we mentally justify our actions.

I would have you to know that I am the father of five young daughters, and with them in mind I wrote this series as a warning. I am also the father of three sons, as a preventative resource, I wrote Infallible to teach them the consequences of unfaithfulness. I also wrote Infallible for you.

Hope you enjoyed.

TJ SPENCER JACQUES
www.tjnovels.com